S
Norton

Norton, Andre.

Beast master's
circus.

DATE			

BEAST MASTER'S CIRCUS

TOR BOOKS BY ANDRE NORTON

BEAST MASTER
(with Lyn McConchie)
Beast Master's Ark
Beast Master's Circus

The Crystal Gryphon
Dare to Go A-Hunting
Flight in Yiktor
Forerunner
Forerunner: The Second Venture
Here Abide Monsters
Moon Called
Moon Mirror
The Prince Commands
Ralestone Luck
Stand and Deliver
Wheel of Stars
Wizards' Worlds
Wraiths of Time

The Gates to Witch World
(omnibus comprising
Witch World, Web of the Witch World,
and *Year of the Unicorn*)

The Solar Queen
(omnibus comprising
Sargasso of Space and *Plague Ship*)

Grandmasters' Choice (Editor)
The Jekyll Legacy (with Robert Bloch)
Gryphon's Eyrie (with A. C. Crispin)
Songsmith (with A. C. Crispin)
Caroline (with Enid Cushing)
Firehand (with P. M. Griffin)
Redline the Stars (with P. M. Griffin)
Sneeze on Sunday (with Grace Allen Hogarth)
House of Shadows (with Phyllis Miller)
Empire of the Eagle (with Susan Shwartz)
Imperial Lady (with Susan Shwartz)

THE WITCH WORLD
(Editor)
Four from the Witch World
Tales from the Witch World 1
Tales from the Witch World 2
Tales from the Witch World 3

WITCH WORLD: THE TURNING
I *Storms of Victory* (with P. M. Griffin)
II *Flight of Vengeance* (with P. M. Griffin)
III *On Wings of Magic* (with Patricia Mathews & Sasha Miller)

MAGIC IN ITHKAR
(Editor, with Robert Adams)
Magic in Ithkar 1
Magic in Ithkar 2
Magic in Ithkar 3
Magic in Ithkar 4

CAROLUS REX
(with Rosemary Edghill)
The Shadow of Albion
Leopard in Exile

THE HALFBLOOD CHRONICLES
(with Mercedes Lackey)
The Elvenbane
Elvenblood
Elvenborne

THE OAK, YEW, ASH, AND ROWAN CYCLE
(with Sasha Miller)
To the King a Daughter
Knight or Knave
A Crown Disowned

THE SOLAR QUEEN
(with Sherwood Smith)
Derelict for Trade
A Mind for Trade

THE TIME TRADERS
(with Sherwood Smith)
Echoes in Time
Atlantis Endgame

A Tom Doherty Associates Book

New York

BEAST MASTER'S CIRCUS

Andre Norton and Lyn McConchie

BEAST MASTER'S CIRCUS

Edited by James Frenkel

A Tor Book
Published by Tom Doherty Associates, LLC
175 Fifth Avenue
New York, NY 10010

www.tor.com

Tor® is a registered trademark of Tom Doherty Associates, LLC.

Library of Congress Cataloging-in-Publication Data

Norton, Andre.
    Beast master's circus / Andre Norton and Lyn McConchie.—1st ed.
       p. cm.
    "A Tom Doherty Associates book."
    ISBN 0-765-30042-7
    1. Storm, Hosteen (Fictitious character)—Fiction. 2. Human-animal communication—Fiction. 3. Life on other planets—Fiction. 4. Circus performers—Fiction. 5. Space colonies—Fiction. I. McConchie, Lyn, 1946– II. Title.

PS3527.O632B57 2004
813'.52—dc22

                                                                        2003060697

Printed in the United States of America

0 9 8 7 6 5 4 3 2

Dedication

To the cats whose lives have enlivened my own reading for so many years. To Midnight Louie, and Carole Nelson Douglas. To Koko and Yum Yum, and Lilian Jackson Braun. To Solomon, Sheba, Sealy, ShebaLu, and Saska, and Doreen Tovey; and to the many cats, real and fictional, of Andre Norton (Chang-Un in particular).

May they find Prauo a worthy successor.

—L.M.

Acknowledgments

To Jim Frenkel, Tor editor, who edited this book with considerable patience despite dealing with an author who can't spell or punctuate, and has no computer-savvy whatsoever. Thanks.

To the computer-repair firm of StanCo, who rushed out several times to fix my printer on the spot so I could produce this work. Thanks, Stan and Andrew.

And to the one, the only, the ubiquitous, Premier Ocispot Tigerman—my Ocicat—on some of whose traits and abilities I based the character of Prauo, and without whose loving assistance this work would have probably been finished a lot sooner.

Thanks, guys, I couldn't have done it without you.

BEAST MASTER'S CIRCUS

Chapter One

Laris crouched over the new animal. It was gasping for breath still, but that would not last long. The shock of its injuries and the pain of losing what meant most to it were draining both its strength and will to live. Even as she worked, it gave one final, long, slow breath—and as that was released so was the poor beast's life. She felt tears come to her eyes. She'd tried. She had. But that would buy her nothing from those who employed her.

Nor did it. A moment later a whip sang, the lash burned across her thin shoulders, and she cried out, twisting away.

"Dedran, no! I did my best. I can't work miracles."

She glared up at him. "If your people brought me anything but damaged goods mind-broken by the way they were taken, I might have a chance."

The Circus Master glared down. Dedran was a lean, hard-looking man. His hair was that odd shade of blond that looked almost white but his skin was a weathered brown. He'd fought with the Ishan forces until his planet was destroyed almost five years earlier. What he'd been before that no one knew—although they made guesses which could well have been right.

Dedran had never given anyone the impression he was rigidly honest. The Ishan forces had not cared, their leader had taken the man in to fight, not to attend league meetings. In fact, Dedran had been a criminal already allied with the rising Thieves Guild. He was a clever man with ideas. One of which had been that it was safer to be given a weapon and encouraged to fight against the Xik than to hide without arms and wait to be slaughtered. He'd bided his time, survived the destruction of his world, and made sure of some very portable and valuable loot as he escaped the ruins of his planet.

He'd set up the circus after Ishan. Spent the two years before the war ended sorting out acts and people to work for him. He seemed to have enough money to do it without problems. Within the circus though there were hints that he owned only a part of it—that others had funded the business as a cover. Laris could believe that. The circus had swept her up four years ago. She'd been a starving refugee from one of the worlds cleared by the Xik, or so she believed. She'd been barely twelve, and remembered little of her first years. The years after the loss of her home had been filled with dimly recalled moves: being bundled into a ship and dumped on another world with no more than the clothes she stood up in and her mother, who wept. She thought she might have been four or five then. Another move and another, and her mother was gone. Another and still yet another until at last she was twelve and in a camp with many others, none of whom she knew and most of whom spoke other languages or the one-speech with strange accents. She'd fought first to survive, then to escape, sensing that if she stayed within the camp she would become as hopeless as they.

Laris had a keen intelligence but had learned enough by the time she was alone to hide much of what she knew. She looked younger than her true age and could appear younger still. People were more careless around a child—both with talk and small change.

She'd found part-time employment in a pet shop run by an old man. He wasn't unkind but he expected a full day's work for his credits. Sometimes the work was almost too much for the light-boned, underfed girl but she always managed. She loved the beasts, and when he saw how well they responded to her the owner gave her more responsibility. Then he died and her way of escape appeared closed.

There were other roads open but none that she would willingly take. At twelve she appeared to be only nine or ten, and in any great city there was a market for that. Had she agreed, there were several, including Mercer, the camp boss, who'd have found her employment. Laris was small and appeared fragile. Yet for all that she showed promise of becoming not so much pretty as elegant. Her movements were graceful, her cap of dark hair complemented the dark brown of her eyes, and her skin was a warm, creamy, faintly olive shade. Her manner was self-contained and she unbent to few.

Why bother? Camp after camp had swept away her mother, her memories, and any earlier friends she had made. Now she walked alone but for the one friend she'd kept these past few years. Prauo, whom she cherished and trusted, loved as she'd had none to love for so long.

Dedran was back. "Don't sit there dreaming, you fool. Get that carcass cleaned up, take samples for me, and make sure no one will find it afterward." He turned to leave, then swung back. "Your cat, he'll be well enough to perform tonight?"

"Yes—at least—here?"

Dedran smiled hungrily. "Elsewhere, a climb maybe."

Laris considered. Prauo had been ill from another growth

spurt but he was recovering. "So long as the climb isn't too exhausting and he can rest once it's done."

Her employer nodded. "It's a straight job. If you and the cat do it well I may even toss you a half credit or two." He laughed and strolled away, ignoring the look Laris gave him. Even after four years she sometimes wondered how well she'd done to sign on with Dedran's Circus. But she'd had to get out of the camp. With the pet shop owner's death her one obvious avenue of escape had closed.

She'd despaired; then Mercer, the camp boss, had come to her smiling and she'd cringed. It meant no good for someone when the boss of the camp grinned so cheerfully. But, incredibly, it had meant good for her. He'd towered over her, smirking down.

"You Laris? The one who's good with animals?" She'd nodded. Mercer nodded back. "You don't look like much. Maybe that's an advantage. Come with me." She followed, hiding the inward sneer at his pretense of not knowing her. He'd remembered her well enough last year when he'd wanted her to accept work in a city place. He'd thought she looked like a lot then, a lot of credits. Now what did he have in mind?

He'd taken her to Dedran. Both men had eyed her coldly. "This! You reckon this miserable thing'll be any use to me?"

Mercer nodded. "She's been working in old man Plaistrin's shop the last year. He told me once she was real good with the beasts. He was considering a contract. Reckon he'd a done it if'n he hadn't died." Laris felt her heart jump. So near to escape and the old fool had to go and die. But what was she doing here, another job with animals?

Dedran snorted. "All right. I'll test her. If she passes I'll take her on." He smiled viciously. "Five-year bond and you get the bond money. I suppose she's yours to bond?"

Mercer looked at her and Laris understood. In the camp there was always talk; some escaped it in various ways, and sometimes they returned to see friends or family. From them and their tales she had learned all she could about conditions of freedom. What it meant to be bonded. If she were ever in that position she must know what she would receive and what she could legally ask for. Here and now she could speak out. Deny that Mercer had the right to give a bond for her. Dedran would walk away and once she was back in the camp, she'd pay. But if she agreed she might have hope. She'd be out of the camp, employed even if she was under bond. After five years she could leave with an honorably canceled contract saying she'd had a good job these past five years. Or she might be able to stay, with a new contract and good pay if she'd proved her worth.

Better yet, under bond she must be decently fed. Given respectable clothing. A bond-servant could not be summarily judged or too badly beaten. There were always those who'd use too clear evidence of abuse against the abuser. None of these things were hers in the camp; she'd be better off bonded.

She'd looked up innocently. "Yes, Honored Sir, the Noble Mercer can sell me if'n he wishes. I work hard an' I'm good with the beasts."

"You'll sign the bond?"

"I'll sign," Laris agreed. And she had. In front of an over-stuffed pompous official, whom she guessed was collecting his share of the money. He'd attested that she appeared to be sixteen. Laris knew that for a lie, but she had to be sixteen for the bond so she signed where she was told and agreed when she was asked, that yes, she was sixteen years old.

After that she went with the two men to a building. She

could feel her nerves tightening as they approached the door. It was possible that the talk of animals had been a trick. That Mercer had sold her for another purpose. But the smell as they entered reassured her, as did the animal sounds which rose in the rank air. Mercer led them to a cage at the back. He gestured at the inhabitant.

"Lereyne tigerbat. The brute's gone into a decline and I paid high. Get in there and rouse it, make it eat."

Laris sucked in a silent breath and bit down on a grin. The tigerbat had a very nasty reputation on its home world which was quite justified. Tigerbat swarms had stripped humans to the bone in minutes, even through reinforced clothing. In swarm, the beasts had no fear and would continue the attack despite heavy losses. Lereyne settlers had almost wiped them out over three generations and now they were seldom seen, although the stories remained.

But somewhere along the line, she didn't quite recall where or when, she'd learned to read. Old Plaistrin had owned quite a library on other-world beasts. He'd loved to talk too, and he'd been both fond of his merchandise and knowledgeable. She'd read and listened, soaked up everything she could. She knew something about the tigerbats. She glanced around. The two men shifted to block her path and she snorted.

"I'm not trying to run. I want a brush."

Dedran looked blank. "A brush? What kind of brush?"

"A grooming brush," Laris snapped. She saw one tossed on the top of another cage and reached. Dedran allowed it. With the brush secured she turned back and looked at the door.

"Am I supposed to walk through plasteel bars or something?"

Dedran's look halted Mercer even as he snarled and drew

back his fist. "No, I want to see this. If she's as good as she thinks she is I want her in one piece."

He swung the door open and his eyes were amused. "In you go, Gracious Lady. You leave once that brute has eaten—you or its food, I don't much care which."

Laris ignored him, stepping quietly toward the huddled animal. It whimpered quietly in its sleep. Tigerbats were swarm animals. To keep one alone was to watch it die of loneliness, something Dedran appeared to be unaware of. Moving slowly and quietly Laris swept the brush down the matted fur. She worked gently, untangling the long pelt, grooming until the tigerbat lifted its head to stare at her. Then she took up a piece of the meat. The tigerbat opened its mouth, revealing the massive fangs within. But the feeling it gave off to her was one of pleasure. One had come to relieve its solitary state. One who groomed the matted fur as a swarm member should.

As the men waited she fed the animal until it had eaten enough. She knew she must not overfeed one which had not eaten well in too long. She returned to the grooming while the tigerbat lay there blinking blissfully. When she stood it moved to cling to the bars, wings furled over its narrow shoulders. Yellow eyes watched her hopefully.

She patted it. "Don't worry. I'll be back, I think." Dedran nodded at her before turning to Mercer. He counted out credits into the camp boss's eager palm.

"She'll do."

The camp boss hurried away, leaving Dedran to look at Laris. "You know animals, it seems. What else do you know?"

"I can read an' write," Laris told him, watching his surprise. "I work hard. And I can keep my mouth shut an' my eyes an' ears open."

Dedran grinned briefly, a mere twist of his thin lips. "Then you may do well here. What do you read?"

"Books about animals. So's I can learn more about them."

He nodded thoughtfully. "I've got no objections to that. Do your work and when it's done you can access the library."

Dedran had been as good as his word. In the last four years Laris had read freely, more freely than her master had known. There were ways to earn a credit or two as the circus traveled. And ways on-planet to untraceably access information once one had those credits. With the war over, Dedran had purchased an old cargo ship, packed his beasts and staff within, and upped ship. Laris guessed he had other reasons beyond the claimed one of bringing entertainment to the human-settled planets. Sometimes they stopped so briefly they could manage only a handful of sold-out shows. Clearly they could have stayed at a profit, but they moved on. At other times they played to half- or quarter-filled houses and must have lost money, but they remained several weeks. It wasn't a large circus. There were some thirty beasts, many which were no bigger than a Terran dog. In fact, they had two of those who did an act with two Trastorian carra. Later the carra did a clown act with their trainer and the dogs often joined that as well.

Dedran saw to it that mostly the animals were decently fed, housed, and well-treated. On her own initiative Laris had taught herself and the carra a trapeze act. Dedran had been pleased with that and her hard work, so he rarely struck her. He wasn't as kind to the forty or so people who worked for him. Often they left when and as they could, and were quickly replaced. Some seemed merely to vanish with no prior word of their intent to depart.

Laris had swiftly seen that some of those who left were the

ones who talked too much, who nosed into Dedran's business. But not always. Once they began to travel there were frequently people who'd do anything to escape their world. Dedran would take them on, for a trip to the next. By that time they had to have worked out a dangerous act to perform. On the new world they would be expected to appear twice a day. Most took too many risks and died or were crippled. They would be left behind when the circus moved on.

But it was good business. The crowds came to watch someone die. Dedran took them on without pay until they had proved themselves. There were always two or three on the ship working hard between planets to earn a place. Over four years many of his staff had come and gone. Some others left because they would not bow to Dedran's blows. Laris had no option in that, so she remained. But the blows weren't that regular, and the food was good, the provided clothing respectable. The girl had grown and filled out. Still others came and went and she made no real friends. Laris knew only one other who'd been there longer than she. That one approached her now.

"Did we lose it?" His foot stirred the stiffening body.

Her voice was steady. "Of course. It was too damaged to survive."

"Yes. A pity. We needed it."

Neither said more but both understood that the damage mentioned had not been that to body alone. He took a container from his pocket and drank. The scent of oranges drifted to her; Laris kept silent. If Cregar wanted to preserve himself in Naranje that was his decision. Dedran never seemed to care. And for all he drank—and it was a lot—Cregar never became less than stolidly taciturn before others.

Once she'd tried to talk to him. She'd been with Dedran

only a few months, and watching Cregar she'd guessed he'd had training with animals. She'd asked about it and he'd turned to look at her, a terrible stare compounded of such rage and pain she'd never asked again. Over the years she'd watched him and wondered. He seemed to have no connection with beasts, no desire to touch or love, yet he knew the way they thought and would react. He was capable of training them to do things which appeared impossible.

He'd trained many of the animals they had now. And unlike humans, the animals did not hate or fear him. This new one had been brought in after midnight. Cregar had dumped it in a sack by her tent and woken her to tend it. He'd been a little drunk and a lot angry. He muttered about stupid fools who couldn't obey a simple order. Then he'd snarled at her to do what she could, and stamped away. She'd lost the fight. She ignored him as he stood drinking. She had to take the samples of tissue Dedran had ordered. She took them gently, mourning over the body.

Cregar was often away, traveling ahead of the circus. When he met up with them again he often brought a new beast. Those he brought rarely survived their abduction and always it was her job to care for them, take samples when they died.

In her reading she'd come across word of beast masters. Those who had the gift of communication with animals. Terra had taken and trained the human halves of the teams, and had bred genetically altered beasts to match with the chosen humans.

Laris suspected Cregar might have been a beast master once. What had happened, she did not know. She knew only that now he seemed always to be in pain, not of body but of mind. Both she and her cat could sense it dimly whenever Cregar was around. She finished taking her samples and struggled to lift the beast. The circus had a simple method of disposal.

The ship's engines were typical of older freighters. They had no real speed but were far cheaper to run than the newer models. Ideal for a circus with its tons of litter each day. They would run on any form of matter fed to them. This carcass would become atoms just as soon as she reached the ship. Laris suspected that a few people had gone the same way. She was sure she would have been one had she failed to pass the tigerbat test and been killed.

Cregar walked away. She glared after him. If he must steal these beasts couldn't he at least see to it that his hirelings took more care? Bad enough being snatched from their human, to whom they were bonded deeply. But this one had been brutally struck about the head and would likely not have survived those injuries. Nor had it wished to. She'd felt its pain, the emptiness, and guessed Cregar's men had killed the human. She swore bitterly under her breath as she carried the body to the ship.

According to her reading the beast master teams were few and far between. Maybe fifty had been trained at first. Another dozen or so in training had broken free before the final Xik thrust which had left Terra a smoking cinder. Most of the trained teams had perished in the hard fighting shortly before that time. But even the partly trained teams were bonded. That intimate emotional and mental connection was set before the physical training began.

In fact, with the later teams the bond had been set far more deeply than with those first used. It was an experiment which, Laris felt, had been folly. The novice teams were bonded until death, but they lacked the military training which would help them resist Cregar's attack. Thus it was that Cregar targeted them, but also for that reason that he lost beast after beast to the trauma of its master's death.

She shivered as she placed the animal in the matter chamber and activated the turntable. Dedran was determined to have live beasts from such a team. They had proved over and over that they could not use beasts from the trainee teams. She was afraid she could guess where his eyes would turn next. But surely there were none left of the trained teams which had fought and mostly died for Terra.

Behind her Dedran spoke. "Prepare for departure, girl. I won't be needing you and the cat after all. Get the cages in. We up ship tonight."

"We have a show booked for tonight. They'll talk if we cancel." She paused then added, "Do we want talk and attention drawn to us?"

His eyes narrowed thoughtfully. "True. All right. Start preparing after the show. We'll leave tomorrow morning as soon as we're packed up."

For a moment Laris wondered if this was the time to jump ship. But it wasn't a good planet on which to take that chance. Lereyne would be better. In her mind another's eyes opened and looked out on the bleak, chill landscape. Agreement came. There was always time to consider. But to act hastily could mean unnecessary suffering.

As she bustled about making ready for the show and then departure, Laris allowed that other to see through her eyes. Cregar didn't know how far they had come since Laris had found a tiny, shivering, starving cub three years gone on a world far off the beaten track. She'd taken the poor beast in, cared for him, loved him, and then found in him growing abilities which mixed strangely with the girl who loved him. Nowadays Prauo and Laris were useful to Dedran. The circus boss had many irons in the fire. They'd taken minute tissue samples from Prauo several times; Laris had been forced to permit that. But she smiled secretly on overhearing Dedran's rage.

"They can't produce anything. Damned beast we grow ends up mindless over and over. And it doesn't grow larger." He'd ranted on and Laris had slipped away in silence.

After that she'd carefully hidden other advances between herself and her friend. After his last growth spurt some eighteen months back Prauo had begun to be able to use her eyes. Not merely a bond, but a direct linkage. Shortly thereafter Laris had found she could do the same and see what the young cat saw. It had enabled them to please Dedran to a larger extent and he would suffer no interference by others in case his valuable asset was damaged beyond further use.

Laris did her show in the first half of the performance, a flamboyant turn on the trapeze with the carra. The act was half serious, half clowning, always skilled, and greeted as ever by loud laughter. Then she changed into a boy's costume and disguise to enter the tigerbat cage. Dedran had found four more of the creatures in the intervening years but her special friend was the oldest and largest of the tigerbats. He ruled the miniature swarm.

As part of her act they acted out a tiny play of a lad who found one of the creatures trapped and aided it. He was then rescued in turn when a swarm struck. Throughout her act there were gasps and cries from the audience. She finished, sent the tigerbats from the center cage, and turned to bow deeply. The applause was generous and Dedran nodded approvingly as he passed her. She'd been an excellent investment.

Laris watched as he ran lightly into the ring. She knew what he'd thought. She made sure he felt that way by keeping her head down, working hard, and being utterly discreet. What he did not know didn't hurt him. He did know of the small amount of quarter and half credits she had hidden in her cabin. Dedran would not have been pleased to learn that she had a far larger stack of credits saved about which he knew nothing. Enough to keep her and Prauo for many months at the subsistence level of most worlds should she decide to flee.

He'd have been still less pleased to know that she read as widely as she did. She regularly invested a credit here and there in unmonitored library access. Using her reading, overheard comments, newscasts, and the work Dedran sometimes required of Laris and her cat, she'd started to build a theory—that Dedran worked for the Thieves Guild. The war and destruction of two planets, the devastation of many others, had not been good for guild profits.

And even worse had been the patrol, a neutral force to monitor human-settled worlds and crewed often by ex-military and survey officers. It had been started soon after the human race had exploded outward. When war began it had been scaled back. In the three years since war's end though, it had grown again, and with such a reputation that even some worlds with races other than human asked for the patrol's intervention at times. As a result a trickle of people of other races were being accepted for patrol training. And the patrol did not like the Thieves Guild.

Laris changed to her ordinary clothing, spent time with Prauo, and then left reluctantly. She must begin the pulldown. She got it started but managed to disappear long enough to access a newscast. Her mouth stretched in an unpleasant grin.

No wonder Dedran had tried to call off tonight's performance. The headlines were screaming about a murder.

Since the murdered man had been not only an ex–beast master trainee but also the nephew of a very influential member of the government, the local surface patrol were out in force. Laris slid through the crowd and returned to her work thinking hard. She dared not let those here find the tissue samples. She'd be implicated. Dedran and Cregar would bribe their way free and up ship. She'd be the one left and blamed.

But she could not allow Dedran to know that she knew of the hunt. Nor could she hide the samples in any place which might alert him that she had other hiding places he had not found. She drifted onto the ship unobtrusively, retrieved the samples, and placed them on the matter turntable under a heap of cage cleanings. Then she went back to her work. It was close to dawn when spaceport security descended upon the *Queen of the Circus.* Whoever Dedran usually paid off, it hadn't worked this time.

They began at the entry port and worked forward using some instrument which they clearly expected would tell them if anything was to be found. Laris glanced at Dedran. His face was blank but his body language, to one who'd known him four years, bordered on desperation. He caught her eye questioningly. She allowed her lip to curl a fraction in reply. His tense posture slacked a fraction as he nodded at her.

She relaxed. Good. He'd accept the samples' destruction. It was what he wanted, given this over-thorough search. She opened the tigerbat cage as requested, persuaded the four to move to a second enclosure while security began to check the first cage. The fifth tigerbat caught her tiny hand signal. He spun on wing-knuckles and fled down the corridor. She raced in pursuit. They spun past the engine-room door; she slowed, glanced back, good, they were out of sight for a few seconds. Her hand shot out, palmed the door ajar, pressed a switch, and thumbed the door shut again.

Then she was back into their view and she moved up, cornering the animal at the end of the corridor. She pretended to strike him several times while he uttered pitiful cries. It was part of one of their acts and he trusted her. He cowered as he had been taught. Laris led him back to his cage. Security got to the matter chamber and found what they had found elsewhere— nothing. Laris breathed out. Their machine could find no trace of samples, now only component atoms. She watched them leave, Dedran ushering them politely. She'd have to admit what she'd done but she thought he'd accept the loss of samples at this time.

Chapter Two

Dedran was coldly furious, but not at Laris. His anger was reserved for those who'd taken his money and failed to keep port security from his ship. He'd lost the samples, and worse, the authorities were still suspicious of him even though nothing had been found. He raged at Cregar in a corner where only the girl could overhear.

"You deadglow, I wanted the man knocked out, unconscious, not killed. That way we could have had a live beast."

Cregar's voice was cold. "Don't be more stupid than you can help, Dedran. He was a beast master. Alive, you couldn't have hidden one of his animals from him anywhere. That's what being a beast master is."

"You could have left him injured. Head injuries would have stopped that."

Cregar snorted. "Fer Crats sake, Dedran. Injuries would have stopped it so long as he was sick. His uncle would likely have been even quicker to start searching with a half-dead nephew urging him on. And I can tell you somethin' else the doctors here would have told Uncle. That the boy would get better faster if the animal was found. And if we killed it and just took samples once they started searching, the boy would have felt it die. He'd have gone crazy. So don't call me names. You were the one who insisted we try here. I told you it was risky."

Laris saw Dedran glance around; she shrank back further into the tigerbat den. "Sure it was risky." Dedran's voice was lowered. "But you know who gives the orders. Want to argue with them?"

Cregar's reply was brief. "No."

"Right, then we try Lereyne. There's one of the original lot there. He was left with only two of his team and he recently lost a beast in some accident. The boss says we try now, before he loses the last one. There's another on Arzor and we do that next."

"Isn't that gonna be a touch obvious? Our ship lands on Meril and a beast master gets killed. Our ship lands on Lereyne, and a beast master's animal gets snatched."

It was Dedran's turn to snort. "No one's that stupid except you." He was half turned from Cregar as he spoke. He saw nothing, but Laris, peeping from the den saw the other man's face. If that was her, she wouldn't be talking to Cregar like that. The man was a killer and right now he'd like to kill Dedran. She drew back deeper into the den. If either knew that she was listening, her life wouldn't be worth a tenth credit.

Dedran continued. "The guild says that with all the fuss on Meril there's been a plan change. We go to Arzor for a few shows, get the lay of the land there. We'll go on to Trastor and set down there for a couple of months. We'll skip Lereyne until afterward."

Cregar nodded slowly. "And I go solo to Lereyne and Arzor and use local talent to help with the snatches."

"Smart man, you got it. And just so's the trail breaks, you leave when we lay over at Port Bhaiat on Yohal for a couple of days." He turned to leave. "An' this time do a proper job. No deaders behind you; in, out, and off-planet while the local yokels are still sucking their thumbs."

Laris drew back as far as she could, putting her eye to a crack in the den wall. Dedran walked away; Cregar was looking after him with a thoughtful look on his face. Laris had seen that kind of look in the camps. It was the slow, careful consideration of one predator wondering if he could, or if the time was ripe yet to take a competing predator down. She shivered. In her mind eyes opened and watched Cregar with her. A thought formed.

He waits. He may challenge when he returns if he has succeeded. That way he will bring good news to sweeten Dedran's death.

Laris was stunned. The touch of the mind was familiar but not the blurred mix of picture and emotion she usually experienced *Prauo?*

A feeling of laughter. *Who else, sister-without-fur?* The presence was gone again and she blinked.

After that she hurried through her chores and returned to her cabin. Prauo lay along one of the two bunks, great purple eyes surveying her with calm amusement. For a moment as Laris stood in the doorway it was as if the sight of him was new again. She admired the sharply delineated black-on-gold markings. Prauo's body was gold, lean, with long, thick fur. His face, tail, and legs were sheathed in shorter black fur and light purple eyes looked from the black mask of his face fur.

When Laris had found him he'd been the size of a half-grown Terran kitten. She'd assumed that's what he was, some mutant coloration of one anyhow. Four months he'd remained unchanged, then he'd taken to her bunk and appeared ill for several days. But during those same days he'd eaten and grown hugely. By the time that spurt of growth had halted he was some thirty pounds, long and lean with developing muscles and claws of which no tigerbat would be ashamed.

The second development had been unobtrusive: the ability to look through her eyes and allow her to see through his. That, she had been able to hide from Dedran and Cregar. The next growth spurt had again put weight on him. He'd attained a little over fifty pounds. And to her amusement he could slide through almost any small gap by flexing his shoulders together. Dedran had found a use for that, and for the odd sucker-pads which had opened from small round growths on each of Prauo's mid-leg joints.

The cat could climb even an overhanging plascrete or clearplas wall, and could slide through small gaps. He was intelligent enough to bring back anything of which he'd been shown a picture, just so long as he was bringing it back to Laris. She'd obeyed Dedran's orders on that. It was safer and it allowed them to build up their small savings. A Dedran pleased was a man who tossed her the odd half credit, a handful of quarter or tenth credits. It was these she saved in an obvious hiding place.

But the first time Prauo had been out with her he'd also brought back a cheek-pouch filled with full credits found while he hunted the item he'd been shown. He didn't find the coins every time, but often enough to build her savings to a respectable sum. And now, with Prauo's loot from that first haul, was hidden a rag-wrapped bundle of small pieces of jewelry. Nothing too large, too valuable. All unidentifiably mass-produced but easily sellable by a girl who appeared respectable and without bringing suspicion down on her.

That was something else Dedran had not discovered, that Prauo had cheek-pouches which he could keep tightly shut. He could eat and drink without revealing the items carefully stowed. The first time it happened Laris had been both surprised and amused. The big cat had shown nothing, returned with her, accepted food and drink while Dedran examined the stolen item with smug approval and then dismissed her. Once back in their cabin Prauo had made odd retching motions and deposited seven credits on her bed.

After that he rarely returned from one of their forays without offering her some small gift. She'd examined the pouches. They weren't large but they would hold a small Astran apple at need. Laris often wondered what purpose they served. She'd never seen Prauo use them except when they were out with Dedran. But they hardly could have appeared for that purpose. She looked at the big cat now and moved to sit by him, her hand scratching around his ears as he purred.

"So you've found something else you can do." It hit her then like a blow. He'd spoken in her mind. He'd been Prauo, her friend whom she loved. But he wasn't just a cat, he was an intelligent being. Her hand halted, fingers buried in the thick fur as she stared down at him. He looked up, purple eyes meeting her dark brown ones. He yawned widely, teeth closing with the snick of a steel trap.

"Prauo?" Her voice shook. Was he still her friend or would he change now, see her as unimportant?

His head thrust hard against her. *Never, sister-without-fur. We are kin. My life is yours. And besides,* the mind voice was warm with amusement. *How well do you think we should do if you appeared with me at some human office to say that this animal who lives in the circus is an intelligent being?

That it should have citizen's rights? Better that Dedran and Cregar do not know. In time one shall come who will understand and listen. Until then let us wait and be silent.*

Laris covered one of his paws with her hands. "That's smart. But listen, brother-with-fur. Do you remember anything now? Where you came from, how come I found you?"

Nothing. Only terror, then cold and hunger. So cold, so alone until you came. His head thrust into her hands.

She hugged him savagely. "Not alone, not ever again. We stay together so long as you want. We don't tell anyone what you can do. Maybe as you say, we find someone who'll listen and believe. After that who knows what will happen. But until then we keep silent."

That is wisdom, and on keeping silent, my sister, there is no need for you to speak aloud. One might overhear. Speak with your mind to mine. I shall listen.

Laris concentrated on forming words silently. *Like this?*

Exactly like that.

She muffled giggles in her hands. *It feels strange.*

You will come to find it natural and it is safer—for both of us. With that she could only agree.

Doesn't it feel odd, one day you can't understand what I say, the next you don't just know, you can speak to me?

I have always understood much. But now it is as if whatever muffled my mind is gone. Think of it as if you learned a new language. At first you must think of every word, understand only a little of what you hear. Then after a time you begin to think in that tongue. Words flow freely, understanding comes. It is so with me. I have been able to do this for many weeks but I wished to wait until I understood more.

Laris nodded. *I understand. And since you have learned now, there are things I would discuss with you.*

Purple eyes gleamed at her. *Cregar and his killing of beasts. Dedran and his links with the Thieves Guild. I have seen and heard much these past few weeks. Who hesitates to speak before an animal? More, Dedran hopes to use us for his own ends at Yohal. He came upon me in the corridor yesterday and talked to me of his plans.* The cat purred as Laris grinned.

If he knew what we know he would not have spoken so freely. But he did. He intends to steal plans. One on Yohal has discovered a way to secure knowledge more safely; it is an advance which will bring wealth and complications for the Thieves Guild. Therefore we are to steal the plans so the guild may be forewarned and find a means to break the codes on this new knowledge, so that they can sell or use it themselves.

Laris considered. If they failed in the task Dedran would be furious. If he guessed that the failure was deliberate he'd regard them as tools which had turned in his hand. Both of them would disappear and no one would ask questions. Best, then, that they succeeded. But best too, that they be ready. Once the beast masters on Lereyne and Arzor had been plundered the hunt would be up behind them.

Maybe she could aid that hunt. It might also be possible to turn Dedran against Cregar. If they killed each other she could escape in the confusion. After that who would notice or care that some bond-servant had vanished? Her bond would not last much longer. By the time they cleared the sector it would have less than half a year to run. She shared that thought with Prauo.

Your hoard grows. What if you bought yourself free? That too is something on which to think.

Laris blinked. It was indeed. Dedran would never agree, but if he was no longer alive, then her bond reverted to the government of whichever planet they were on when her bond-master died. With only five months to go few would wish to purchase it. And then too, she had a choice. Under the law on many worlds she might choose which of a number of bond-buyers she would accept once the original owner was gone. If she had the credit to buy herself free there were none who could prevent it.

Prauo's thought held savagery. *That is very well, sister-without-fur. I would have taken out the throat of that one before. Save that I would have been slain and you left little better off.*

Laris was practical. *He doesn't beat me, only hits me now and again. The food is ample and he obeys the law and clothes me well enough. Many bonded have far worse conditions. At least he does not use me as a woman.*

The cat snarled softly. *That is so,* he sent. *But I tasted his mind while I lay watching you as you talked together. I did not like the taste of his thoughts. You are valuable as a beast trainer; what if he persuaded you into an open bond which could be kept or passed to another?*

I would not sign.

There are those who would happily fake such a bond, and who would listen to you?

And then?

Your bond to the circus is over in less than one year. An open bond would keep you here until death claimed you, or if another paid high enough you could be sold on.

She saw the idea at once. *There are those who use beasts

to fight for amusement.* Her thoughts darted. Dedran had contacts, friends, power. He could take her to a place where officials would swear she had signed a bond herself. The circus boss knew she would never willingly train beasts for an arena, but once Dedran had an open bond he could sell her, the arena master would break her to obedience.

Thus far she'd been of more value as she was. She recalled his words to Cregar. The circus boss might be getting out, leaving to take up some place of power in the guild. What matter then if she was of no more use to the circus? He could sell her as a trainer, or kill her to see her mouth stayed shut. He'd kill Prauo before that. Dedran was no fool, he'd know he could never abuse her in any major way while the big cat lived.

Or worse, he could drug Prauo and sell him to some planetside zoo. Put him in stasis and take regular samples, try to clone more of him for thief training. In her mind she felt the cat following her thoughts.

Best we are gone before he decides that his time has come, the cat sent slowly.

Or if he is dead before that time. Then his plans die with him.

You think of Cregar?

He hates.

Then let us help that hate. But for now, best we sleep. Tomorrow there is always work to do. Laris smiled. That was all too true. They slept and with morning both moved toward their new plan. Subtly they strove to widen the breach between the men. Laris dropped half sentences, apparently repeating things Dedran had said to her. Prauo allowed Cregar to follow him twice, each time he warned his sister-without-fur. The second time it prompted an open quarrel.

Cregar was due to leave the ship when it landed in the morning. The beast master who had retired on Lereyne had teamed with a pair of wolves. One had died. Fortunately a genetech had arrived about that time, or so Dedran's contact reported. The man had successfully cloned a replacement beast from the body. He had gone on to build other wolves from tissue samples taken from both. Now Lereyne had a small pack of the animals in a large preserved wilderness area.

As the only wild Terran creatures the human-settled planet had, they were much prized. But there was a catch—the wolves in a beast master team were genetically augmented to be more intelligent. The authorities had not wanted a pack of those wolves freed, so the genetech had reverted his end-products back to ordinary wolves. Hence Cregar could not simply steal one of the pack, a far easier task. Instead he must steal away the only wolf left with team gene-augmentation.

Since the beast master lived on the outskirts of a large city, that meant many watching eyes. Cregar would have problems. Laris snickered quietly with Prauo after they overheard a discussion on the difficulties.

I hope he gets caught. He won't keep silent and take all the punishment. He'd spill on Dedran.

And the patrol descends on the ship, and us as well. Better Cregar returns and we can set him against Dedran. Now, when they are both about the ship, is a fine time. Cregar is one who holds a grudge well.

After that the maneuvers were complicated but ultimately successful. Laris mentioned to Dedran that she was worried about one of the carra. It had appeared sluggish when they practiced in the empty training hold. Perhaps she should ask Cregar to look at it. He trained so well. For that last comment she adopted a rather dumb and admiring voice and expression. Dedran, busier than usual with the landing, and annoyed by the look, snorted and spoke without thinking.

Prauo had trotted past Cregar, carrying something in his mouth. He was ordered to stop, to hand over his trophy. He'd given the human a smug defiant look and ignored the order. Cregar had pursued grimly. He arrived at the last curve of the corridor in time to hear Laris's suggestion and Dedran's savage reply.

"Cregar! High Command tossed him out. If he was that good he wouldn't have ended up taking my orders in a . . ."

Cregar exploded around the bend. "In a run-down circus in a broken-down ship, bossed by a man with a fat price on his head," he finished.

Dedran's eyes glittered. "I wouldn't talk about prices if I were you."

"Wouldn't you? Then perhaps I should talk about a man who pretends to be an owner when he's more of a hired hand."

Dedran opened his mouth to speak as his hand dropped to the stun gun at his belt. Then he saw Laris listening open-mouthed. Cregar's gaze followed.

"Get the kid out of here."

Dedran waved her to leave and she obeyed meekly—as far as the bend. Then she leaned on the bulkhead, sliding the nearest door open about a foot. But to her exasperation the voices around the bend had dropped to a vicious muttering. Still, from the tone it was no friendly conversation. She shut the door again and padded silently away along the corridor. The low snarl of the sounds followed her.

She busied herself in cleaning the tigerbat cage and jumped when Cregar spoke quietly.

"You watch yourself, lass. I may be a lot of what he claims

but I'm not a man to work the arenas." He gave her a half-grin as he walked away, leaving Laris gaping after him. Perhaps it had been because he'd heard her admiring him, she thought. Or perhaps he was merely enjoying spoiling Dedran's plans. For whatever reason he'd said it, he'd confirmed her own fears and Prauo's belief. She would indeed watch out.

They landed on Yohal and Cregar slid into the port-side crowd. He gave her a tiny nod as he went and she nodded back. It wouldn't hurt to keep him sweet. Prauo wouldn't be working with her in any act. Not when Dedran planned a theft. He wouldn't want anyone to notice the cat. But she rode in the opening procession, swung out on the trapeze with the carra, and acted out the tigerbat play.

The audience departed, leaving Laris to clean the cages and settle the animals in for the night. After that, in the ship lights she was surprised to notice men approaching the ramp. One look and Laris recognized their strut. These men had some sort of authority. They were used to obedience. She fled for Dedran, dropping into the slurred ship slang so any stranger who overheard would be less likely to understand.

"There's men coming, look like law 'a some kind."

"Crats, why now?" He moved quietly to the ramp door and looked around the edge of the opening. "Authority, maybe." He shrugged and strode down the ramp. "Can I help you, Honored Sirs?"

"Do you have a man named Jas Cregar aboard?"

"No, may I know why you ask?"

"That is not your business. We will look on your ship."

"Now, hold on there . . ."

His protest was cut short as one man produced a paper and displayed it. "We have the right. Step aside."

To Laris's bewilderment look was all they did. They asked no questions even when she made sure they would see her working. But she did notice something interesting. One had an earpiece. He glanced at a wrist dial now and again and she wondered if his asking for Cregar hadn't been a ruse, if they weren't looking for something else. If so, they didn't find it. They departed and Dedran stood on the ramp top wearing a thoughtful expression. She guessed he was wondering too. And what about tonight?

Chapter Three

Once the invaders were well and truly gone Dedran turned to Laris. "What did you see?" She recounted the earpiece and the impression that one had been spending too much time looking at a wristwatch.

"I thought I heard something too. So high it was more like an air vibration." She hadn't but Prauo had. He'd alerted her in the first place.

"A watch." Dedran understood. "I see." His voice came slowly, thoughtfully. "No, they don't make a sound like that and one doesn't keep looking over and over to see the time usually. Either they had a deadline—or that was not a watch." He stood a moment and spoke to himself, not the listening girl. "And why Cregar? They knew his name, what did they want with him? Maybe tonight would be dangerous." He turned briskly.

"Laris, wait here, see to everything. I must make a comcall."

She looked after him as he hurried down the ramp. This was becoming dangerous for her and Prauo, as well as Dedran. If she jumped ship here the authorities would probably pick her up at once. Something made her feel that while the officials might have left, eyes were still on her and the ship. Dedran didn't return until the setting up was complete. Then he had only time to fling a hurried word at her as he passed.

"Be ready after midnight."

She nodded meekly.

The performance was well received, the audience in this backwater enjoyed the novelty and afterward the crowds on the midway were in a spending mood. Optional extras or not, the circus would make money here if they didn't overstay their welcome. To make sure however, the sideshows had been set up and already the holograms danced and coaxed passersby to enter the curiosity tents. In the game tents barkers called the wandering crowds to roll up and try their luck. It was a charming scene—if one didn't know, as Laris did, that all the games were carefully rigged, and most of the curiosity tent attractions were cunningly faked.

Prauo's mind voice came to her as she moved in the shadows. *You were right. Others watch. There is a ring about us.*

Where is the nearest?

Walk toward the tigerbat cages slowly. Be casual. I will direct you. I cannot probe their minds but I can feel their attention like a light directed upon us.

She obeyed, wandering as if checking on the circus animals. Yes, a watcher there, and another further along. A third near the ramp noting all who came and went from the ship. She stretched, allowed her shoulders to slump wearily. Then she plodded up the ramp. Once out of sight she trotted in search of Dedran.

"There're spies outside. They're watching everyone."

His face twisted in fear and fury as she spoke. Then he fought for calm. "Well done. But I must get out of here again for an hour or so. Let no one know I've left." He considered. "Go to the tent of Good Fortunes. Set it up so that it blocks the alley between beast cages. The carra have the end cage, do they not?"

"Yes." She saw his plan and grinned, a quick flicker of amusement.

"Well? Hurry, girl. Hurry!"

Laris did so, appearing back down the ramp minutes later with two of the men carrying a light tent and a large case. She'd done this before, usually to take messages for Dedran—the sort of message he didn't want others to know he was sending or receiving. Not that she was able to read them, of course. Dedran wasn't that silly. He trusted her more than most, which was to say, only a little.

She oversaw the setting up of the tent and dismissed the men. Then she vanished inside. Moving swiftly she unfolded the table, placed the crystal ball on the tabletop and laid out the cards. From a pocket in the case she retrieved a long brilliant robe, wig, face veil, and several other items. She donned the wig and clothing then moved to the door to place a sign at the entrance. It took little time before seekers after knowledge began to drift her way.

For several hours she told fortunes, amused the customers with her wit and insight. Three years back a real teller of fortunes had traveled with the circus. Shiira had an empathy rating and had been very good. In Laris she'd detected another who could read the emotions and hopes flung at a teller of fortunes. She'd liked the child and quietly, patiently, she'd taught Laris all the girl could learn. Shiira had left after a few months. Her abilities had warned her it was best to be gone, and she had listened. Fortunately she had said nothing of Laris's small talent to Dedran.

Almost a year later when Dedran had needed a back door

Laris had suggested she become a fortune-teller. It had worked that time, and other times subsequently. Moreover it was a useful supplement to the circus income at leaner times. After all, Laris was a bond-servant and the money she made went into circus coffers. However, to Dedran she was merely a good talker giving the fools what they wished to hear. She talked on until midnight had come and gone. Then a man paced into the tent.

She knew the feeling of Dedran but he would not be pleased to know it. He'd donned the mask and the light, toe-to-throat coverall worn by members of the Casran sect, an offshoot of the main religion on Yohal. The watchers would still suspect. The disguise was too basic. Too obvious. She went into her routine and was hushed.

"Enough. It's Dedran. Now, do you have the things?"

She produced the items she'd laid aside ready. He stripped coverall and mask then settled the wig and overcoat into place. Quick strokes with plastiflesh stick, a lightening of his eyebrows, contacts slipped in, and he was a different man. It had taken only minutes and thus far she'd taken care to give each fortune seeker a good long fortune. The watchers, if any had concentrated on her, were already used to seeing those who entered stay for a length of time.

Dedran raised the rear of the tent, moved out unobtrusively, and hurried down the narrow alley between cages. Laris watched. He slipped through a panel at the back of the carra cage and would emerge unobtrusively on the other side. The watchers would start to wonder when he did not reappear but she'd dealt with that too. A short time later one of the women scratched at the tent back. Laris lifted the material. The woman walked in, donned mask and coverall, and left openly through the front of the tent.

Let the watchers see that, and not know the person they had seen enter Laris's tent was not the same person as had just departed. The sect's costume had been of use to Dedran before now—and had likely been useful as a disguise to many involved in both intrigues and other acts, Laris thought. The Casrans were an equal opportunity sect. To that end, while light, the coveralls were designed to hide any gender differences. One never knew if one spoke to male or female until the one addressed replied. Even then, most who'd belonged for any length of time had been trained to speak in a flat neutral voice which made it hard to tell male from female. Laris shared her thoughts with Prauo.

All that is true, furless-sister. But what interests me more is Dedran's errand. And why those men sought Cregar.

Laris told another fortune while mulling over those questions. She was interrupted by giggles outside. Someone speaking in accented one-speech was insisting that she be taken inside to learn her fate. The hair on the back of Laris's neck rose. She could feel danger here. The voice sounded like that of a young flighty girl, indulged, spoiled, and from some rich planetside family. But there were undertones only Laris, and through her, Prauo, could detect.

Leave, sister, quickly. Go openly before they enter.

Laris leapt for the tent entrance. All her instincts were shouting that she should not allow herself to be trapped inside where none could see. She was barely in time. Her slender body brushed past the girl who would have entered and the girl staggered sideways with a gasp. Laris caught only an impression of her. Apparently young, richly dressed—and with the most coldly vicious, experienced eyes Laris had ever seen.

The man with her matched well. If he wasn't heavily

armed, then Laris was a carra. He appeared young and from some wealthy provincial family but his eyes too did not match the outward picture.

Strip your veil, Prauo sent. *Make them believe they are dealing with a child.*

Laris paused to wipe her forehead as she stood outside the tent. She removed the veil, lightened her voice, and shifted her stance to the slightly angular hip-shot way of standing of a younger girl.

"I apologize, Gracious Lady, Honored Sir. But I am weary, the tent grows stuffy, and I feel unwell."

The girl surveyed her. The air was one of spoiled irritation but the eyes showed only calculation. "I wanted my fortune told. I demand it. That's why you're there, isn't it? Tell her, Baris. I'm the Lady Ideena, and it'll pay for her to do what I want."

Laris concentrated, letting her body sag a little, her voice waver. "I'm sorry, Lady. But I really do feel unwell." From the corner of one eye she could see Dedran approaching, or at least someone who looked the way he had when he had departed her tent. She raised her voice, thinning it to a more childish note.

"I feel siiick. Oooo!" She retched realistically.

Dedran had slipped behind a cage. He wouldn't want this pair—whoever they were—to get their hands on her too long in case she talked. His current disguise would take only minutes to remove. She must play for time. The man took hold of her shoulder.

"If you feel sick then you should go back inside your tent, my dear. You can lie down in there. We'll stay with you. Maybe you'll feel better after a while." Somehow Laris doubted that. She doubled over, holding the tent rope in a ferocious grip against his urging hands. Her voice came out in a piercing wail.

"I feel so sick." She swallowed again and again, forcing her stomach to react. She'd eaten only a couple of hours earlier. One of the circus women had brought her the food and the portion had been generous. It was always easier to be sick on a full stomach. She swallowed again. Where was Dedran? They were beginning to attract attention but the grip on her shoulder hurt. The girl, hands screened by their bodies, was trying to make her let go of the tent rope.

Laris felt her fingers pried loose one by one. They'd have her in a minute. She wailed again. Her stomach finally cooperated and she was lavishly sick over the girl's expensive cloak. The girl snarled.

"Get her into the tent, Baris. There's gossip about this outfit and I want to find out all I can. There could be credits in it for us."

A voice came just as Laris was running out of strength. "Gracious Lady, Honored Sir. May I aid?" Dedran moved to block the tent entrance.

Laris took her cue. "Oh, Master. I'm so sorry. Maybe it was something I ate, an' the tent being so hot. I came out to get air an' these gentlefolk wanted their fortunes told. I was afraid if I went back inside I'd be sick but they kept pulling at me, an' then I really was sick and now they're mad at me . . ." She let her voice—which had gradually become louder, attracting the attention of many close by—trail off into childish sobs.

Dedran drew himself up. "I apologize for my bond-servant. But she is very young."

"Too young to be in bond, surely?" The man's tone was acid.

Dedran raised his eyebrows, lying smoothly. "On Meril one

may set a bond providing the servant is ten. And the girl has only been with me two years." His voice became silky. "If it is any of your business. It is not I who has been frightening the child."

Laris swallowed a grin. She'd been bound on Kowar where the bond age was sixteen. Although it was true Meril permitted a far lower age. And she'd been with the circus more than two years. But then she'd also been bound earlier than the law allowed. Oh, what a tangled web was being woven. But that precious pair had just noticed that people were gathering, drawn by the commotion and raised voices. They wouldn't like that much public attention, she was sure. They didn't. Her would-be abductors were muttering explanations and allowing the crowd to close about them until they were gone.

"Who were they?" Dedran hissed.

"They called themselves Baris and Lady Ideena," Laris hissed back.

He nodded, apparently recognizing the names. "Scavengers seeking pickings and information. Scavengers—with a touch of the tigerbat," he added as he helped her with mock solicitousness to walk toward the ship. "What did they ask you?"

"Nothing. They just tried to get me back into the tent. She said there was gossip and where there was talk there were credits."

Dedran grunted. "She'd be the one to hear any talk too. Crats! Have we drawn the attention of every nose on a dozen planets?" He focused on Laris. "You'd better not be really ill. We've a job to do tonight still." She gasped. That was madness with so many watchers. He shrugged.

"I know. But there's no choice. We do it tonight. I've been given a security-breaker and copier. It will take time but should break the security coding and copy the information. Then you can put the target back in place and no one will know. We leave in a couple more days and they won't know what happened." He snickered. "Not until they find copies of their fancy protections being sold all over."

Laris hesitated to argue but she had to say something. It would be Laris he turned on and her at risk. "Surely they'd have the information protected by their own new codes."

He chuckled harshly. "It should be. But money buys favors. It bought that one. There's an assistant who thinks he should be more."

"Then why doesn't he just sell the information?" She'd noticed that he seemed to be talking freely and she chilled. That wasn't a good sign.

"None of your business, my dear. You and your clever cat just get the thing to me outside. I copy it, and you return it." His fingers dug into her arm as he shook her slightly. "Understand?"

"Yes," Laris muttered.

"Good. I'll have the tent packed up. You go and sleep, eat something but not too much. We don't want you being sick in the wrong place." He laughed and pushed her toward her cabin. "Go on. And be ready in a couple of hours. I won't want to waste time."

She nodded, trudging for her cabin. She liked none of this and danger signals were nudging her harder and harder. She slid her door aside and joined the big cat where he sprawled comfortably on the bunk. No one could hear anything but within the cabin the two were at once engaged in intense discussion.

They came to no conclusions, only questions. Who were

the searching men, why did they ask for Cregar, and for what were they searching? Then there were Baris and the Lady Ideena. Dedran said they were scavengers. Presumably they'd have asked questions of Laris. But what would they have wanted to know? Were they members of the Thieves Guild and if so, did they have any standing? If they did, how high was it in comparison to Dedran's status?

They considered that for some time. There'd always been thieves, even on Terra. When Terrans broke into space, thieves had gone with them. Gradually they'd organized into a guild which now stretched across the settled planets. They had their own organizational structure—that much was known by ordinary people who kept their ears open for the gossip, although little else about the shadowy group was public knowledge. It was known that the guild had a system which allowed the more important members to be recognized by their own people on any human-settled planet. That, Laris believed, applied to Dedran, which suggested in turn that either he himself was important, or that he was commanded by one who was of power in the guild.

Finally, tired out, girl and cat slept. The alarm woke both at three A.M. planet time. Yohal's rotation being slower, there were still some six hours until daylight. Laris yawned, stretched, and sullenly climbed into a dark blue jumpsuit. Prauo trotted silently beside her as she left her cabin. Dedran was waiting, dressed in a dull dark-green coverall. One side of it bulged slightly and from the way one hand shifted Laris was sure he was carrying a stunner as well.

He made for his cabin again, locked the door, switched on a light, and dropped down a desktop. On that he laid out plans and several gadgets. Laris had grown used to using the items and to learning plans within minutes. Once he'd finished the explanation she asked only one question.

"Security in the area?"

"All taken care of. Now, come with me and don't speak again until I say you can. No matter how long that may be." He beckoned and set off toward the ramp.

She and the cat fell in behind obediently. They traveled in silence until they reached a hovercab stand. The cabs were robotic and accepted tokens. Dedran signaled her to remain silent as he fed tokens into the fare slot. The cab lifted, and they were on their way. Some twenty minutes later they arrived, exited, walked around a corner, climbed into a second cab, and rode again before finding another. They left the third cab and went on foot a while before Dedran halted at a corner.

From one pocket he took a small rod and extended it to a right angle. Placing his eye against one end he peered in. "Right, be ready." He waited, "Wait . . . wait . . . now, around the corner." Laris obeyed. He pointed to a wall cloaked in heavy shrubbery around the base. "Into there, now." She scurried into hiding, Prauo close on her heels. Dedran paused, looking out over the street. All was quiet and empty. On a post above them a scanner revolved slowly.

Laris had noted that in one swift glance as she dived for cover. It was slower than those normally used to cover the wealthier residential streets. It also seemed to halt in its circuit earlier and return. It looked as if the last part of the missing arc would have covered the house wall. Now it didn't. She guessed someone had been here before them. Some kid working his passage for the guild by slowing and aborting a portion of the scanner's movement.

But there was no time to think about that. She had to keep

her mind on the job. Prauo was scaling the wall, a fine rope trailing behind him. He reached the top, folded his shoulders together, slid between bars barely a hand's length apart, then walked briskly around one to anchor the rope. His mind voice reached her.

Climb, sister-one. None stir here.

She climbed, leaving Dedran below. Once balanced on the window ledge she was able to cut the center bar and bend it outward. She slid adroitly through the narrow gap and joined the waiting cat. Her hand smoothed the ruffled fur over his shoulders.

Just as well for us that Yohal has little of the inner world's technology. Their security is laughable.

Not so laughable that they cannot invent the thing we seek.

Having technology and having brains are different things.

She felt his amused agreement as they moved silently through the building. Dedran had shown her a plan of the place. It was simplified but it had all she needed to find the safe. A small instrument given to her before she climbed would deactivate the alarm. She had the security codes after that. The guild would hold their stolen knowledge until the new invention was in widespread use. Then, little by little they would sell the code-breaker.

They would make millions of credits from the sale, garner a hundred favors owed. This theft of the breaker's plans and technology, if successful, would probably gain Dedran more guild status. If he failed it might gain all three of them an early, unlabeled, and unlamented grave. Laris moved more carefully. She'd gain nothing from a successful theft but she had no desire for the possible results of a theft foiled by discovery.

Ahead the big cat moved on silken silent paws. They accessed the safe without difficulty once it was found. Laris shivered with nerves the almost sixty minutes it took to crack the technology and make the copy. With all the information safely in her hands she returned it, closed and re-coded the safe. Then, she carefully reset the alarm.

Half done. She moved quickly back through the building. Hissed the all-clear to Dedran and climbed through the window bars. With the miniature heat device she re-welded the bar shut; below, Dedran was waiting when she descended the rope. Together they watched as the scanner circled slowly, halted, returned, and set off again.

"Now." They trotted quickly around the corner into the darker alley. Laris heaved a sigh as they reached it in safety. No alarm. With luck they'd be home free. It seemed they were, since in another hour they were drifting, darker shadows among shadows in a deserted circus ground, up the ramp to their respective cabins, and still in silence.

After that Laris waited. The performances went by, there was no sign of Baris and Ideena and after another week of ordinary events the circus's ship requested takeoff clearance. It was granted casually. They lifted from Yohal and no one below was the wiser that the departing ship was now worth a million times its previous value.

Chapter Four

The circus landed on Arzor with the minimum of official fuss and the maximum glare of publicity. Not since the half-forgotten days before the war had there been such an event. Some of the oldest families at Arzor Port liked to consider themselves sophisticated. But sophistication is in the eye of the beholder. It pleased the first-ship families to decide that a traveling circus was sophisticated and to have their entire families attend in their best clothing.

With them, as Dedran had expected, came the beast master here. Laris was watching when they arrived.

"Is that them?"

Occasionally Dedran enjoyed showing off what he knew. "Yes, see. The man at the end with the woman. That's the beast master and his wife. His name is Hosteen Storm and she is Tani."

"Who're the others with them?" Laris was peering at the distant figures with fascination.

"His stepfather and younger half-brother. Storm only joined the family after the war. He was raised apart. But the stepfather is from a first-ship family. He doesn't make a parade of it but there's some wealth and a lot of influence there." He studied her briefly. "I'd have no objections if you spoke to them. With you handling the animals here they may well wish to talk with you." His fingers bit into her arm. "Just be very careful what you say, my dear. We wouldn't want them to be warned in any way, would we?"

"No, of course not. I'll be careful."

But he'd put the idea into her mind and she thought about it all through the performance. She gave it up reluctantly. If Dedran thought she'd let anything slip it would be her body on the turntable; what would Prauo do then? Even as her mind flew in search of ideas she soared on her trapeze. The carras soared with her, tumbling like the happy beasts they were, whirling about her, clowning to her serious act so that Arzor Port alternately gasped at her skill and laughed as the carras foiled her attempts to be a serious artist time and time again.

She caught glimpses of the family as she swung. They were laughing as hard as anyone, all but the beast master and even he wore a half-smile. Somehow it pleased her, that they should admire her. She pushed her act to the edge and brought gasps from below. She ended the performance by dropping lightly from the trapeze to land bouncing in the safety net, the carras dropping with her, chittering merrily.

The family was clapping for her as she swung down, to turn, bowing to the audience. She scampered with the beasts from the ring and Dedran watched her take up the carras. That had been an interesting display. The girl had pushed safety to the limits and given an act that had brought the audience halfway to its feet in horror and then applause. But how much of her daring had been a determination to show her skill before a beast master, Dedran wondered.

His mind paused at that thought before following the path. How much had been admiration for beast master skills?

Maybe a desire to see the man's animals remain where they were? Dedran was not a fool. He knew the girl was more and more unhappy over the stolen animals that died. So was Cregar. Could it have been one of them who had brought down those spies from the authority, and later, Baris and Ideena, upon the show? He'd have to think about that. Cregar and Laris could be replaced. Not easily on the part of the man but for the girl, there was the De Pyall camp where he'd first found her.

His lips twisted into a sneer. In a refugee camp there were always those who'd take any job, accept any condition to be free of the place. He'd known the girl's fears. But she'd still followed him. Signed a false closed bond and held to it. His glare became a scowl. He hoped to leave the circus behind if his patron's plans worked out well. He would take the girl—someone with her skills was worth real credits to arena buyers if he faked her signature on an open bond. He had to be careful there. Between officials, the patrol, and do-gooders who checked on bond-servants, he dare not make the wrong move. Not yet. But the closed bond under which he held her did not allow the bond's sale to someone else. An open bond would permit that.

He wanted the money he could get for her. But the guild had no time for what its members wanted. He had a job to do and until it was completed he dare not take time for his own wishes. Not that it mattered anyway. There were months yet before her bond was completed and where would she go then? No, she'd sign for another year. Surely by that time he'd have taken a few live beasts. He must.

A small shiver ran down his spine. The guild was becoming impatient. The latest message from his patron had indicated that Dedran's position could be in danger if he didn't produce something soon. And the guild had a simple way of seeing that an out-of-favor member told no tales. The lean man shivered again as he ran into the ring, spinning to bow and garner the audience's attention in his upraised hands. Cregar had better not fail or it could be the death of all of them.

He switched off his thoughts, concentrated on the clapping fools around him, and signaled the next act. He had a show to give and that too was part of it. Lull the idiots, then strike. He'd use the girl to open a gap in beast master armor. She was quick. She'd make friends. Then return to give him what Cregar needed to take the animals once the circus was safely away. He settled to the whirl of acts about him.

Laris came on again in her boyish guise as the tigerbat cage was pushed in and connected to the larger cage where she'd display their play. Her old friend was first out and she saw the crowd stiffen. She faced it, then turned her back as it ran on its wing-knuckles to lie on the ground, pulling the light branch across its lower body.

She turned back, miming her shock, her fear at the sight of the deadly beast—and tigerbats were deadly, in that there was no fakery. To the Terran eye they looked like an amalgam of tiger and large bat, hence the name. They stood some five feet tall, and one on the attack appeared to be all reaching teeth and long sickle-like claws. They'd been a horror to the settlers on their original world, although by now they had been almost wiped out there. Still, enough people on other worlds had seen depictions of them and their depredations to know how truly dangerous they were.

Laris mimed her fear, showing to the crowd then her growing realization that the savage beast was trapped and no threat to her. She was triumphant, raising her weapon to kill, then slowly finding sympathy for the injured beast, freeing it, and standing to watch it dart away.

In the front ringside seats, a ranger leaned over to speak to Storm. "He's clever, but aren't those things dangerous?"

"Dangerous enough alone and lethal in a major swarm. I doubt they'd have that here. A real swarm has a hundred members or more."

The man returned to his seat and Storm concentrated. Beside him he could feel Tani doing the same as her hand slid into his. Her whisper came to his ears alone.

"That's the girl from the trapeze act, isn't it?" She caught his nod. Her senses extended to touch the animal in the cage. "Friendship. It trusts her. She is kind."

"How many of them?"

"I feel five, no more."

Storm nodded slightly. That was the number he could feel as well. Enough to tear the girl to pieces in seconds if they attacked in swarm-rage. But he sensed no anger. Only anticipation, enjoyment. They liked what they would do. He watched the act. It was clever. The whole tiny play was a timeworn idea, the person who saves an animal only to have the beast save them in turn. But it was well done and tigerbats could be genuinely lethal to the person who acted with them. She was skillful. From his ringside position he could sense that she was in no danger from these.

She took her bow and the tigerbats ran down the tunnel to the smaller cage. It was rolled out and the carras returned with two Terran dogs to put on a clown show which had everyone laughing as the main cage was swiftly dismantled and removed.

Storm and Tani came out after the performance still smiling. His father looked at him in resignation.

"I suppose you want to see the girl and her animals. Go on then. I'll get a ride with Put Larkin. He'll drop me off. It's a fine night. I can walk down our road."

Tani fidgeted and Storm gave one of his rare smiles. "It looks as if I should. Tani wants to see the animals." He glanced at Logan, his younger half-brother. "And I suppose you do too?"

"Darn right." He showed off a little. Storm and Tani weren't the only ones who could see through a disguise. "Except that it's the girl I'd like to see. Anyone who can sit around in a cage full of tigerbats and look casual is someone worth meeting."

Tani giggled. "She isn't bad looking but don't you think she's too young for you?"

Logan flushed. "I think she may be older than she looks, and anyhow, I'd just like to see her act again. She's good." His voice went up enthusiastically. "Did you see her on that trapeze?"

Tani nodded. "She was good. You're right. And I loved those little animals with her in that act. Storm?" She turned to her husband. "What were they?"

"Carras. They're a bit like Terran monkeys, aren't they? They have similar habits too, but nicer natures." His voice lowered. "What did you sense from them?"

"Pleasure," Tani said softly. "They like the girl and they enjoy their act with her. They were having fun in that clown act too. They aren't abused, Storm. They're working for the fun of it and the food treats."

Her husband nodded. It was something Kelson, head of the ranger group, had asked them to find out. He looked down at Tani. They'd been married only a few months and he was still a little incredulous at his good fortune. After so long walking alone save for his beast master team he'd never thought he'd find someone who would slip into place with them all. But Tani had. She was not officially trained but her gifts were, if anything, a little stronger than his own.

Her team, together with his group, had been left at the main Quade ranch. Tani wanted to walk the animal cages, study their inhabitants, and maybe arrange to take samples from some of them to send on to the interstellar ark her aunt and uncle ran. It preserved species against permanent destruction and the Terran dogs should be immortalized in its tissue-sample banks.

They made their way slowly through the crowd. It was a good-natured bunch here this evening, Storm thought. But then with some of the port VIPs present, the rangers and security were also out. Few of even the most enthusiastic brawlers would be silly enough to start trouble here. Tani danced ahead and his face softened again as he watched her. It had been barely six months since the end of Arzor's problem after Xiks had seeded the deadly flesh-eating swarms of clickers in Arzor's lands of the Big Blue.

He knew she still had nightmares sometimes about the clickers and no wonder. He had a few himself. But Tani had almost recovered from the trauma the clickers had caused her. Last week she and Storm had been off hunting with the Djimbut tribe of the Nitra, the Arzoran natives with whom Tani had made such firm friends while she and Storm sought out the origin of the clickers. The swarms had slain natives and settlers alike and in the end, both peoples had combined to destroy them. Tani and her beast team of coyotes and Mandy the Ishan paraowl had accounted for a full bag of grass hens on the hunt last week.

Storm's team had remained at home. Surra, his dune-cat, was in heat. She had not become pregnant last time. But this time he was sure she would. After that she'd bear the first dune-cat cubs to appear in the three and a half years since Terra's destruction. Baku the African eagle might take longer to produce her eggs. But she'd accepted the mate Tani had given her from the ark's tissue samples. Hing, the meercat, had had no scruples about a mate. She'd taken one look at the male offered and accepted him with churring approval.

The meercat group of Hing, her new mate, her four adult offspring, and their mates, were producing a meercat population explosion just at present. Not that this was a problem. The all but extinct Arzoran rinces had occupied an important ecological niche on the planet, since it was they who helped keep several desert species of large insect and small lizard under population control. They also ate the eggs of the big solitary venomous yoris lizard, when they could tease a female from her nest in safety.

The rinces had almost died out after human settlement and a rince plague which followed two generations later. Even scientific intervention had failed to improve their survival rate. The meercats were moving into the rince niche and doing it in style.

Hosteen loved to see them. After so long without a mate Hing was making up for lost time. The original group with added mates had been ten. All had mated and produced so that now the group numbered almost thirty. Normally only the dominant female would have bred, but this time at least, they had been encouraged to ignore custom.

Hosteen and Tani had chosen a second site for a meercat home. Once the babies were adult they'd move half of the group there. Later the meercats would move on to form their own new groups. In time they'd spread across Arzor's desert lands. Both settlers and natives would approve of that; the yoris were having a population explosion of their own and needed the meercats to cut back on the big lizard's numbers.

Up ahead of him he felt a surge of excitement from Tani. She turned to beckon him. He reached her and looked in the cage. He blinked as he studied Prauo.

"What on Arzor is that?"

"I thought you'd know."

Logan joined them. "What's that?"

Hosteen snorted. "I've seen many animals but not that one." He studied the longer gold fur, the gleaming black of the shorter, plusher fur that clad the creature's legs, face, and tail. "I really don't know. It's beautiful but I'm certain I've never seen one like it before. I wonder where it came from."

Laris had been listening quietly, unobtrusive around the cage corner. She allowed herself to be seen as the question was asked. The younger man saw her and nudged his brother. The three of them turned to look at her. Prauo was in her mind.

Good scent, he said sleepily.

Don't distract me. They're the kind who'd notice. Aloud she spoke politely. "You like my cat, noble visitors?"

Logan spoke first. "He's beautiful. None of us have ever seen one like him before. Were did he come from?"

"Fremlyn," Laris began.

The other man cut in. "I've been to Fremlyn. They don't have an animal like this."

Laris eyed him coolly. "I never said they did. I said he came from Fremlyn. Where his home world is, none of us know. I found him as a tiny starving cub when the circus was there. He was on waste ground at the edge of the port. He's been with me now for a long time. For all I know he was some experimental beast and has no breed."

The girl grinned. "My name's Tani, this is Storm, my husband, and Logan, his brother. I'm pleased to greet you."

Laris nodded. "I'm Laris. You seem to know animals?" Her tone was a question.

Tani laughed softly. "Storm is a beast master, if you've ever heard of them."

"I've heard." Laris closed her mind tight.

Logan smiled. "You should have been one as well," he said cheerfully. "That act with the tigerbats was wonderful. But the stuff on the trapeze had my heart in my mouth." He laughed suddenly. "When that carra caught onto your foot just as you swung, I've never seen anything so funny."

Laris found she was smiling too, seduced into verbal carelessness by the honest praise. "It's part of the act but they enjoy it so much. Sometimes we just add in bits. Everyone does. Particularly if we need to stretch the acts because one's missing."

Tani looked interested. "What act was missing, what happened to it?"

"Nothing much." Darn, it was Cregar who was absent and she shouldn't have mentioned it. She covered quickly. "The trainer has a bad cold. He's resting until he gets over it. He doesn't want to give it to anyone else."

Storm said nothing but he'd heard enough lies in his time to know one when it was thrust at him. So did Tani. She changed the subject with more admiration and speculation as to Prauo's origins. Laris could lose herself in that very happily. But she was careful to suggest nothing of the big cat's other talents. These people weren't fools. She thought that Storm had guessed her to have been less than truthful over the missing act she'd carelessly mentioned.

She showed them around the other beasts, accepted an invitation to eat with them, and found she was enjoying herself. It had been so long since she'd had free time. Afterward she returned alone and walked toward her cabin. Prauo's mind voice broke into her thoughts.

Dedran waits for you. His mind churns. With that warning she did not jump as she rounded the corridor bend to find the man waiting. She took the initiative swiftly.

"I've made friends with them as you asked. I think I can get them to invite me to their ranch in a day or two. How hard do you want me to push this?"

His posture relaxed a little. "Don't be obvious. But as quickly as you can apart from that."

Laris wanted to keep him pleased with her. Perhaps the possibility of more information would do that. Technology had advanced in the ten generations since Terrans had first settled another planet. She remembered where she had seen one of the tiny card-sized voice and picture recorders. One of those could tape some five hundred hours of recording, for replay on a larger machine.

"What about taking one of the mini recorders? Cregar had one I could use if he's left it behind."

She saw the last tensions leave his body. "Too dangerous. If they spotted it they'd ask questions. Do nothing to alert them. If they ask you to stay a few days, you may. Don't tell them you're a bond-servant either. I want you to get a look at their security precautions if they have any. See as much of their land as you can."

"I want to take Prauo."

His body tensed again. "Why?"

"Because they're interested in him. The girl wants tissue samples." Dedran snickered at that but said nothing. "And I can use him to check out security more thoroughly. They'll think it natural I have him. The man's a beast master, remember. He's inclined to believe that someone with an animal is more trustworthy." She wasn't at all sure that was true but Dedran would believe it. He did.

"Very well. Prauo can go with you if they ask you to visit and if they're happy with that. In the morning you can drop the news that I've decided to stay a while longer. We'll be performing here for a couple of weeks. After that I plan to rest the animals and performers several more weeks before we leave. See those people as often as possible until the season is finished. After that, hint that you'd like to see their ranches."

"Ranches?"

Dedran grinned nastily. "I said your friends have money. There's the main Quade ranch in the basin. But the old man has land in the Peaks country about five hundred miles away, and Storm and his wife have more land running alongside it up there. Quade mostly lives in the basin, but the other three all spend time at the second place. There's some strange tales about that family." Laris flicked a look at him. He was standing there and she could tell that he'd stopped being suspicious of her and was wondering about Storm, Logan, and Tani. She prompted him.

"Strange tales?"

"Some gossip about Xik holdout groups. Apparently Storm found one and brought in friends to destroy it. The rumor was that he had native help. After that there was a hush-hush deal in the desert. Some high muckymuck got lost there and Storm went in to find him at a time the tribes were up in arms. All of that story was hushed up by the patrol, or so talk has it." Laris shivered. "Yeah. I don't want them around, myself. After that there's a tale about some kind of plague that killed natives and started in on humans. I heard that Storm and the girl stopped it cold somehow."

Laris stared, stating a common belief in all Terran space.

"Diseases don't cross species. If it killed natives surely it wouldn't harm us?"

"I know, I know. But that's the rumor." He pushed off from where he leaned against the wall. "You get to bed. Just remember: Tread carefully with that lot. I want you in there with them thinking of you as a nice little girl with a cute pussycat."

He turned away abruptly and walked off, leaving Laris looking after him. She knew the way he thought. He was wondering if she'd find the Quade family so much to her liking that she'd be too talkative. She'd reassured him for the moment. But she'd have to be wary. The problem was that she did like what she'd seen of them. But if Dedran decided to be rid of her they'd be of no use to her and in danger themselves. Better she should stick to what he wanted. She plodded wearily to her cabin, moved Prauo over, and slumped down. She was asleep almost before she pulled the hotcover over herself.

For the next twelve days she obeyed Dedran's instructions. She was openly delighted to see any of the family whenever they appeared. She arranged for Tani to have tissue samples from the dogs. She talked by the hour about the circus, Prauo, and the other beasts and acts. All without saying anything which would anger Dedran. She listened in turn to Logan's tales of the natives, and Arzor. She noticed that despite his apparent openness as well, he said nothing of the rumors Dedran had heard. At first she had seen all three of the younger family. But by the time the circus was due to close it was Logan she saw most often.

He found her by the carra cage. "Laris, I see the show's shutting down. When do you leave?"

She smiled at him. "Not for weeks yet. Dedran says we're all tired. We're to take a break. We'll stay here for a few weeks and rest up before we go on to Trastor. We have quite a long season there."

Logan studied the ground. "Do you ever get any real time off? I mean, can you leave the circus?"

"Not for good." Her reply was quick.

He looked up. "No, I mean, could you spend time on our ranch? I could teach you to ride. Would Dedran agree to let you come and stay with us for a few days?"

"We could ask him." She wasn't sure how to play this. Let Dedran give her the cues. Logan led her in search of the circus boss and once they found Dedran, asked straightforwardly.

"My father would be pleased if Laris could stay a while with us. We'd show her Arzor. She'd be quite safe." Yes, but would the family be safe from her, Laris thought sadly. Dedran was considering.

"I have no objection. My ward is a sensible girl and I'm sure you would see she came to no harm." He watched Logan react to the words. The boy was becoming attracted. All to the good. He'd be less on his guard, and the others, seeing him so, would accept the girl more swiftly. He glanced kindly at his little piece of bait. "When would you like to leave, my dear? I can have Girran take your orders. Tell him anything he must do to care for the beasts."

"Is it all right if I take Prauo?" He nodded and she turned to Logan. "Will anyone mind if I bring him?"

Logan grinned. "Storm said you'd probably want to. He won't try killing anything without your say-so, will he?" She shook her head firmly. "Then it should be fine. Be ready the day after tomorrow. I'll come with the crawler to collect you about midmorning." His smile widened. "It'll be great to have you at the ranch, and don't worry. You'll have a wonderful time with us."

He left Laris with Dedran and hurried away. The girl kept her face blank knowing Dedran was looking at her. "You know what to do?"

Laris nodded. "Check out all the security systems," she recited for him. "Map the layout of both places. Learn the routine and who's where and when. What if they have a safe or something? Should I try for the code? It might help if Cregar can confuse their local patrol about the real target."

Dedran looked approvingly. "Well thought. Yes, if you can get the safe code do so. But take no chances. Besides, even on these rural planets, many these days have security systems that are quite sophisticated. Not around their property but certainly protecting a safe. If it's that secure, then Cregar will have no time to play about."

His last words were emphasized and Laris hid another shiver. She knew the guild methods of opening such security. It often required only the hand which would make a print. More technical systems required a live hand. That too could be arranged, as could the owner's voice. Few refused to cooperate when shown a family member and told the alternative. The guild was known for its ruthlessness.

But she would enjoy this brief time away. She could pretend that she was an ordinary girl visiting friends. Prauo could run free, be happy, and hunt where permitted. He'd never had the chance to do that before. Logan was on time and she seated herself with him while Prauo jumped easily onto the back of the crawler.

"Do you have many of these?"

Logan shook his head. "Nope. Just this one for hauling loads. Arzor uses a minimum of technology. It breaks down, has to be fixed, and it's very expensive to import. On the ranches we get around on horseback. The rangers and security have copters. But only a few."

"Security, that's what you call your local patrolmen?"

Logan looked a little surprised. "Men. What about women?"

"Oh, on Kowar they'd never have let a woman join. They only have patrolmen."

"Kowar? Is that where you come from?"

"Sort of." She changed the subject. "What's that bush? It's so pretty."

He started to tell her about the plants they passed. Then the land. By the time they were almost at the ranch he'd forgotten the question she'd never answered. But Laris felt she must decide. Should she tell them the truth if they asked again? She could do so safely. The only thing she had to hide was her exact status with Dedran. He'd claimed her as his ward with the Quades. That was respectable. Some planets didn't hold with the bond-system.

She thought Arzor might be one of them. And still more worlds did not approve of bonding underage children. She'd keep silent on all that but if they asked again she would tell the truth about the little she remembered of the times before Meril then Kowar's De Pyall refugee camps. She had just made the decision when the crawler passed the Quade ranch gates and halted at the top of the rise. Logan pointed.

"Home," he said softly.

Chapter Five

Laris seemed to drop into the Quade ranch as if she had been born there. She learned to ride with a speed that made it seem as if she'd had only to be reminded of her skills. That did her no harm with Storm or his father. Prauo was aloof but sensible with the other beasts of Storm's team. His longer legs and rangy body carried him miles alongside Laris's mount as he hardened to the exercise. He hunted with her, the two so clearly attuned that Storm nodded approvingly.

For Prauo it was all delightful, but it was the girl whose soul expanded in the freedom. She reveled in being able to ride down the miles; in the new sights, sounds, and scents. And in the quick give and take, the clatter and chatter of family life. Logan was with her everywhere. It was he who taught her to ride, accompanied her on those rides, and who sat beside her at meals.

They talked, sometimes casually, sometimes with more seriousness, discussing events on other planets as seen on the newscasts. Laris started to realize she had a good mind. She could argue a point and make her reasons plain. And from the camps and overheard conversations at the circus on an assortment of planets, she had a hard-headed appreciation of what could be contributing circumstances to the problem as disasters unfolded. She'd been there five days when her own origins came up again.

"Logan said you came from Kowar?" Brad Quade looked at her kindly. Laris heard the unspoken part of the comment, that she did not look like a Kowar settler. They'd mostly been from the Asiatic parts of old Earth.

"I said 'sort of,'" she noted. "I don't really remember. Dedran adopted me out of the De Pyall refugee camp on Kowar. I'd been in camps for years. That was just the latest. But I was at the camp there for the last two years so I think of Kowar as where I came from, I guess."

Brad looked interested. "What do you remember from before that?"

Laris leaned her chin on her fists. "Not a lot." She thought back. "I was on a ship with others. No one I knew. I was eight or nine. We landed at Meril and I was there maybe a couple of years. Before that another camp. Ermaine I think. The camp before that they called De Pyall as well. It might have been on Yohal. My mother was still alive. I think I might have been four or five."

Storm looked up. "What happened to your mother?"

"She died," Laris said briefly. "She got sick. I think there were a lot of deaths in that camp. A woman looked after me for a while. She went to a different ship when they moved us again."

Brad's voice was gentle. "Don't talk about this if it distresses you."

The girl shook her head. "It's old. It doesn't bother me."

"Then, what do you remember about your mother? What did others call her when they spoke? Did she ever tell you stories of some place?" Brad leaned forward. "Do you remember any names, words that don't match other places you've been?"

Laris looked back—into the blank times. The times when she must have been loved and protected. When maybe she'd had a family of her own. They were still as they had always been for her ever since. Blank.

"I think I was sick when my mother was. I don't remember much about her. No names or people. Sometimes I think I dream. But I can't remember anything when I wake." She shrugged. "It doesn't matter."

Brad nodded. "But you know your name," he said quietly.

She answered without thinking. "I'm Laris. I've always been Laris."

"Yes." The tone was contemplative. "Yes, you are. Your name is the first thing you learn as a child and probably the last thing you forget. If it could be discovered where you come from, would you like to know?"

She thought about it. Knowing wouldn't cut her any slack with Dedran. But it would be nicer, good to be able to say that she was Laris of a particular place, not just a camp stray. She felt a sudden surprising flare of hunger. She'd like to know. She said so and Brad nodded.

"I'll make inquiries."

It was two days later before something dawned on the girl. If Brad started at the De Pyall camp on Kowar, the records there would show that she'd been bonded, not adopted. She thought of trying to persuade Brad to drop the idea, but it was probably too late. Anyway she could always say she'd just signed papers. That she'd thought it was an adoption. After all, she'd been twelve. Uneducated, ignorant, straight from a camp. Brad would believe that.

She was wrong but it would be months before she found out how wrong. It wasn't spoken about again until she was due to return to the circus for a day.

"Laris, we'd like you to come back to the ranch once you've seen the animals are well. Would you like to do that?" Brad's smile was gentle.

"Yes. If Dedran says I can. It's fun on the ranch." Her rare grin lit up her face. Beside her Logan bit back a sigh. He loved to make her smile. Laris smiled seldom and often tentatively, as if she wasn't sure she should. Considering what his father had discovered so far that wasn't surprising. Camp records had disclosed that the girl had been about ten when she arrived on Kowar. No known family. She'd left again at twelve.

Brad had checked how it was that a twelve-year-old had walked out of a refugee camp. He'd found her bond registered with another office. Except that the bond claimed her as sixteen. All of them could guess the reasons for that. Logan would have discussed their discoveries so far with Laris but Brad forbade it.

"I believe Laris knew she was bonded but hopes I won't have discovered that. She lied, probably out of shame; being bonded is quite a stigma on some planets. A child learns pragmatism in a refugee camp and accepting a bond was probably her only way out. Letting her know we've found out would spoil her time here. She wants to know where she came from and who she is. Leave it lie, son."

Logan had. At almost twenty-one he was discovering reasons why people could be fragile, but it had made him gentler with her. Storm, guessing at more than Logan could know of what Laris's life had been like, remained suspicious. A child growing up in the camps learned to care about their own needs first. Ethics would have gone to the wall as Laris fought to survive. He watched her with Prauo and later with the meercats and Surra. She was a natural. The animals liked and trusted her and she seemed to know by instinct what they wanted. After that thought his gaze on her sharpened; it could be he was right in his belief, that she had the true beast master empathy as well.

Maybe that was why the circus boss had bonded her. Anyone whose livelihood or passion was beasts would pay highly for someone that good. Perhaps his allowing her to visit the ranch was simply an employer making sure a valuable employee was content. He let his suspicions lapse temporarily and rode out with his wife, his brother, and Laris the next day. Tani was on Destiny, the silver three-quarter duocorn mare which was her usual mount.

Her coyotes put up a merin deer and all of them chased it laughing, not too serious in the pursuit. Minou and Ferarre joined in the spirit of it as the deer ran, their tongues lolling out in amusement. The deer doubled, twisted, and finally shook them off. She paused to look back at them from a small rise as her pursuers halted. Laris started to laugh.

"She looks so surprised. As if she thinks we're all mad." Her laugher was infectious and even Storm chuckled.

"It will keep her in practice."

"Oh," Laris said in mock-amazed tones. "So that's why we chased her. We're exercising the wildlife. Maybe we should find a few more. After all, Logan said that it's the growing season. The animals could be getting fat. Don't you think it would be a kindness to keep that from happening?"

"Couldn't we just set up a gymnasium for them?" Tani murmured. "That way they can exercise and we don't have to do half the work."

Storm looked at her. "Deer, deer. Aren't we lazy."

Logan groaned at the pun. "Puhlease. I only had breakfast a while ago. I may be sick." Laris was laughing again, a joyous carefree sound which somehow warmed them all.

"It isn't breakfast," she said sweetly. "It's as I said. Logan's just exercising the wild . . ." she paused and added the final word, "life."

This time they all moaned. Tani snorted. "Laris, you're being corrupted. That has to be one of the worst puns I've heard in years." Laris giggled. Storm studied her from the corner of his eye. She looked like a child when she was happy. But she wasn't. Brad said from the records she must be somewhere between sixteen and seventeen. So far he'd traced her to Ermaine. Still no more name than Laris. No planet of origin. No family listed.

He knew what it had done to him to be alone before he found his stepfather and half-brother. What had it done to her? It hadn't broken her. But things like that could warp and twist in ways which often weren't apparent to an outsider. Then too, small children could be amazingly resilient. Maybe she'd come out of the camps mind-whole. Brad thought she had, and his stepfather was a shrewd man. Storm sat back as his mount ambled after the others. Logan liked her. But Storm was very fond of his younger half-brother. He didn't want the boy hurt.

Ahead, Laris dropped from her horse to reach out slowly within a small jumble of recently cracked rock. Prauo came trotting back to stare at her find. She cradled it in her hand and showed it to them, eyes wide with pleasure.

"I saw the sun catch it. Look, isn't it pretty?"

Storm glanced at the cat's-eye gem. "It's valuable too."

"Oh," she hesitated then held it up to him. "It was on your land."

Storm realized that both his wife and brother were glaring at him. He shook his head. "Finders keepers."

Logan took it from her carefully and turned it over in his fingers. "That last frosty night, it would have split the rock this was in." He touched her arm. "Storm was teasing. It's pretty but it's the green ones which are really valuable. This is gold. It isn't a large stone either. It would take ten or twelve of them to make a green one's value. But it's yours. You found it. Just don't start digging holes like a Djimbut to see if you can find more."

Laris took the gem back. She admired the gold color with the black line like a pupil which split it in two. She pointed. "Is that why they're called cat's-eye stones?"

"Yes. Look." Prauo had moved to her side and was looking to see what his sister-without-fur had. "It would look just like one of his eyes if it was purple," Logan pointed out.

Laris nodded. "But I'd rather he had his own eyes than I had this. It's very pretty though." It was, she thought. And Dedran would have it from her as soon as he saw it and once they were away from Arzor. "What's a green one worth?" If this one was still quite valuable it might give her a chance to escape. She could keep Dedran from knowing about it if she was careful.

Logan thought a moment. "Don't see many green cat's-eye stones. But I think the last good-sized one went for about five thousand credits on the market. That gold one would be worth around a hundred credits maybe, considering the size."

Laris kept her face blank but Storm saw the sudden glitter of her eyes. That had surprised her. To a camp child a stone worth only a fraction of the value Logan had quoted on a green cat's-eye gem was still real riches. He was right. To Laris it meant jumping ship and still having enough to survive at least a half year on the stone's price. It could mean safety, freedom from Dedran and the guild. The guild wouldn't look for her. And they might keep Dedran moving on, too busy to turn back and seek her out.

Smiling, she dropped the stone in a pocket. She nudged her horse up alongside Logan's mount and continued an earlier conversation. Tani dropped back with Storm.

"Has Brad found out any more about her?"

"Nope. He's still chasing through Ermaine's bureaucracy. They closed the refugee camp they had there about seven years ago. Just over a half year after Laris was shipped out. They claim that a lot of the records were dumped after five years."

"Claim?"

"Uh huh. Brad thinks they're holding out for a bribe to look."

Tani smiled unpleasantly. "Let me at the com when we get back," she said, referring to the ranch's method of communication, not only locally, but also planet to planet. "Aunt Kady would enjoy lighting a fire under a few bureaucrats. The ark's important to most planetary governments. Aunt Kady asks, Aunt Kady gets. And if I can tell her we've got tissue samples from two Terran dogs she hasn't found before, she'll get those records if she has to go there herself. I don't think she has many carra samples either."

Storm knew Tani's Aunt Kady. She was a scientist. Nothing deterred her when she was on a trail. And it was true she'd be delighted about the dogs. He touched his mount into a canter to catch up with Laris and Logan. He addressed the girl.

"Would Dedran mind having a scientist take tissue samples from your carra as well?"

"I don't think so." Laris frowned. "Why would they want to?"

Tani had caught up with them. She explained how Terra had created a space-faring ark with beasts and embryos in stasis, with huge tissue banks, all to save Earth's flora and fauna if the worst happened. "And it did. But the ark was safe," Tani said softly. "Now my aunt and uncle seek out other Terran animals or rare ones from other worlds and take samples to hold. She'll be so pleased about the dogs' samples you got us already but carra are quite rare too."

"What if something happened to the ark?" Laris was fascinated.

"Then we'd still have the samples. They split those into three. Two others go to planets with groundside storage facilities. They're held in those as well. Lately Uncle Brion's been talking about increasing the groundside places to five. That way it would be even less likely everything could be destroyed."

She started to tell Laris about her days on the ark. Then how she had come to Arzor. The girl listened, wondering if she should say anything about the rumors Dedran had heard. But she didn't know who'd told him. Maybe he wasn't supposed to know. Tani and Storm had said nothing and it sounded like an exciting tale. Surely if it was all right to tell it they would have. In the end she listened with interest but asked few questions and those carefully chosen.

The next week passed quickly. Then there were only a few more days. Dedran had commed the ranch to say they would up-ship in five days. The call had come in late one afternoon, insisting Laris must be back well before the ship's departure to see to the animals. Few of them enjoyed takeoff. Some started becoming agitated early as they understood that the time was coming. She could have another three days.

She hoped Brad would hear from the Ermaine camp

before she had to go. Tani had taken samples of tissue from the carra and sent those and the dog tissue to the ark. Kady hadn't received them as yet, although she had mentioned getting the message asking her to interrogate Ermaine's people. She'd replied she'd do her best and that was the last they'd heard.

Laris sighed. Perhaps even a scientist who knew people still hadn't enough influence to open those files. She dimly recalled some strange events at the camp shortly before she was transferred. It was likely that there—as in many places during and after the war—there'd been corruption. The people involved wouldn't want records found. And others wouldn't want such events exposed. It could reflect badly on the current government. Besides, would all of this be worth the effort? She was in the ranch house the next evening when she decided to ask the one who'd know.

"Mr. Quade, if Tani's aunt does get the camp records opened, what could you find?"

"Your full name for a start. I had a search done in Kowar. They have no record of you as other than 'Laris.' No last name in their records. But many of the camp's records simply list the adults of the family who arrived and note 'with three minor children,' giving only the children's first names.

"If we had your full name we could track that. Once we had the full records we could trace how you came there and from what planet." He looked at her kindly. "It takes time to do that sort of thing, Laris. But governments thrive on records. They're there somewhere." He paused. "I know it seems like a long time to you. But it's only ten or twelve years. A few seconds to a planetary government."

The girl twisted her hands together. "There were some

things that went on . . ." Her voice trailed away and Brad Quade understood.

"In the camps? And you think some people in power now might not want to remember them? That's very likely. But I can make it clear to them there's no legal trouble in mind. Don't worry. I know you have to leave soon. I'll get the circus schedule and spacegram any information that comes in. Or won't Dedran like that?"

She thought. "I think he won't mind. But maybe if you sent it to the port office for collection. I could just pick it up there when we land."

He nodded. "I'll do that."

He returned to the book he was reading and Laris departed quietly. She adored the excellent library the ranch owned and understood that a reader liked to read in peace. She read late most nights in her bedroom and her companions were amused at the wide variety in her reading.

The three days passed. Laris sat down to her last meal at the ranch and was conscious of sadness. Prauo sprawled behind her. He'd eaten earlier but preferred to stay with Laris. She kept her face blank but the others were beginning to know that look. It meant that emotion lurked and the girl was determined not to show it. They combined to make her laugh, sharing old jokes and retelling amusing incidents.

Finally she excused herself. If she didn't leave she was going to cry. Laris, who hadn't cried since she was six and had learned she would never see her mother again. That she must move on alone.

You are sad, sister-without-fur.

I won't see them again. Dedran's going to do something awful to them and they'll never forgive me.

You could warn them.

She sent nothing in reply. Better he not know that Dedran had once made a threat which had turned her heart cold with terror. But the big cat had learned. He picked it from her mind in part, guessing the rest. *You keep silent for my sake. Well, they have each other. We have only the two of us. But if there is a chance, if we escape, then warn them.*

I will.

She read late that final night. Losing herself in the adventures of another. She rose to eat and then to take one last ride with Tani and Logan. Only Logan was there.

"Tani had to talk to people at the Peaks ranch. It'll be just the two of us. Do you mind?"

She shook her head. How could she mind a few hours alone with a man she was coming to care about? But she mustn't think of that. Once Dedran struck, Logan would hate her. A hopeful part of her mind pointed out that Logan might never know she'd been involved in whatever Dedran did to the Quade family. She could get away from the circus boss. Use the cat's-eye gem to buy passage back to Arzor.

And what, the sensible part of her brain pointed out, what would she do if she got back and found Logan had just been being kind to her? How would she feel if he was surprised to see her? If she was just a nuisance coming back where she wasn't really wanted? It wasn't Logan's ranch. It belonged to his father. Mr. Quade had been nice and he was helping find her background. But then by now he must know a few things she'd rather he hadn't discovered. He wasn't likely to want her back either, even if he was being nice about the records.

She rode with Logan, laughed, and galloped her pony. She hid what she felt and concentrated on enjoying her hours before she must go. Live for the day. It was all she had. She had no way of knowing how her eyes mirrored her thoughts whenever she remembered she was leaving, even as she twisted her face into a smile.

They turned back to the ranch house in the distance. Laris halted her pony for a brief moment. She sat looking at the only place where she'd been happy in so many years. She wondered if her own home, wherever it had been, had been as nice. Had she had family there? Been a happy child surrounded with love? She shrugged. What was gone was gone. She heeled the pony into a gallop and forgot her sorrow briefly in the joy of speed.

"Laris?" She turned to Logan as they slowed, trotting the ponies into the big corral.

"Yes."

"You can come back, you know. Anytime the circus is on Arzor. You'd be welcome here."

"Thanks. But it's the only time we've landed here since I've been with them. I guess we may not be back for years." She held her mouth in a firm line. She would not whimper like a motherless cub. She would not!

Logan took her hand, glanced quickly around. No one in sight. He tipped her chin up with the other hand and brought his mouth down on hers. Her lips were warm, sweet with a startled half-shy response; then she freed herself quietly.

"Maybe I shouldn't have done that," he told her. "But I'm not sorry."

"Neither am I." Then she was running for the ranch door. It had felt strange. She'd fought in the camps to stop anyone touching her and succeeded. Not until now had she understood how that had deadened her emotions. For many years she'd touched only Prauo and the animals. With Logan it had felt good. No coercion. Just safety, warmth. A melting inside.

Her mouth went wry. Logan hadn't said, "Come back." Just, "Stay with us if the circus is back on Arzor." And if Dedran knew how she felt he'd never trust her again. But she couldn't let him harm her friends here. Yet how could she stop it? She did her best as they dropped her at the edge of the circus area.

"Storm." She held his eyes with her own, willing him to understand. "Tani's aunt can take other samples if she meets the circus. Sometimes tissue samples can be worth a lot. There's always someone who wants to use things. Other samples, other reasons." She turned away, hoping he'd understood enough to take care.

"Logan, I'll miss you. Thank you all for letting me stay at the ranch." She spun, hiding her face as she ran. By the time she and Prauo reached her cabin she had herself under control again. It was just as well. Dedran met her.

"There's been a message from Cregar. He was successful at Trastor and he's going on to Lereyne to meet us there. Get the hidden cage ready. We'll need it for the wolf he's got. Get on with your work now that you're back." He paused as he studied her face.

"I hope you learned plenty. You'll have to tell it all to Cregar. Did you get to their place in the Peaks?" She nodded. "Good. What about security systems?"

"Only coms and computer lock-codes. No security in the houses apart from the animals. There is a safe. Lock-coded. I couldn't get the code." That was a lie but it was a secondary target. Dedran probably wouldn't care much. He didn't.

"Too bad. But Cregar should be able to get in, gas the beasts, and get out again. What's he likely to find?"

"That depends on what's there on the day he picks. Unless he's very unlucky there should be several animals."

"Right. Go and fix that cage. We up-ship in a few hours. I've decided to leave a day earlier and I let you stay longer. It does seem to have been worth it but I need you for the animals now." He gave her a shove. "Don't think you can come back and be idle, my dear ward." The last words were a sneer as he turned away.

Laris nodded. No, she wouldn't make that mistake. She plodded in the direction of the animal hold. She was leaving, she could never return, and all her world was dark right now. Nothing mattered anymore.

She worked hard for the next half day as she reassured the beasts, prepared the hidden cage to receive Cregar's victim, and now and again listened to conversations. They were taking on two new people, desperate men from the port who'd never quite settled on this new world. They were already planning an act on the high wire. They'd seen it done, thought it looked easy enough. The girl sighed.

Others had thought that. It was one of the things which brought crowds. This pair would end up on a new world. But at least here they'd been whole, undamaged. On Trastor once they'd failed it would still be a new world but now they'd be injured as well, maybe permanently crippled or dead.

In which case they'll have no more problems, Prauo sent.

Laris grinned. The big cat was such a realist at times. She waited until no one was about and moved to where the largest cage stood in isolation. It held the five tigerbats. They sometimes reached out for those who passed and most people in the circus gave it a wide berth. Just as well. It had secrets other than the inhabitants.

She drifted around to the rear of the cage, pressed two places on a panel, and leaned hard. A door-sized piece of the back slid aside. Laris entered, stooping through the entrance, light already in her hand. She turned slowly. It wasn't dirty; she could sweep it though. There was a little dust. There were built-in containers for food and water. She would bring bedding.

If there is anything left alive to sleep there, came to her. She had to agree. Cregar and his abductions certainly hadn't been so successful in the past.

I'll clean it and put down bedding anyway.

She found she was thinking of Storm as she worked. He was so calm, so self-contained. How would he react to the disappearance of some of his team? She wished she didn't have to know about that. Or to be involved. It was betraying the people who'd been kind to her. Then camp life came back to her. None of them were her kin. They had no claim on her.

I too am not kin to you, sister-without-fur. Yet our hearts are bound together. What of Logan?

Within the hidden cage Laris paused in her sweeping. The name conjured up the touch of his hand on her face, his lips warm and gentle on hers. Sorrow swept over her.

Logan will never forgive me if he finds out. And if I ever see him again I think he'd know just by looking at me. Our only hope is to get away before they take Storm's beasts. There was a long silence while she finished her work. She peered through the tiny viewer in the cage panel, then the viewer which looked out through the tigerbat portion in the front. No one was about. She slid aside the panel, stepped out, snapped it shut swiftly, then emerged from behind the cage.

Dedran caught up with her a short time later. "Is the cage ready?"

"It's clean. I've put in fresh bedding. The food and water containers have been scrubbed. I can fill them when the wolf arrives. Everything works well. The viewer lenses are clean. The panel moves easily and without making noise."

"Very well. Cregar has messaged. He's coming here. He'll land before we leave. The wolf will be transhipped to the circus and you'll get the animal under cover in the cage the minute Cregar is up the ramp. Understand?"

She nodded. Why the change of plan? What had happened on Lereyne that Dedran would turn everything on its head and leave earlier than planned? Had Cregar started some kind of trouble and had to run? She asked no questions on that score. By the look on Dedran's face it would be unhealthy. She could ask one question safely.

"What about food for the animal? I could give it some of the carcass the tigerbats have."

Dedran's reply was a snarl. "Give it whatever is suitable. Damn thing may not be eating anyway. Just be ready to help once Cregar arrives. We could have to delay liftoff." He departed, walking in a way which showed he would like to stamp but didn't want to draw attention. It looked as if things really had gone wrong somewhere, Laris thought. Cregar coming here. Liftoff first advanced then delayed. She wondered if those at the ranch knew about the abduction of a beast master's wolf.

Chapter Six

On Quade land, Storm entered the ranch house to find his father coming to look for him. His face was hard with anger.

"*Asizi?*" Storm used the Navaho word in reaction to that anger. "What is it?"

"Kady Carraldo has just spoken to the ranger station at port. They linked coms so she could speak directly to us. There's been a beast master murdered on Lereyne. An old employee of hers talked to her from there."

"A beast master," Storm muttered, shocked. "Murdered how, why?"

"Apparently to take the remaining member of his team. Kady says the man was supposed to be in the city all day. His wolf was left at home. Those who took it probably knew all that. The trouble was that the man came home early. They think he tried to prevent his animal being taken and someone hit him too hard in a panic." Storm considered that.

"It sounds likely." But his father's anger was too great to explain it as just the death of a man none of them knew. "What else?"

Brad Quade stared at the silent com. "Kady says she has been told by authorities there that it fits other abductions of animals from teams and the murders of their beast masters. She has no idea why it's happening but she can now list seven separate occasions beside this one. There could be more which haven't been passed on as yet."

"But . . . but. That must be almost every beast master left alive after the war."

His father shook his head. "No. Most of the dead were trainees. They had teams but they had never been in the fighting. Maybe that's why they're being targeted. They're easier to take than you veterans."

Storm's mind was clicking over. "Get me a list of names and where they were when they died. How long they'd been there and any other details you can find."

"No need. Kady downloaded all that over the link. Here."

He handed over a sheaf of paper. Storm reached without looking for the nearest chair, dragged it to him, and sat, already reading. At last he looked up.

"What do you think, *Asizi?*"

"You first."

"It seems clear to me. The first killing was a man I served with. He was no pushover and his team was trained. I'd say the animals fought, he picked up on that, and came running. He killed a couple of the kidnappers, the animals got a third and the leader of the kidnappers made a clean sweep to avoid witnesses. He couldn't get the bodies away so he picked them clean of ID and left them. The authorities say the dead men were port scum, they'd do anything if they were paid."

Brad sat back. "Uh-huh. Go on."

"After that whoever was running this operation decided that us veterans were too tough. He started trying for trainees.

It looks as if he got away with a few animals but it wouldn't do him any good."

"Why not?"

Storm's mouth twisted as if the words tasted sour. "Because with the trainees High Command was trying something different and more advanced. They were mind-bonding the trainees' teams to them. Not just a mental link of the kind I have, more of a complete bonding. The communication between leader and team was clearer and could reach farther when they were apart. High Command believed it would work better out in the field. They found instead that it didn't work as well so they stopped it after that initial group had been bonded. If the war hadn't ended they'd have gone back to the way they used with me."

He paused and accepted the drink Brad offered. "Thanks. Sure the bonding made for a closer team. A good team could be used almost like your own extensions. But it was more trouble than it was of use. If a beast master was injured, his team went berserk. If he was killed, his team would die. They found that out after there were a couple of training accidents. If some fool tried to kidnap a trainee team they'd fight like the possessed. If their leader was badly injured they'd go crazy. If he was killed they'd die within a few days too."

He sat thinking. "What do we know? That someone somewhere is trying to steal beast master animals. If the beast master tries to prevent that he's killed. It's possibly one man doing it under orders and using local criminals as gun fodder. But why? It doesn't make sense."

"Would animals like that breed true? Maybe they're setting up teams of their own."

Storm eyed him grimly. "They'd breed true if they could keep them alive. Setting up teams would be harder. But who and for what purpose?"

Brad stood. "I'll talk to Kelson. He's head of the ranger divisions here, and he can reach security on other planets and be listened to. So can Kady. We'll alert everyone we can. High Command should have a list of surviving beast masters and where they went. Brion can talk to them as well." He turned to reach for the com then grinned wryly at Storm. "At least it isn't Xiks this time."

Storm snorted. "Makes it worse, not better. Xiks don't know us as well as our own do. I'll go and find Logan. He can take Surra and the others up to the Peaks ranch. I want them out of the way just in case." He strode out, leaving Brad looking after him. Storm still hadn't grasped Brad's fear. If the trainee beasts all died or were killed as had already happened to some of them, the hunters would return looking for the veteran teams again. Storm could be next on the list.

But Storm had understood very well. He spoke to Logan, then to Kelson. A copter landed a day later. Surra and her mate were loaded, along with Baku and Lazo, her mate. Hing came scampering to Storm's call bringing her tribe. They too were loaded. Logan went with them. He leaned out before the copter lifted.

"What about Tani?"

"She's with the clan. If you think some port filth could casually drop in there and kill her, steal the coyotes, Mandy and Destiny, then she's in danger." His tone was slightly sarcastic.

Logan grinned. Half a year ago Tani had ended a menace to the natives. Not the more civilized Norbies alone, but also the savage Nitra tribes of Arzor. She'd been adopted into the

Nitra's Djimbut clan as one of them. It was only the second time in the history of human settlement on Arzor that it had happened. The Nitra were warriors, frequently at war with each other. Constantly alert, and honed into fighters without betters on Arzor. No criminal from the port would sneak up on the clan. If they thought to do so they'd have a rude awakening, and a very unpleasant death.

Storm pushed his hand at his half-brother. "Go, go. I'll talk to Tani when she gets back but she'd planned to be gone a tenday. Just take care of yourself." He watched the copter lift off and then felt a chill run down his spine. Maybe he'd take his stallion Rain-on-Dust and ride out to the clan lands. Tani had taken the small comunit but the ride would be pleasant. Talking at length on the unit was still not being with her, and he wished to be.

She and the clan should be warned too of a possible attempt on Tani and her team. She was beast master in abilities and in her bond with her team, but she'd never been trained in war. There were things he could say to the clan warriors about the abductions of beasts and the killing of beast masters which would put them on their guard.

He smiled a little to himself, and his face warmed in a way seldom seen by any but his family. He'd still pity a man who tried to separate Tani from her beasts. His wife might not be trained but there was warrior heritage there. She would not submit easily. He entered the house again just as his father clicked off the comceiver.

"That was Kady and Brion. They say we're to take care of their niece." Storm nodded, waiting. "Brion talked to High Command. They'll com every beast master they can reach. Several veterans went into the new survey department that started after the war. They should be safe, half the time that lot don't know where they are themselves. We can add another death to that list of Kady's. A trainee again. And another body they've traced to their port."

"How long ago?"

"The bodies have been there for weeks." He stopped Storm's exclamation with a raised hand. "Not incompetence. The man went off into the bush somewhere, built himself a hut, and started acting as a ranger for the native wildlife. It was all on a voluntary basis, he was living on his veteran's pension, so he had no regular reporting schedule. They only saw him two, maybe three times a year. He'd left a message on his com asking callers to call back in a few weeks. He said he was off on a survey of wildlife numbers."

Storm swore bitterly. "Either someone knew that or they were just lucky. I suppose someone wanted to talk to the man and couldn't wait, or he'd still be out there."

"Us, we started it. High Command passed on the warning. One of his ranger friends in the wildlife department thought he should know at once. When they kept getting the same message someone else remembered they'd called him a month back and heard it before. His friend went out just in case and to pass on the warning. They found him dead with another body, and signs others had been hurt. His beasts were all dead as well, killed apparently while fighting to protect their master or to keep from being taken. They can't be one hundred percent certain but they think the deaths occurred thirty-five to forty days ago."

Brad and Storm sat thinking silently. At last Brad spoke again. "I'd say that it might be a good idea to ride out and talk to Tani and the clan about all of this."

"I'm going in the morning. I'll suggest either she stays out with the clan or she goes up to the Peaks ranch to stay with Logan."

His stepfather rose slowly. "Well enough. Get some sleep then." He remembered something. "Wasn't Logan going down to the port to see that girl leave?"

"Uh-huh. He's catching a ride with Kelson. The man's running around holding meetings about frawn numbers just now. Some of the ranchers are risking over-grazing their land up there. Then Kelson will take him back to the Peaks later on. Don't worry, *Asizi*. Everything will be well." But he felt again that small cold shiver and wondered.

In the ship Laris finished tucking the wolf away in the hidden section of the cage. It was breathing badly and she was concerned. Cregar stood beside her looking down at it.

"It isn't injured."

"There are different kinds of injuries," Laris said sadly. "I don't think this one will make it either. Tell Dedran I'll do my best but it's samples he's likely to be sending on. Not a live beast." From the corner of her eye she caught a half-satisfied look on the man's face. Didn't he want the guild to succeed then? Cregar grunted and walked to peer from the viewer.

"No one is about. Make very sure no one sees you coming in or out of that cage. There are half a dozen governments who would hang us all if they ever find out we're responsible for kidnaping Terran animals and killing beast masters. It's only a matter of time too before the authorities on one of the planets who've lost animals post a reward." He saw her flinch. "Once that happens everyone in any port will be on the lookout for something odd to use to try and claim a reward. You know Dedran. Bring him down and he'll make sure we all go with him. Only way for us to be safe would be if he's dead before the authorities find him." The last words had been spoken almost to himself.

He slid the panel aside and stepped through, closing it with a quiet click behind him. Laris stared after him. Now what had that last comment meant? Was he suggesting she should kill Dedran? Or that Cregar might? She sat down beside the sedated animal and smoothed its fur. Poor beast, it hadn't asked to be kidnapped and brought here. She'd try to keep it alive, but was that right? Would it want to live without friend or kin?

She turned the thought aside. She couldn't kill it. Humans had done enough to cause it distress. Not that it would matter. About her she could feel the small sounds which indicated liftoff shortly. She must go out. Dedran would want her to pass on his orders, check other animals. She hoped that Logan might find time to see her before the ship lifted.

Dedran did want her. He kept her busy until suddenly Logan appeared. Then the circus boss smiled. Laris eyed that look suspiciously. It boded no good for someone when the man looked that pleased with himself. He placed a heavy hand on her shoulder.

"Take your friend into the small group cabin. You have half an hour to say your good-byes then he'll have to go."

The small group cabin, Laris noted. And that's bugged. He'll know every word we say. But if we don't go then I'll pay later on. There'll be a chance on the way back though. I can say he grabbed me, kept kissing me and wouldn't let go. That's if Dedran realizes we took a while longer to get to the ramp after we left the cabin. She'd chance that. Although maybe she could encourage Logan into suggesting a side trip somewhere. To see the animals again perhaps.

They reached the cabin, she slid the door shut, and Logan started talking. Laris bit back a groan as she saw where his warnings were leading. He was afraid for her. But he was revealing at the same time just how much was known. Dedran would be interested, furious, and afraid. Someone out there was stealing animals. The smart ones. Prauo might be taken, or her tigerbats, Logan insisted. She must be careful. These people had killed again and again.

She couldn't shut him up too abruptly. Dedran would listen to this. If he was suspicious of her she could do nothing and might not survive. Laris waited until a suitable place in Logan's warnings.

"So I had to let you know before you left." She laid a finger softly against his lips. He had more to say but she'd prefer Dedran didn't hear it.

"You're kind. Thank you but I'll be safe here." She pointed at the door, raising her eyebrows. Now if only he didn't say the wrong thing. Logan assumed she wished to show him the animals to demonstrate their safety. He nodded.

"Of course. It's unusual for anyone to have five of them." She had the door open and was leading him out quickly, before he opened his mouth again and said something Dedran could use. She was too late.

Logan halted in the doorway to talk again. "You will be careful. Storm's got me tucked away up at the Peaks ranch with his beasts. Tani's with the Djimbut clan in the lower foothills. We're safe but I worry about you."

Laris kept her voice steady with a huge effort. He'd just

told Dedran everything the circus boss would need to know in order to find Storm or Tani's teams. "Don't worry. I'll be all right." Too true she would be. Because Cregar was going to be at High Peaks just as soon as the circus was on Lereyne and innocently doing shows for the local population there.

Logan gathered her into the circle of one arm. "Are you sure? There'd be no objections if you wanted to come back with me." He stopped abruptly. Damn. She couldn't do that. Brad had said the girl was bonded to Dedran, no matter that the man had referred to her as his ward.

Laris was thinking quickly. Dedran wouldn't release her. The bond had several months yet to run. The circus boss would see to it that Laris didn't take Prauo. She had no proof of ownership and he could delay legal attempts to repossess Prauo, up-ship, and then claim Prauo had died on the trip. Apart from that, Cregar was planning to steal Storm's or Tani's beasts. If he succeeded she might be the only one standing between Dedran and a dead team.

She remembered Hing and her troop. Small, merry, and so charming, Laris had been constantly giggling whenever she watched them. Surra, beautiful in her pride and dignity, so gracious toward her mate. And the eagles, Baku who had unbent sufficiently to accept a piece of meat from Laris's hand. No, if Dedran succeeded she must be at the circus. Her presence might save them still. She mourned inside but she must not show that.

She smiled, her mouth stretching upward but her eyes miserable. "No, I couldn't leave the circus. I have a place here. And anyway, I'm quite certain I'll be safe. Now come and see the tigerbats before you have to leave."

Logan followed her. He admired the five carnivores who watched him sleepily. The largest came to be stroked.

"It's amazing how gentle he seems when you know what they can do."

"They aren't vicious," Laris objected. "They're just predators. Kreel is quite clever." She sighed. "I wish one day they could go back home. I know they couldn't ever be free to swarm again. But if they had a really large pen so they could have a few babies . . ."

Logan gaped. "Some are females in there?"

"Of course." She pointed at the two smaller tigerbats. "They are. I have to put a contraceptive in their water so they can't breed. We've only had them a year and they're two. Too young to breed safely as yet. But it would be so nice for them if they could have a family one day."

Without thinking Logan hugged her. "You have a good heart." Laris stiffened then relaxed in his arms. He lowered his mouth to hers and for long seconds they clung. Then she freed herself gently.

"I have to take you down the ramp. Dedran will be expecting to see you leave." He allowed her to walk with him to where Dedran was indeed waiting. The tall man glared as they came in sight.

Logan took her hand and held it briefly. "We shall look forward to seeing you again if you land here." He nodded politely to Dedran. "You too, Honored Sir. But I must hurry, there's always work." He turned to look at Laris, his face hidden from the circus boss. Out of the man's sight Logan's lips framed words. "We have a place for you always." Then he was hurrying down the ramp to where Kelson waited impatiently. The ship's ramp whined as it was raised to close. The last sight Laris saw was Logan's hand waving as they drove away. She made her face blank as she turned.

Dedran caught her by the shoulder. "Don't get ideas, girl. That fancy first-ship family would never touch you if they knew what you were."

Laris spun. "What was I?" she snarled despite herself. "I was an orphan like a million from the war. I was bonded illegally and we both know it. I've never done anything to be ashamed of."

Dedran smiled at her furious face. His own eyes were cold and dead. "Dear, dear. Is that what you think? And how would your fancy friends like to hear that you've been up to your little neck in espionage, theft, and murder? I can prove you've helped me often enough with the first two. And you knew what Cregar did on his trips. It was you who cared for the animals and took samples when they died. Try convincing any authority you were innocent." He smiled again as her defiance wilted, shoulders hunching in surrender. She'd showed signs of becoming too interested in the Quade boy. It felt good to remind her that she was merely property.

"Get on with your work. We have clearance to lift." He walked arrogantly away, pausing at the end of the passage to make sure she was obeying his instruction.

She kept her cowed look as she headed for the animal hold. Let the circus boss believe he had convinced her there was no hope of using the Quades to escape Dedran's grip. But inside she was recalling something she'd accessed in the library at Yohal. There was a law on all Terran-settled planets stating that a bond-servant could not be held accountable for her master's misdeeds or her own under orders if she had no opportunity to inform, she feared crippling reprisals if she attempted to inform and failed, or—if she was in danger of death, or if she was saving another under that same threat. Laris could plead three of the four; the last for Prauo.

She'd also been bonded illegally young as she could prove with the camp records. She could claim duress on a minor which would be even more convincing. Cases she'd read showed that courts tended to look even less favorably on punishing a child forced into crimes. She set about her chores with a lighter heart. Her reading skills might save her yet.

Chapter Seven

Laris worked on, knowing that Dedran would be listening to the record of her talk with Logan. In a few days he'd ask her to expand on the Peaks ranch. Her bond-master and Cregar would want to know all she could tell. Well, she had an idea there. She started to think it out as she cleaned cages, fed and watered their occupants. What she had in mind just might work. It would delay an attack on Storm's beasts *if* some of the things Logan had told her were true.

She smiled savagely to herself. It would take careful handling. She'd have to make Dedran think it was his idea. But if she said just the right things the circus boss could take the bait. Cregar was under orders and why should he know any more about Arzor than the circus boss knew? She'd accessed the information available in the ship's library often enough to know all the library had about Arzor.

Laris had listened to Logan as he talked about the natives of Arzor. He'd told her old stories, native customs. And something of the vast and often savage desert lands in which the wild Nitra clans lived. The ship records had said almost nothing about Arzor, save to note that the natives were mostly friendly. The men would accept that.

Eyes opened behind her own. *Be cautious, sister-one. Too little said is better than too much.*

Come with me and listen when he calls me then. Maybe you can think of something to say. Prauo was not a talker without cause but his advice was good once he did.

I will do that.

The intercom on the hold wall began to whistle her name. Dedran wanted to speak to her. She obeyed, trotting from the hold with deliberate haste. Let him also believe that she was eager to be cooperative in the face of his threats.

Dedran eyed her prompt arrival with approval. Bond-servants. They all needed a touch of the whip occasionally. The girl was more valuable to him than she knew but if she did not bend to his designs, then he'd have to break her.

He addressed the small figure as she stood before him submissively. "Sit down." She obeyed. "Now, I've listened to your talk with this Logan. So he's going to High Peaks ranch. Tell me about it."

Laris talked, making the difficulties sound just a bit greater than they were.

"So they send few copters up there," she informed him. "The winds as they come from the peaks are dangerous. Logan will have coptered to the lower reaches of their land, then ridden the rest of the way." She watched as he absorbed that then shifted to prattle about the animals.

"And they have coyotes. They're so cute, and smart—why once I saw them . . ." She recounted a hunting story making much of the animal's intelligence. "They're a mated breeding pair too. It's a pity, but they won't be at the Peaks. Storm's wife took them to some native camp to hunt again. But you want the others, not a pair of coyotes."

"Don't tell me what I want," Dedran said absently. Laris kept her face bland and submissive. Had he taken the bait? He looked at her. "Tell me about this Tani. Is she a trained beast master?"

He had! She shook her head. "No, Storm said once she has the abilities. But the war ended too soon. She was never even in the services. Her aunt and uncle are scientists and she worked with them. Mostly washing bottles and lab equipment I think." She mustn't make him think Tani worth taking or killing. "She's only about nineteen I think." A lie but Dedran might not know, she thought. Tani didn't look older and he'd only seen her briefly a couple of times. Dedran equated age with wisdom, youth with stupidity. Let him see Tani as no threat.

Dedran scowled thoughtfully. "Tell me about this girl and the coyotes."

A mind voice came, *Quickly, protest their importance.*

Laris wrinkled her forehead. "But she's not even trained. And if you take one of the coyotes it would pine away like some of the other animals you've brought in."

"You said she has the abilities, and so do her animals, yes?"

"Well, so Storm said. But he's her husband. He could have been just, well, bragging about it."

Well done, sister-without-fur. Gently, not too firm.

"I don't know. Anyway, Tani and her team are over on the fringe of the desert. It'd take longer to get to them." She allowed her face to frown a little. "Of course Storm did say it was easy to get there in a copter. There isn't the same wind gust problem as they have at High Peaks . . ." She allowed her voice to trail away.

Dedran nodded once in decision. "I'll want you to speak to Cregar tomorrow. Tell him all you know about this girl and the coyotes. I presume you have some idea of where the natives she's visiting are camped."

Laris agreed. Logan had talked about the Djimbut clan and their lands enough to allow her to give some direction to Cregar's search.

"Then get out and check that wolf. Is the stupid brute going to survive or are we talking samples from another dead beast?"

Laris mumbled that the latter was probable and fled. To her distress that information was almost certainly true since the will to live was broken in the large gray animal. It lay there refusing to eat or drink. She could provide nourishment intravenously but when she'd tried that before, the wolf had roused as soon as she left just enough to rip the tube free each time. She was using stimulants but they had worked with less and less effect. She had kept it alive for several days but she was losing the battle and knew it.

Inside herself she raged at the necessity of torturing the animal. But if she didn't Dedran would see that someone else did who would be less kind. She counted. Five days since liftoff. If the wolf died now Dedran wouldn't blame her. She'd kept it alive long enough to show she was trying. She removed the tube, cut off the trickle of stimulant, then stroked the harsh pelt. She bent over and whispered softly into one furred ear.

"Go free, friend. Run free. I give you leave to go."

The lungs heaved up, hesitated, and then the breath went out slowly. The body seemed to flatten. She waited a few minutes to be sure before taking with a steady hand the samples Dedran would require. She placed those in the chiller, labeled them, added a warning to the lid, and went to find the circus boss.

"The wolf died. It tore out the tubes again while I was with you. I've taken the samples. They're safely in the chiller. Three sets."

He hurled a paperweight at the wall. "I had it! It wasn't even hurt. Damned beasts, damned beast masters." His eyes suddenly looked frightened as his voice dropped to a hoarse whisper. "I have to get one that stays alive. Maybe a beast would stay alive if its mate was with it." He turned on Laris. "Get out!" She edged to the door as he slumped in his seat. Her ears caught his mutter as she slid the door shut.

"Nhara will kill me if I fail."

Nhara? Laris drove the name deep into her mind. It sounded like an inner systems name. She wondered if Nhara might well be Dedran's mysterious patron and backer. She'd long since deduced that Dedran owned only a small percentage of the circus. It was a decoy, used as a screen, as through it moved people and animals which would have been noticed as illegal in some way without it.

Cregar came to talk about Tani and the coyotes just before the Lereyne landing. He listened to all Laris could say. Dedran was there as well and the men talked over the girl's head.

"Coyotes are smart even without genetic enhancement." That was Cregar.

"So why did the beast master HQ switch mostly to wolves?"

"I'm not certain. I think they may have found coyotes more independent. Wolves are pack animals."

Dedran was onto that. "So coyotes are less likely to suffer separation trauma, and with the girl not having been trained at all they may be less strongly bonded." He smiled nastily. "Think of it, Cregar. You could even end up with them bonded to you." He turned to Laris. "You say the girl went to this native camp alone? None of her family are with her?"

"She went alone but," Laris said, choosing her words carefully, "there's nothing to say one of the family won't go after her. Although I did get the impression she was to stay there alone several weeks. But I could be wrong." That should cover her. If anything happened then she could quote her own words. She hadn't been sure and had said so.

Dedran discounted her warnings as she'd expected. He had fastened onto this idea of a young harmless girl unable to protect two enhanced beasts. Two animals bonded to each other as a mated pair. He discounted the natives too. Dedran came originally from a long-settled inner planet. Any native race there had died out long before humanity lifted its face to the stars. He despised native races as primitive. He'd never been called on to live as they did and had no idea of how much intelligence and ingenuity—and ferocity—such a life could take.

They were only a step up from the animals they used, he thought. Cregar could copter in, sneak up after dark, stun as many as was necessary, and escape with the stunned coyotes. He could pick up assistance from local criminals as always. Make sure they had no ID. Hire the copter under a false name. And anyway, one thing he had found about Arzor: The native lands were theirs by treaty. The natives had no copters and by government decree no one over-flew tribal lands. It would take them days to get a message out about his raid. By then Cregar would be long gone.

He waved the girl to the door and gave Cregar his orders. "I want both coyotes undamaged. Stun them. Try not to kill any of the natives or the girl either. The Quade boy was talking to Laris in one of the bugged rooms. Too many people are beginning to put two and two together and they're getting a conspiracy against beast masters as their answer. Take as many men as you need and stun the whole camp if you have to. Set their horses free, and stun everyone again before you leave. It should give you enough of a head start."

"Uh-huh. Baris and Ideena were heading here the last I heard of them." He gave a hard grin. "I had a contact of mine keep a watch on what they were doing. You know, Dedran, I could use that scout ship of theirs. If I offer them the right to loot the camp before we get out they'd take me in and off Arzor again without declaring a passenger. If Arzoran security start looking for anyone it would be for them."

"And if they get themselves killed you could fake voice-prints and lift off with a sweet ship to add to our outfit. They aren't guild." Dedran agreed slowly. "I like it. Talk to them. Offer them anything but let them set the price." His eyes met those of the man opposite him. "And if the natives don't kill them, maybe they still won't make it back."

"I think that's possible. I'll look for them as soon as we land." He stood and left the cabin. A man couldn't choose the ones he worked with. A pity. But the money was good and the chance of beasts again sounded even better. But he'd see to it that his hirelings didn't harm the Tani girl. She wasn't a real beast master. Not one of those who'd stood by and let him be dumped like rubbish. He'd allow her to live. Since she wasn't trained the loss of her team wouldn't be so bad anyhow. He went to his cabin, laid down, and dreamed of days long past when one was many and all were one.

He was near the cages the next day, gazing at the beasts as Laris scurried to and fro in her work. He noticed her struggling to move a larger box of supplies from the top of several others, and moved forward just as the box began to to tilt dangerously downward. It had been heavier than Laris expected as it slid toward her. Cregar jumped forward, realizing if it fell on the child she could be injured. His hands closed on the box's handles and he caught it before lowering it down safely with her help. He glanced at her.

"Be careful, if you are hurt Dedran won't be pleased."

Her mouth twisted into a wry smile. "I know." He turned to leave and without thinking she spoke. It was the old custom of the camps binding her to a fair exchange. The man had maybe saved her from injury, a favor of the same kind was owed.

"Cregar?" He turned to listen. "Don't discount the natives on Arzor. Logan told me they're warriors. A clan can fight like a tigerbat swarm." He said nothing, only nodded in reply before he left again, but Laris was satisfied he'd understood her warning.

They touched down on Lereyne to find that Dedran's forerunners had whipped up crowd enthusiasm to almost a frenzy. Cregar faded into the crowd seething on the port periphery, watching the circus set up on the back lot. He found Baris drifting quietly along, eyes flicking from side to side. Cregar could have taken the idiot right there. But he wanted to use the pair as long as possible. And it would fire the other man's touchy pride.

Cregar half turned away and waited. Crats, but the man was clumsy. He'd sensed him sneaking up minutes before he closed in to hand range. He encouraged his body to flinch when the hand tapped him lightly on the shoulder. Turning, he had time to see the gratified look in Baris's eyes. The man had been a skulker, a scavenger, and a hanger-on during the war and in some ways he'd never gotten over not being a real fighter.

Now it delighted him that he'd successfully surprised one

who'd not only been a warrior, but one of the elite. Cregar allowed him his moment of triumph before beginning negotiations. Ideena was more suspicious.

"What's in this for you?"

She was sniffing at the bait. Now to set the hook. "We'll both do well," Cregar told her calmly. "For us, I get the beasts Dedran wants. You'll be transporting me and them free. I'll split the cost of those we hire. For you, Dedran had his little snooper staying with the family there for weeks. She says that the Storm woman is off visiting with a native clan." He leaned forward and splayed a set of photos across the table. "Ever seen something like this?"

Ideena gaped. "Cat's-eye gems." She stared at him, her tongue flicking out to lick her lips. "Where?"

He smiled. He had her now. "Where'd you think? Arzor, where I want to go. That's the world which produces them. The Thunder-talkers there wear sets like this. Thunder-talkers are their witch doctors and they always wear the most valuable green gems as their symbols. Some of the wealthier clan people would have lesser jewels. The ones in gold or red maybe. Those photos are from the early days. Now the planet holds a native treaty in place. They don't go onto native lands, they can't hunt there or even fly-over without specific clan permission." He added one further comment, his voice stressing the words slowly.

"And the clans have only bows and arrows. They ride horses. No guns, no copters, no nothing."

Ideena's eyes were glittering. "And any clan would have a Thunder-talker."

"And any Thunder-talker would have a set of gems like these, maybe better," he confirmed.

She exchanged looks with Baris. "We're in. But we get to check the whole clan if there's time."

"There should be. If there isn't we can just stun them again." He watched her. Ideena looked at Baris who signaled acceptance.

"All right," she said. "We're definitely in. But any tricks, Cregar, and Baris'll feed you to those damn beasts you're snatching."

"I'm interested in the animals, and getting in and out with my hide and no peacekeepers on my tail. That's all. But while you're giving out warnings take one for yourself." He fixed her with his eyes until she nodded. "Good. When can you lift off?"

Ideena consulted Baris in a low mutter as they walked to the ramp. Baris seemed to be protesting. She overrode that and turned to Cregar. "Tomorrow morning at the earliest. We need supplies, and Baris has something he wants to do."

Cregar would have bet on it. At the very least Baris would be planning some way to make sure they weren't tricked. Considering the man, it wouldn't be anything too subtle though. And since neither of this precious pair would want anyone knowing their business, they'd be unlikely to be planning the timeworn "leaving an envelope with someone to be opened" routine. There was always a chance that trick would go wrong, and the envelope used to convict them of something.

He waved graciously. "Tomorrow morning then. And I'll contribute to supplies. That's fair." He handed over a hundred-credit note, contriving to brush against Baris's sleeve as he did so. The tiny bug should stay there long enough. He'd planted two larger bugs already. One under the table here, and another by their ship's ramp. Ideena would expect that. She'd look, find them, and be satisfied. But they were meant to be found. Now he flicked three more from his fingertips when neither quarry was watching.

One bounced off and was lost. The other two clung to Ideena's clothing near the hem. Not an ideal spot but they had good amplification. He should be able to hear what this pair said. He left the duo with protestations of comradeship and hurried to a secluded place behind a shed. Then he thrust the receiver into his ear hastily. Baris was complaining.

"Why can't we just murder the creep once we lift off? We can dump his body into the sun and keep going."

Ideena's voice would have etched steel. "Baris, you idiot. If we do that how are we going to find out where this clan is?"

"Who says we need that particular clan?"

"I do. If we get picked up for any reason before we're clear, well, we're just innocent traders accepting a hired collection job. We had no idea what the man was doing. When we found out, we were out over the desert in a copter filled with his men. You get us new IDs in some unlisted name before we lift. If they run us they find nothing. If they run Cregar they get . . ."

It was clear that a great light was dawning on Baris. "Oh, I see. That's clever of you, Ideena. They'll get his record and then they'll believe us."

"Riiight," Ideena drawled. "So we dump him after we score and get clear. He thinks we're going in without listing him as a passenger, but we do more, we list him as having hired us. If nothing does go wrong Dedran will likely pay well to have these animals back even if Cregar doesn't come with them. Just see to it that Cregar can't steal the ship and we'll make out like pirates."

"What do you mean 'like pirates'? We *are* pirates." There was a lot of chuckling and Cregar removed the receiver. He took a small flat object from his belt, set several buttons, hooked it back, and strolled into the port crowds again. He'd let the recorder pick up anything else they said for a while, and he'd play it back every few hours. But Baris and Ideena would be busy most of the day. It would be later when they had their errands out of the way that what they said might have some bearing on him again.

He reported back to Dedran. "They're not intending to do anything until we leave Arzor. But I need a clean ID for myself and a set of theirs with their true identities. I'll plant theirs somewhere half smart. If we get picked up by any authorities I'll be clean and it'll be that pair who'll have to be answering questions."

He smirked. "There's times when I can hardly keep track of who's double-crossing who in this game. Hang on a moment." He activated the recorder and listened. "Nothing, just supplier trading. Listen, we'll be using their ship to get to Arzor and do the grab on the animals. One thing Baris and Ideena will do is try to fix their ship so I can't lift off on my own without them. Any ideas how they might be able to do that?"

Dedran considered. "Nothing you shouldn't be able to counter if you drop them at some stage and can pick over them and their gear for any lockchip. They'd probably use one of those to freeze their ship's controls. But if you have to make a run for it and lose them . . ." He thought. "Take an all-purpose memorychip. If they take a chip out of the navigationcomp the ship won't lift. Or if they run a null program to keep the programming wiped. Put a memorychip in and it bypasses the null program or the lack of a proper chip."

Cregar nodded. "Sounds okay. But keep thinking. I'll see you before I lift. If I don't come back neither do your animals."

He didn't have to mention that if the authorities collected him because Baris and Ideena had been able to dump Cregar first, then if Cregar was still alive he'd have no reason not to talk to the Arzoran authorities and save his own skin. If he gave them someone higher up the chain they'd give him immunity and a new ID. He'd talk selectively of course. Enough to have them out looking for Dedran the mastermind.

Not enough to encourage a guild contract. But that would still leave Dedran doing several lifetimes—depending on the planet which caught him and for what. Some had the death penalty for many of Dedran's activities. And Dedran had no one farther up the chain he could talk about. Too many of those were heavy into the guild, who'd forcibly resent it. Not that Cregar had to say any of this, he didn't have to, it was what Dedran would do if he was the one caught first. His smile was bitter—what a life. Turn in your companion before he turned you in. Trust no one, make no friends, never stay long in any place. How had he come to this?

Cregar spent much of the day on the move, but he sat in to watch the afternoon show. It went well and the crowd stood to applaud at the end. Judging by the number of people turned away at the door, Dedran would be able to stay here for weeks without suspicion. He checked out the recorder as he checked back with the circus boss. Neither had any more worth hearing. Cregar headed toward the ramp, then halted.

There was one other thing which bothered him. But there wasn't much he could do about it. He turned away and stood looking indecisively into the animal hold. At the far side he could see the girl grooming a tigerbat. They'd be setting up for the evening show soon. Cregar cursed in a soft, tired voice. He was a fool. But he trusted Laris more than he did any other person, and she'd warned him. He'd understood her earlier comment to him about the natives, they weren't quite as passive as the ship's library made them out to be. With that warning in mind he'd added a precaution or two for his trip into the clan lands.

Dedran had talked recently about his plans for the child. Here on Lereyne they had the arenas as they had on several other worlds. In them, beasts fought for their lives. On Lereyne the sport was frowned upon socially although it was not illegal. However, the nonacceptance meant that it was very difficult to acquire good beast trainers. Dedran would like to sell Laris for that purpose, unless her bond expired before he could do so, or the child found enough credit to escape. And if she thought what he would tell her now was only about money—the child was as honest as she could be with Dedran as bond-master.

He caught her eye and signaled her to come to him in silence. She obeyed, then stood listening as he spoke in the camp slang he'd learned in low ports, using a very soft, carefully blurred voice. None could lip-read that or even pick it up understandably with a wall bug or directional mike.

"If I don't come back, I gotta a stash 'a credits. Want you ter have them. They behind a panel, room next t' mine." He gave swift directions and waited to see she understood.

"Why'n me?"

"If 'n I don't need them 'ny more what matter. Take 'em and get out. Swear oath, no touchin' 'til it's sure I'm gone. Then use 'em to leave. Oke?"

She met his eyes firmly. "Swear oath," the same carefully blurred voice repeated. She put out a shy hand and brushed her fingertip over his arm. "You'm take care 'n thanks." She was gone, back to her tigerbat grooming and Cregar was left shaking a little. He forced calm and left without meeting Dedran. He found himself wondering, if he'd stayed in the service, if he'd married, if he'd had a daughter, would she have been like that one?

He hoped so. Then he scoffed at himself. He was getting soft in his old age. Laris was just another camp brat, but—she was better than most. The girl had warned him, risking the circus boss's anger if he'd heard that, and Cregar had heard her tell Dedran earlier that Cregar was a fine trainer. Something inside of him was warm remembering her words. Let the kid get out if she had the chance; if he went down on this trip his credits would be no use to him anyway.

He turned into the street where the shop should have his requirements, his thoughts returning to the circus. If Laris stayed there Dedran would fake an open bond and sell the child to be a beast trainer for one of the arenas. She would fight that— and her new owners—and be broken, something he didn't wish to happen. He put it all out of his mind as he entered the store and settled to bargain for one of the all-purpose shipchips. They came high and he wasn't wasting credit.

Fortunately he didn't have to. Lereyne was a fishing planet with a number of ports—and all the shops which catered to them. On the huge inland sea there were canneries, fish-drying factories, and a host of fishing boats, along with the people who worked on the boats and in the factories. The volume of foreign cargo ships which ported on Lereyne not only made it an excellent place to stop for a circus, it also made it a good place to buy small, normally high-cost, portable items. Cregar bought an all-purpose secondhand shipchip for a price which made his smile stay in place all the time he searched for Baris.

Chapter Eight

Cregar found Baris. The man was gambling again but with skill. From what the ex–beast master knew, Baris often supplemented his and Ideena's income with some clever cheating but only on planets not sophisticated enough to have checking programs in place. The penalties for being caught cheating ranged from forced bond to death depending on the world and its laws.

Nor would Baris bother with the inner worlds, where monetary systems were mainly on personal or general memorychips. They depended on IDs which were almost impossible to forge, and their gambling payouts were transferrals from one chip to another. Baris wouldn't gamble on such worlds; they gave nothing portable and anonymous. Computer winnings on such worlds could be too easily tracked from planet to planet. He signaled Baris who raked in a stack of credits and nodded.

"Thank you, friends. I must go now as I warned you." He flicked a couple of credits across to the dealer. "Drinks on me." He bowed to the gamblers around the table. "I salute you. It's as well I'm leaving before fortune frowns and I lose my very boots."

Cregar noted the grins. So, Baris had been cheating a bunch of rich amateurs. A good touch. He'd warned them he'd have to leave when a friend showed up. Paid for drinks, and left them with a compliment. By their looks, they had no suspicion they'd been done. They thought of Baris as a nice man and merely a good gambler with luck on his shoulder. Cregar made a mental note of that. Baris was a better psychologist than he'd thought. Judging by the stack of credits he'd scooped up he'd sheared this bunch and left them liking it.

Baris joined him. "Nice people, terrible gamblers." His smile was satisfied. "Ideena will be pleased. I made back everything we spent on supplies earlier."

Cregar hid a wince. "How long were you at the table?"

"Five hours. Come on, Ideena wants us back at the ship. She plans to lift off as soon as we get clearance."

Obediently Cregar hurried. Five hours, he was thinking as he trotted along. Baris must have tossed in the occasional hand and built up a slow but steady trickle of hands won. No huge pots. No obvious runs of too-good fortune. Just a quiet bleeding of credits across the table in Baris's direction. He'd have used sleight of hand to drop credits into his pockets. No buildup of those on the table. With them out of sight and Baris not seen pocketing them either, there'd have been nothing to remind the others that they kept losing.

Cregar wasn't a gambler himself. Most professionals in that field had a touch of ESP. His own abilities didn't lean in that direction, but he knew how it was done. It was one of the first things they taught beast masters, so they didn't get caught in any traps. He'd survived long enough to learn that as well as other things. He didn't realize his lips had peeled back in a snarl. They'd taught him, shown him heaven—then torn it away from him, leaving him empty and bleeding for the rest of his life. They would pay.

At the ship Ideena was waiting. "What kept you?" Her tone softened when Baris grinned and began turning credits from his pockets. "Well done. No trouble?"

He snorted. "Bunch of amateurs. Rich kids wanting to show they knew what was what. I trimmed them good an' they never knew a thing. They'll still be down there drinking the credits I left and saying what a nice guy I was."

Ideena was counting the notes and coins. "This'll cover what I spent for supplies. Nothing like a free trip." She eyed Cregar. "But there's still fuel. You'd better make this worthwhile, Circus Man. Get to your cabin and strap down. I've already got clearance. We lift in a few minutes."

Cregar nodded and left. He opened doors. The first two cabins clearly belonged to Baris and Ideena. The next was empty. He dropped his bag into a chest bolted to the floor, rolled onto the bunk, and fastened the shockweb harness. Just a couple of minutes later the small ship shivered and leapt skyward. Cregar was mulling over something Ideena had given away. She had to have known Baris had met him and that they were on their way to the ship.

Without knowing that, she'd hardly have asked for liftoff clearance. This was an active port. It was the clearing area for the trade of several planets. Ships large and small came and went busily. If Ideena had asked for clearance and then aborted they'd have dumped her to the back of the queue. Therefore she'd known they were on their way. Which meant she and Baris had some way of keeping in contact without the man making it obvious.

He'd better find out what that was. It could be inconvenient at the least to have them exchanging information if he wanted them isolated. At the most it could be lethal. The shivering quietened as the power curve leveled off. Gravity dropped to what felt like a quarter of standard and Cregar flicked the shockweb harness free again. He stood and wandered from the cabin. Time for a quick snoop now under the guise of finding his way about.

He had time for that and more over the time it took to make Arzor. Baris tried to entice him into gambling and failed. Ideena tried her wiles and he allowed it to appear she had succeeded. Not that she'd take it further than sweet smiles. Baris wouldn't like it. But he allowed it to seem that he was softening toward her, perhaps that he was beginning to even trust her a little. He wondered who was fooling who. But you had to play the game.

They landed on Arzor. Hiring a copter and a few career criminals was easy. Baris had the transactions completed by evening. They'd fly out early the next morning. Cregar went to his cabin for a good night's sleep. Judging by the sounds, Baris and Ideena had sought her cabin for a similarly early night, although not to sleep. That was another interesting point. Courting danger clearly excited them. His smile was grim as he made his own preparations. If they tried anything he'd be ready for it and the danger would be more than they were expecting.

The copter was already there by the time they had risen and eaten a light meal the next morning. The hired quartet of scruffy, dangerous-looking port scum were lounging about beside it. Baris was a qualified pilot, but at a pinch Cregar could get the copter up if he had to. He took the seat behind Baris and unobtrusively watched as the big man handled the controls.

The copter circled, drifted in as quietly as possible from an unexpected direction, and finally settled in to land in the rough country past the clan camp. They'd wait until dark then move in. Both Baris and Ideena had slipped dark lenses into their eyes. They would be able to see well enough. The lenses Cregar used were state-of-the-art. He could not only see everything as if it were day, he could also pick up heat auras. He'd know if living things were in hiding behind brush or behind anything else which allowed a heat signature to seep past.

He omitted to mention that. Let them believe his lenses were of the usual kind. If things went wrong he wasn't about to risk more than he had to. The sun curved slowly across the lavender sky. The copter's seven occupants dozed, drank, and ate. Cregar eyed the hired quartet from under half-closed eyelids. An unsavory bunch. Ten-to-one if Ideena found her gems in any quantity there'd be an attempt to dump her, Baris, and Cregar. Probably not until the men had been paid though. If they waited until they were back at the ship they could maybe loot the ship too.

He lay back, allowing himself to fall into a half sleep. He could smell the desert from here where the small breeze lifted to higher land. It was a good smell. Clean, dry, with a hint of the growing brush. That soft smoky scent which would have said falwood in bloom to an Azoran. In the distance a grass hen squawked angrily. Cregar squinted at his watch. He'd keep an eye on their so-called comrades in crime. He didn't think they'd try anything. Not yet. They wouldn't move until there was loot to take. Right now he'd be safe enough.

When he woke completely the sun was almost down. It would take them a couple of hours to walk the distance to the clan camp. Best they had a meal now, then started. Ideena was of the same mind. Once they'd begun the march she ranged up alongside Cregar and her voice came in a low tone none but he could hear.

"I don't trust these men." That was the pot calling the kettle black, Cregar thought. He cocked an eyebrow in invitation for her to continue and she did, dropping her voice still lower. "I've a spare gun tucked in the clump of weeds by the ramp. If anything happens, pretend to fall down there."

"What sort of gun? How effective will it be?" He wanted to know how far she'd go.

"Stunner but it's blast-bolt activated." That told him. She'd go all the way. Activating a stunner with a blast-bolt had been done before, but it was so frowned on that anyone caught doing it would go to rehab automatically. Of course, if it was his life, then he'd risk the illegality first and worry about rehab later. It wasn't likely they'd catch him anyhow. Or care greatly about the death of any of this lot. But it told him more than he'd known about this precious pair. He'd always thought they were small-time. They might still be the jackals he'd believed. If they were prepared to go that far though, they were rabid ones. He spoke quietly.

"What about your own stunners here?"

"They're straight."

That was better—if it was the truth but he couldn't be sure of that until they used their weapons. He plodded on in silence considering all he'd learned of them thus far. He couldn't trust any of the six people with him and he didn't like that. He'd have liked things even less if he'd known what lay ahead.

Tani had returned to the clan. Storm had accepted that when, after ten days, there'd been no sign of trouble. But it was the time between the two major seasons on Arzor, the big wet and the big dry. She enjoyed that pleasantly mild in-between season and had gone back to hunt with her friends another few days. They'd taken two yearling merin deer and a number of the fat grass hens. It was an hour short of dusk. They'd done well enough, now they'd head for the camp to be back before dark.

Jumps High, the first clan friend she had made the year before, had been about to pack the meat onto their horses when Ferarre's ears pricked. He whined. Linking, Tani caught the up and down beat of a muffled copter. She hissed and dropped flat. Jumps High copied that as did the other four natives.

He half turned from his sprawl to hand-sign to her. "Danger, where, what?"

"Ferarre hears a copter. That's not good."

"How so?"

"It didn't head for the camp, instead it's gone in a half circle around and landed beyond. It hasn't lifted off again. You know the law, no copter is allowed over clan lands. I think those who fly it may be enemies." It had to be that. Or some idiot citizen with more money than sense but the rangers would have known and stopped it. The treaty was very firm on over-flights.

If it had been Storm or one of the rangers with an emergency he'd have flown straight to the camp. The Nitra weren't fools. They would have understood if it was truly needful. But the copter had landed in cover; not near the camp. She felt there was danger and these were her friends, she would not have them hurt because she did not make her warning clear.

Jumps High was signing. "Does the copter rise again?"

"No." The coyote's ears could hear no sound. The engines were still off. That probably meant it would stay where it was for a while. She stood, turning, listening. Then her hands rose. "The engine sounds came from that way."

Her friends clustered around their mounts, swiftly field

dressing the dead deer then loading the kill. Jumps High considered. "How far are the copter sounds from here, and how far from our camp?"

"From here maybe a half-hour ride. From camp they may be one hour's ride." And that was what had given the copter away. They'd circled in from the far side of the outer lands. It was their ill fortune that Tani and her friends had been hunting in that direction. Worse luck that Ferarre and Minou could hear even a copter with a muffled engine at that distance. Had it not been for the coyotes, even then the copter would not have been noticed.

She smiled to herself. They'd all been under cover cleaning the game when the copter circled. If it had heat-sensing gear the occupants hadn't been reading it at the time. And neither Tani, the Nitra, nor their animals had been out in the open to be seen by any glancing out of the clearplas bubble. A copter's heat-sensing gear differed. It was possible theirs was of the basic kind which read only that there was a sort of blotch of heat in a certain position. Not the shape of that source. In which case with everyone in cover they could have seen the sources and still mistakenly assumed them to be animals, sheltering from the hotter sun of afternoon.

The deer and grass hens safely loaded, Jumps High was signaling to Tani again, using her native name. "We will go now, Sunrise. Once we are back in camp I will speak to the Thunder-talker of this. She will pray and ask the powers of the Thunder what is the danger to us. Then we can make plans. For now, let us ride quickly for the camp."

His mount leapt away and Tani swung into her saddle. Destiny, the silver part-duocorn filly she rode, followed Jumps High's mount eagerly. Behind them in a scattered group came their friends. The coyotes ranged ahead. Tani wondered if she should mind-link with Mandy. The big paraowl could fly out and look over the area where the copter had landed. But if anyone who knew Arzor saw her they'd know she didn't belong here. It could warn the enemy if that's what they were. Best to take no chances. Not yet.

One thing the possible enemy should not know. Tani smiled, a slow hard grin. She was the only human clan-friend among the dozen clans of the Nitra. Because of her position Kelson of the rangers had granted her a miniature comcaller. When she visited the Djimbut clan it came with her by clan permission. Using it she could report any Nitra problems, anything likely to make trouble between native and settler. There was a built-in scramble as well; that way if the news was bad no one listening in would raise a premature alarm. She nudged Destiny and the filly sped up to canter lightly beside the mount of Jumps High.

"When we come to the camp I'll speak to Kelson. Ask why a copter breaks the treaty."

"That is good," was the brief reply.

Tani rode on, her mind busy. She had to know what to say to the ranger head. She sorted her impressions, ordered them by importance, then rode patiently. As soon as they arrived at the camp she slowed but continued through toward the tent of the clan medicine woman. Once there she dismounted, signing swiftly as her friend stepped from the tent entrance to greet her.

"There may be trouble, I must speak to Kelson. Listen to what I say." She switched on the comcaller and reached Kelson almost at once. As she spoke into the transmitter panel her hands flew, repeating in sign-talk for the benefit of those clan members who did not understand the settler language what she was saying to the ranger head.

"Kelson. Listen. While I was hunting to the north of the clan camp Ferarre heard a copter. It landed about an hour's ride from the camp and hadn't taken off again after an hour or so. I don't like the way the engines are muffled and it circled supposedly out of our hearing before setting down. Could it be a legitimate flight?" There was a gasp, then the sound of a computer beeping. After several minutes the ranger's voice came back, loud and angry.

"No, it is not. There's no record of any request. Our two copters are both out in other directions and I've just checked with port. No copter filed any flight plan even remotely in your direction."

"You're sure? Then what do we do?"

"Hang on. I'm checking." He came back after several minutes. "I don't like this, Tani. The only copter it could be is one belonging to an outfit I don't trust very far. The copter has muffled engines and the pilot filed a flight plan toward the desert fringe on a sight-seeing trip with tourists. My contact at the port says seven people boarded. He knows two of them from the port here as minor but unsavory criminals." He paused. "It should be just about dark where you are by now."

"It is," Tani informed him.

"I can't get our copters back until morning. Tell the clan these people have no rights. If the warriors protect the clan in any way they must, then they are within our laws as well as their own." He paused again then spoke with heavy significance. "In any way. But do your best to see those ways don't include the tourists, who may be an innocent cover."

"And if they aren't?"

"Then that applies to them as well."

Her flying fingers had been keeping up with the conversation as Tani and Kelson spoke. From the growing Nitra circle about her there came soft hisses of satisfaction. If their actions were within settler law as well as their own, that meant that stunners taken were legitimate loot. They could be kept as could anything else taken from the attackers. The Nitra would have no use for the copter, but if they took that they could exchange its price for clan wealth in horses. Tani could guess at their reaction to *that* idea.

"I think you've said the right thing, Kelson."

"Tell them live tourists can be fined and the fine given to the clan as well, but only if the tourists are in one piece," he suggested.

"I'll do that. But you see what you can find out about them. I'll switch the com alarm off. Better our possible enemy doesn't know we have one. It'll flicker the lights if you call. The Thunder-talker's interpreter will stay with it; he's crippled so he isn't a warrior. If there's no attack going on when you call he can whistle me in to answer. Tani out."

She settled in to discuss tactics. The coyotes would eat and drink now then slip into the night. They'd show to heat sensors but as smaller blotches only, not as what they were. With fortune the enemy would assume them to be native animals disturbed by the movement. Jumps High had called in the camp's younger warriors as well. Thrown out in a screen, they would let the attackers through then close in behind. The experienced fighters would be ready, defending the camp and filling in the other half of a surrounding circle of death. The horse herd was loosed to wander about. The more heat blotches the better.

The Nitra medicine woman was signing, "What weapons will they have?"

"They'll have stunners for sure, those are legal and everyone has them. If they really mean this as an attack they could have pulse rifles." She grinned again as the listening warriors hissed in delight. They knew weaponry. A pulse rifle was normally beyond their ability to buy, but if the enemy brought the rifle here it was legitimate loot. Her hands flashed signs as she continued.

"They may have special things for their eyes. Lenses that allow them to see in the night as if it was the day."

The Nitra medicine woman gave a bark of amusement. "Hough! Djimbut are warriors. We can fight in dark or light, do they think we do not know our own lands? These enemies are fools if they think that way. Already we know they are here while they do not know we know. Kelson says their landing is not lawful. They are our prey and their property shall be ours." Tani signed swiftly then. She must make them understand that it would be bad if the possibly innocent tourists died.

The Thunder-drummer nodded, the human gesture of agreement the Arzoran natives had learned from the settlers. "We understand. It is simple, those without guns we do not harm, those with guns we shall kill. If your tourists fight against us, they too shall die."

It was a reasonable attitude, Tani thought, and Kelson could hardly expect the clan warriors to let themselves be shot, whether the shooter was a panicked tourist or not. She glanced from the tent entrance. By now it was about an hour after full dark. The clans tended to sleep about the second hour unless some celebration was occurring. Those in the copter would likely know that. She turned to the com.

"Kelson?"

"Kelson listening."

"I think if they come it'll be in about an hour. The clan's agreed not to hurt the tourists unless they're using weapons too. Then all bets are off. Did you find out anything more?"

His voice was harsh now. "Much more! The copter was supposed to be taking three tourists from an out-systems ship on a two-day tour, with one of the tourists acting as their pilot. The whole things's an orchestrated litany of lies. I checked the ship register. Nothing. But a friend in the patrol pulled a scan of the ship's registration and it's fake. So are the registered IDs of the two owners. She can't be sure who they really are but she'll keep trying to find out. She's found nothing on their so-called passenger as yet, but birds of a feather flock together." He heard her soft gasp.

"No time to talk that over. Listen. One of the port people says there were seven in the copter. That leaves four of ours. Two we knew about as soon as security saw their recorded faces, and port recording has ID'd the other two tentatively. All four are criminals. Never been sufficiently nailed to be forced into rehab but the peacekeepers say they're sure there's a lot of crime the four have been responsible for, it just hasn't been proven against them. All four are nasty pieces of work."

Tani had been thinking quickly, aided by the fast-moving hands of her friend, the Thunder-talker. "Kelson, would any of the four have ridden herd; are they used to outlands or are they city folk?"

There was a chuckle. "Well asked. Nope, they're all from the city." Her hands relayed that. Jumps High twittered a couple of swift orders in his own tongue and two of the warriors vanished. "I doubt they know much about local terrain and so far as I know none ride. They can't have more than stunners and just possibly a selective needler, either," Kelson assured her.

"Certain of that?"

"Fortunately. The port periphery sensors just put in a new weapons system. It lets us know if anyone crosses the port boundary carrying heavier weapons such as pulse rifles or blasters. It doesn't alert the carrier, just the peacekeepers. They can check them out without the one who's caught knowing how he came to be tagged. So, there were only stunners for certain when this bunch lifted from port, but there was a slightly different reading which could indicate a needler, one of the small handheld type."

She seized on the loophole. "But they could have landed and picked up other weapons after leaving."

"I don't think so. I timed your message, added the time they left here, and there's no gap. At steady speed they'd have just been landing when you heard them. We do think the copter may have basic heat sensors. Those would only give them a rather blurred heat signature and the rough size of the target. I'll get rangers to you at dawn. Where's Logan?"

Tani sighed. "At High Peaks with Hosteen's team. Logan twisted his wrist and ankle handling a frawn. Hosteen's riding circuit alone around our ranch. He's got Baku with him but Surra's still bonding with her new mate, and Hing has babies."

"Then neither man's going to be available. Okay, Tani. I'll have reinforcements in by dawn. I'd like some of these idiots to be alive when I get there but if it's you or them, let it be them. Kelson out."

From the darkness outside the tent came a twittering. The interpreter signed at flowing speed and fluency. "They come. Jumps High has put up the bodies of the merin deer on stakes as though they lived. Our scouts waited in line behind them. Our enemy sees beasts only. They see in the dark as you have said. They circled the deer so as not to alarm them." He stopped to listen as the cry of a night bird came. "The enemy approach. They are close to the horse herd." He gave a thin-lipped smirk.

"They see in the dark, yes. But still they do not know what they see. Within the herd other warriors wait and are over-looked."

The Thunder-talker nodded. "Go now, make ready. Sun-rise, walk wary."

Tani smiled at her. "Very wary," she agreed. "You also, wise one." She trotted silently from the tent and went to ground in a small hollow at the far edge of the camp. The chill ground would shield part of her heat signature. With only her head showing she'd look like a rock-rabbit to any heat sensors. The small plump creatures tended to be about in the early hours of the day or during the night, their thick fur shielding them from any chill.

At the edge of the camp Baris halted his troops. "The whole place is asleep. Ideena, you and Cregar go to that big tent, grab all the jewels you can. Stun-spray every tent you pass. You other four, stunners on wide spray. Don't worry, we have additional power units. Walk in line and overlap stun beams in front of us in a semicircle. Make no noise."

They obeyed, setting their stunners. At his word they started forward, stunners weaving in a pattern which should cover and overlap every living thing in front of them in a wide area. Unprepared for this tactic, the Nitra in the van-guard fell silently in their cover and without the attackers even knowing of their presence. Moving in skilled quiet, Ideena and Cregar had circled just outside the stun influence toward the shaman's tent. They sprayed it and entered.

Ideena took one look and swore viciously in a low monotonous voice.

"No one here but a Ghesh-damned comcaller." She touched the panel. "Warm, someone was using it only a few minutes ago. Had to be that girl. Look through the gear here. If they cleared out fast they may have left the cat's-eyes behind." She began raking through the Thunder-talker's possessions ignoring a commotion which flared up in the distance.

"Do you really want to waste time?" Cregar snapped. "The rangers could be on their way right now."

Ideena glared. "No, they couldn't. We paid high for the infocheck. Their copters are on the far side of the area. Even if they were warned just now they couldn't get here in time. But we may have to get back into the port a different way. Move it, Cregar. Check that box!" She gave a subdued cry of pleasure as several bracelets tumbled out of the folded cloth. She snatched up the jewelry, crooning at the play of light over green and sparkling white, before wrapping them again and thrusting them into her pocket.

"Worth a whole packet of credits. Any more?"

"No sign."

Her mouth turned angrily down. "You promised a lot more than these."

"The wretched woman is probably wearing the rest. Get out and look for her if you want them," Cregar growled. It wasn't likely Ideena would find anyone. But it would get her off his back. She scowled and vanished through the entrance only to leap back again.

"What . . ."

"Don't talk. Get out the back under the edge. Fast. We've got company."

Cregar was no fool. He dived for the edge of the tent, levered a peg out, and crawled through the gap. Ideena followed and he turned to re-peg the edge. As he did so a heavy blow to his back spun him partly around. Ideena stunned the warrior who had appeared, then looked down at Cregar.

"I thought you were supposed to be good, Circus Man?"

"I'm alive aren't I?" Cregar shook himself as he rose to his feet glancing at the heavy fighting spear which had struck him at close range. He owed Laris one for that, if it hadn't been for her warning he'd have been wearing lighter body armor under his shirt. The spear would have gone through the lighter level of that.

He took the lead again, drifting through cover to wait and look back once they were clear. Two of their men were down, dead he thought. The third had been struck down and was being tied even as they watched. There was no sign of the fourth. Baris had hung back cautiously behind his small command. Seeing that he apparently used no weapon, the Nitra had ignored him.

Baris put two and two together when he was ignored and fled as if in a blind panic. Ideena and Cregar came up with him two miles out of the clan camp.

"What do we do now?"

"We get to the copter and come back." Ideena was white with fury. "I'll show them they don't beat me so easily." She smiled nastily. "There's a wide-spray heavy-duty stun on the copter. We brought it aboard in that chest Baris carried. We'll lift, come in at about fifty feet, and spray everything for a mile around the camp. Now, run."

They trotted through the brush and over rough ground until Ideena was stumbling and even Cregar was wearying.

They reached the copter, Baris leaped to the pilot's seat and waited, speaking softly.

"Get your breath first. Give them time back there to calm down. Did anyone see what happened to the others? I know some crazy horse killed one. He walked into it around a bush and it jumped him."

"Three dead then," Cregar said. "They've got the other one and he'll talk if they keep him alive."

"So we clean him. Leave him with the others. They'll identify them in time but nobody'll know anything. If we reach the port before daylight we can get to the ship and clear before they can stop us."

Ideena looked mutinous. "Not without my gems."

"Not without my beasts either," Cregar added.

"Okay, okay. Here, take a drink and then we'll go." Baris passed over a flask and both drank. The Fever brandy burned a track clear to their livers and both gasped at the rush of heat. Ideena nodded.

"All right. I'm ready. Go, Go!"

Baris lifted the machine into the air on steady engines, swung it around, and pointed it south to the camp. The return engagement was about to begin. This time . . .

Chapter Nine

Again the coyotes were the first to hear the copter returning. It couldn't be Kelson. He'd said they couldn't get to her until dawn. It had to be the enemy coming back. Tani stared up at the sky. From the sounds heard by Minou and Ferarre the machine was coming in barely off the ground. That was the action of a peacekeeper machine about to stun-spray. These people must have one of those harmless pacifiers.

But why, what did they want? She was standing in the entrance of the Thunder-talker's tent with the older woman. They'd been replacing the tumbled clothing. Tani stood motionless, her mind suddenly racing. The enemy had been here. They'd searched among clothing and taken—what? Her hands flashed into life.

"Elder sister! Those who came, they took what?"

"My bracelets."

"Those of the Thunder-talker's power?"

"Not so. Friends gifted me these. But Thunder-talker gems. I mourn their loss."

Tani put two and two together in one intuitive leap. "I think two of our enemies have banded together. Some come to steal the cat's-eyes. The others come to take my spirit-friends." She reached for the coyotes and Mandy the paraowl, urging the paraowl to be ready, the coyotes to go with the Thunder-talker. Then she turned back to the medicine woman. "My spirit-friends hear them coming back again. Take off your gems of power, hide them well outside somewhere. Quick, be quick!"

She called Mandy as the Thunder-talker swiftly stripped herself of the gemmed belt, the necklace, and items of her calling. The paraowl arrived just as the Nitra medicine woman vanished into the dark to hide her sacred jewelry. Mandy landed lightly and waddled forward as Tani dropped to one knee to stroke the large bird.

"Take this message to Brad," she told her friend, impressing it with both voice and mind. "Brad, I'm with Djimbut clan. We have been attacked and they are returning. Thieves after cat's-eyes and possibly my team. Tell Kelson to close the port." By now she could hear the copter almost at the camp fringe. "Mandy, fly fast. Copter enemy. Fly!"

Mandy was into the air as the last word left Tani's lips. She lined out and fled for the home ranch like an arrow. But quick as the paraowl was, the copter had been quicker. The stun-spray was wide-set and the edge of it clipped the fleeing bird. Only lightly but enough that she went into a temporarily blacked-out tumble. Her wings extended, she planed to a soggy landing in brush several miles from the clan camp. She struck lightly enough but one wing hit a branch within the scrub.

Feathers bent, then broke. It was a painless but exasperating injury. It would unbalance her flight. Mandy crouched, dazed, in the bushes, panting. Her head drooped as the light stun took effect. She slept, safe at least from those who would have stolen her, but her message undelivered.

In the clan camp all was quiet. Nothing moved but the breeze twitching the clothing of those who lay about within its confines. The copter landed. Three humans emerged to begin raking through the camp. Cregar caught hold of Ideena before she could get far.

"People first. Where's that man they took alive?"

Baris was checking limp bodies. "He's here, badly injured but he's still alive." He borrowed a knife from the nearest recumbent Nitra and slashed once. "Now he isn't."

"That wasn't necessary." Cregar didn't care about the man's death, but if he was ever deep-probed by some authority he wanted to be able to say he'd protested.

Ideena snorted. "Save it. We don't have to carry the weight back, and we don't have to pay him. The natives killed the other three, we just say they got him too. Maybe this one will even believe it." She took the knife from Baris, wiped the handle, and pressed it several times at a number of angles into the Nitra's hand. Then she allowed the knife to drop as if fallen when his body relaxed, stunned.

"Let them find that. Now, stop worrying and start looking for my cat's-eyes." They found cat's-eyes enough, but of the commoner type. Red, gold, and the occasional black. But of the many times more valuable green or white used only for ceremony or gifts to a Thunder-talker, they found nothing. Ideena cursed steadily as she hunted.

Baris called from where he too searched. "I think this is their witch woman. But she isn't wearing any gems."

Ideena came running. "Check her."

"I have. Nothing."

"Look around her. She may have taken them off and hidden them when she heard us coming back. She'd have only heard that a minute before. Barely enough time to get them off, alone hide them away."

Baris grunted. "I still can't find anything." He nudged the stunned woman with his foot. "Pity we can't take the cow with us. I'd see she talked."

Cregar intervened. "We don't have time to waste. Pick up anything you want and help me with this pair." He'd discovered the coyotes where they lay in small heaps near Tani. The girl too had wisely stripped her cat's-eye jewelry, gifts of the tribe, and hidden it in a hastily scooped hole just by the tent rim. In the black and white of dark-lenses the minor earth disturbance should pass unnoticed. It had. But Minou and Ferarre had leaped back to be with their friend as the stuns struck. Now they lay where Cregar could find them.

His voice came harsher. "Pick up the Ghesh-damned beasts and get back in the copter. We're going on to that mountain ranch."

Ideena turned angrily. "What? That wasn't agreed."

"You want the credits I can release to your account, you'll do it. Get going."

She nodded slowly. "Baris, fire up the engines. It seems we have one more stop."

The limp coyotes were loaded. The engines sounded their muffled beat, and the machine lifted, swung to the north, and was gone. Below in the camp, nothing moved. Not for many hours. But in the air the copter was traveling at full speed and so was Ideena's tongue.

"What are we supposed to do? Where is this ranch? What are we after there, is there likely to be anything worth having?"

Cregar waved her to silence. "Baris, head north seventy degrees by west five. You'll see lights at a hundred and fifty miles. Stun-spray the whole ranch as we come in. We drop straight down, grab what I want, and lift again immediately. If you can find anything worth having in that time, do it. If not you'll have to leave it behind. First priority is the beasts I indicate. As soon as we're back in the air head for the port with all the speed you can get out of this thing."

"And land where?"

Cregar's smile was hard. "On the port perimeter to the east near the cargo area. I have it all arranged."

He saw Baris and Ideena exchange glances. That would hold them. They knew what kind of an ant's nest they could have kicked over here and they weren't keen to walk into peacekeepers. If he had a safe way into the ship they'd hold off. They could always take him once they were safe—or so they believed. He saw their bodies relax and hid an unpleasant look. They were effective, this pair. But incurably small-time and a little too independent. The guild would never suggest they joined it. He suppressed a bitter smile. He was just as independent. He'd simply hidden it better and the guild needed his skills. The abilities this pair had were a cred a score.

The copter droned on until Baris spoke. "Lights coming up below."

Cregar checked the instruments. "That has to be the Quade ranch. Swing low across it and stun-spray. Then go back and do the same at right angles. It should cover any of them out in the other buildings too."

Ideena nodded. "Once we land, Baris, you stay in the copter. Keep the engines ticking over and watch out for anyone coming in from elsewhere. Be ready to lift off as soon as I say."

The machine was swinging through the second line of stun as he nodded in turn. "All done. Get moving . . ."

The copter dropped like a stone, landed lightly, and the doors slid open. Cregar vaulted out. The door of the ranch opened to his thrust and he darted inside. When the copter swung down Logan had been in the basement. At the start of the Xik troubles his father had lined that with proplas—an application of plascrete and clearplas. Specially treated, it was impervious to stunner and blaster, and if the house collapsed on top, it would hold those within safely.

Logan heard the engines above and headed for the stairs, dropping the basement trapdoor shut behind him. He emerged into the corridor with Surra snarling beside him just as Cregar entered. Behind him Ideena produced a selective needler taken from one of the dead men, and shot in panic; the beast looked like death incarnate as it charged and Ideena had no plans to die here. Surra dropped, blood pouring from a gaping wound across the top of her skull. Logan shouted in anger and kept coming, his hand lashing across to reach his knife. Her adrenaline pumping now, Ideena shot again and Logan fell. Cregar bit back his fury at the possible loss of the dune-cat. It was done and there was no time to fight about it.

He stunned Surra to be safe then snapped at Baris who had followed them in when he heard the needler discharge. "Pick the cat up and get her into the back of the copter. Seal the wound off. If she bleeds to death I'll deduct half the cred. Move it!"

He saw the big cat safely stowed and returned to search quickly through the house. In the main family room he found a stunned meercat curled about a newborn litter. He grabbed the babies and mother and leaped for the copter again. He dumped the box of meercats carefully, then returned to look through the house. Somewhere there was an eagle. He wasn't sure if he wanted to find that or not. But for his own pride he had to know he'd looked. After that he found the safe. It was impossible to open in the time he had but there were a number of small items of value about the room. He returned to the copter with filled pockets.

"Where's Ideena?"

"Looting, of course," Baris drawled.

"Rev the engines."

"That'll bring her." He obeyed and the woman came running, her arms full of small plunder. Baris shifted a hand, the engines rose a note, and the copter lifted. Ideena took her seat and strapped in as the machine fled low and fast for the port.

"I found a few good things. Makes up for that jewelry we couldn't find on the native." She displayed her loot and Baris grunted approval. Cregar leaned forward and selected a ring from the pile. It was from old Earth, Cregar thought. Silver, with a flawed grass-green garnet as the stone. Some skilled gemstone-carver had etched that with the head of a cat in three-quarter profile. It seemed to look sideways at him.

"I'll take this. It isn't worth much and I know someone who'd like it." He saw their sneers. They thought him enamored of some woman. Nor did they recognize the work as Terran. They saw only the flawed stone. He smiled into the dark. Laris would be delighted by the cat's-head ring. He'd give it to her as recompense for his return and the loss of his stashed credits—and for her warning which had saved him a spear in the back. He'd have to tell her not to wear it if they ever returned to Arzor though. He dropped the ring into his pocket and sat back.

The copter raced the daylight as it hurtled across country. It beat the sun by a narrow margin. Dawn was showing dimly as it set down quietly behind the largest cargo shed. Cregar was first out. He peered about. A man approached and hissed softly.

"One is sent."

"One is found."

"Good. Dump whatever you have into these." Two men wheeled in large covered pallets and the raiders got busy. Surra went in, her bleeding stopped although Cregar didn't like the way she breathed. Dedran would be furious if another beast died. After that they loaded the uninjured but still stunned coyotes and meercats. That haul was good enough to temper rage. The meercat female would stay alive to care for her babies, and the babies wouldn't care where they were so long as they had their mother. What was more, the babies wouldn't be even loosely bonded to anyone as yet; he'd claim a pair for himself before any other person reached for them.

The man was nervously tossing them port coveralls. "Here, quick, put these on over your gear. Push the pallets up to your ship. Will it unlock as you get there?"

Baris nodded. "I can voice trigger it when we're close. It'll drop the ramp on command."

"Good. Take the pallets and coveralls with you. No time to leave them." He was checking the chrono on his wrist. "Go that way," he pointed. "Behind the shed and around from the other side. It puts you closest to your ship without being seen until you leave cover. Security will scan anytime now. You go the minute I say. You have one hundred fifty seconds to reach the ship before they see you moving. On my mark—" He held his hand across their path. Then, "Go!"

With Cregar in the lead pushing one pallet, Baris right behind him shoving the other, Ideena racing up to pass both men, they made for the ship. In his head Cregar was ticking off the time. Fifty seconds, a hundred. Baris called a hoarse order and the ramp began to lower. One hundred fifty seconds and from behind them a Klaxon howled. Ideena slowed to scoop up a stunner from the weeds. The ramp hit the dust and Ideena was first up, running for the bridge. Baris shouted an order as he and Cregar thrust the pallets up the ramp.

The ramp began to close behind them and the ship shivered into life as engines obeyed the final order. Beside him Cregar heard a clang as someone shot at the closing ramp. It snapped shut obliviously. He grabbed for ties. They'd have to up-ship right now. No time to sort out the beasts. Just hope they could lift before any heavier port security came into play. There certainly appeared to be a lot of activity in the main building. He could see lights coming on all over the place.

Someone was shouting at them with a loudspeaker. Someone else had fired up a laser cutter on a crawler heading toward the ship. He could see the ruby winking as it lit. Baris and Ideena weren't listening. They'd flung themselves into seats on the bridge, the engines were screaming, and even as Cregar threw himself flat the ship howled upward. Baris must be pulling five gravities, he thought dizzily. But at least he could think. They hadn't been shot down yet. He hoped the big cat would survive such a liftoff.

The ship cleaved sky, higher, higher. A vanishing silver splinter until it was gone. Below the port manager was resolving to make some very stringent inquiries. Her security shouldn't have been that slow. Whoever that bunch had been they'd had help from some at Arzor Port. She'd find whoever they were and make them sorry. The port was autonomous, but for an insult like that she'd work with the peacekeepers. Even the patrol. No one raped *her* port and walked away laughing.

On the High Peaks ranch Logan was drifting into consciousness. He hurt. He crawled bleeding from room to room unable to accept what had happened. Surra was gone, taken. So too were Hing and her babies. What was he going to tell Storm? He heard hoofbeats outside just as he slipped into darkness again.

In the Djimbut clan camp Tani stood shakily. She reeled toward the comcaller and gasped out a message. Then she sat limply waiting for her strength to return a little and her stun-headache to abate. The Thunder-talker joined her. They sat in silence, both outraged, both determined. This insult would be avenged. Neither as yet had realized that the coyotes had gone.

In the basin, Brad Quade finished breakfast and answered a call. He blew out a mouthful of swankee as he heard, dropped the cup, and ran for the door. Moments later his crawler left a plume of dust along the road toward the port. He drove with a reckless disregard for the road or his own safety. Kelson's copter came in overhead and settled on the first suitable spot. Brad's vehicle raced up.

"Talk fast, Kelson. What's going on?"

"You've been raided. I'm on the way to the Djimbut camp. Tani called from there. She says some copter came in during the night, attacked the Nitra. Stunned everyone, stole her coyotes, as much cat's-eye jewelry as they could find, and left again." Brad opened his mouth and was waved to silence.

"That's not all. The clan got four of the raider's men. I want to go there first and see if we can ID any of the bodies. They went on to hit your place at High Peaks. Storm commed in. He got back after line-riding to find Logan hurt bad; Surra and some of the meercats are missing." Brad sat. Then he spoke quietly.

"There's more, isn't there?"

"Yup, we lost the damn raiders too. Somehow they got back into the port and managed to up-ship. Port manager's going crazy. She swears they didn't do that without someone helping them and she's going to bring in the peacekeepers." Kelson eyed the big rancher. "Keep it together, Brad. Logan will be okay. Tani isn't hurt. We'll find out who it was and get the animals back."

"This ties in with those other reports."

"Seems likely. I have one of my men alerting other planet ports. We may pick them up elsewhere. The city security knows too." He grinned wryly. "I gather they aren't any happier about this than the port manager. Their officer here has made an offer to the port manager to bring in a deep probe and operator. Last I heard she was thinking about it. That's how serious she's taking everything."

"Guada's First-ship family too," Brad said absently. "Our families have been friends since then. I'd do the same for her." He lapsed into brooding silence again as the copter hurtled on.

It all fit together somehow. The dead beast masters, the missing beasts. The way in which the raiders had been able to arrive unnoticed and lift off again despite a closed port. They'd had a copter, he remembered. And left four men dead in the clan camp. Those would be places to start. With his teeth in the beginnings of a solution he'd not let go. A small deadly smile quirked his mouth. Nor would his kin.

Storm was a trained fighter, a beast master who'd fought the Xiks across a dozen worlds. Tani, small, slender, untrained, was still in many ways Storm's equal. They'd stood shoulder to shoulder against the enemy before. And Logan, his wild-blooded son who loved the wilderness more than civilization. Logan who'd lost his half-brother's beasts and a fight against the raiders. They were three to take up a war trail indeed. And that they would do. He had only to find the trail head for them. That was his work.

He set his teeth and willed calm. He'd be of no use if he allowed his anger to rule. First let them land at the clan camp and see what they could do to help there. He leaned forward to touch Kelson on the arm.

"The Nitra, they know we're coming?"

"The Thunder-talker has spoken. We are welcome to land and collect the dead. Tani's coming back to High Peaks with us. Jumps High and a couple of his people will lead Tani's mount back to the basin."

"Any word of the paraowl?"

"Not when I left."

Brad fell silent again. If his young daughter-in-law had lost not only her beloved coyote friends but also Mandy she would be utterly devastated. When the copter sank to a landing the girl was the first there. She was leading Djimbut warriors who carried four bodies, one trampled and hoof-slashed almost beyond recognition as human. Brad grunted. That would be the work of Destiny, Tani's filly, three-quarter duocorn and wholly ferocious to any she deemed a threat.

Tani was everywhere now: guiding the bodies into the copter cargo hold, finger-talking rapidly with Jumps High, then the Djimbut medicine woman. Finally she came to stand looking at Brad.

"*Asizi.*" She used the ancient word of address. "We have none of our own dead. The Nitra will leave vengeance to us unless we ask. Of what lives were taken none were theirs, by the Thunder's will." The Thunder-talker moved up to stand by the girl. She spoke and her interpreter's hands flickered with quick fluency.

"The enemy would have taken the gems which mark my power. But for the quick thinking of my younger sister all would have been lost. Her spirit-friends twice heard the enemy and twice that aided us to be ready. The clan stands with their clan-friend. If there be anything in which we can aid in return, let it be known." Kelson gave the bow over linked spread hands which was the Nitra acknowledgment in all formality of the Thunder-talker's power. Then he lifted them to sign.

"Gratitude. The enemy evil ones were ours. To ours the law which judges. Our clan is greatly angered, we ride in war. Yet if there is need, be sure we shall ask."

She made the small cupped-hand gesture of acceptance and turned away. From where Tani stood, there came a loud cry and the girl was running. Both Brad and Kelson jumped from the machine to follow. They reached her as she halted, half laughing, half crying.

"Mandy. She's all right." From the brush along the camp edge stumped a weary, still almost flightless paraowl. She had flown where she could, walked where she must, and Mandy had not appreciated the walking part of the journey. Tani dropped linked arms to make a bridge and the tired bird clambered up to sit on a padded shoulder. There she rested, drawing her beak gently down Tani's cheek and crooning softly as she sent a series of pictures. Tani examined the indicated wing and sighed before turning to the men.

"I sent her to take you a message, Brad. The copter came in faster and spray-stunned farther out than I expected. The stunner fringe caught Mandy as she flew, and knocked her silly. She landed several miles away without breaking more than some of the flight feathers in one wing. So she couldn't fly more than a few yards at one time. She's been flying and walking back here ever since."

Mandy made a disgusted spitting sound and there was laughter. Kelson had been translating Tani's words into sign-talk as she went. Even Nitra faces broke up in amusement at Mandy's obvious disgust at having to walk.

"She has very good hearing though. The copter came back very low still past her and she heard a few words. Say them for us, Mandy." The ferocious beak opened and an incongruous voice sounded. It was female, the accent was inner-systems and over-cultured.

"... men. Oh, all right ... go to this place. But there'd better be something there worth having besides those stupid animals. Your boss won't thank you for more of them dead either ..." Mandy stopped and waited for the generous praise she promptly received.

Kelson looked at them. "That might be useful. We can't run a voice scan on an imitation but it's so good to a human ear I'd bet experts at the school can tell us which world the woman comes from. Maybe more. Right now, we'd better head for High Peaks." He waited for Tani to settle Mandy before leading the way back to the copter and ushering them inside. He leaned out to sign to Jumps High.

"What do you want of us?"

"The bow hands of the enemies who do this," was the swift reply. "If that cannot be done, then bring us sure word of their deaths. Bring us a death-trophy we can hang in the medicine tent." Kelson's hands moved in acknowledgment of that. Then he slid the door shut and started the engines. Tani glanced at the paraowl as they lifted. Mandy's feathers could be fixed as soon as they reached the basin ranch and had a night's rest. She hoped Logan would be well. Brad had mentioned only that he'd been hurt.

Logan had been more than merely hurt. Storm, when he came running into the house, had found his brother lying in a spreading pool of blood. His eyes opened as Storm knelt by him and he tried to rise.

"Lie quiet. I'll get this bleeding stopped. Think about what you want me to know." He worked for several minutes before sitting back. "That's well. Wait now." He turned to slide open the door in a cupboard. Behind that was a small chilled area with a palm-lock. From it he took medical items and used them quickly. "Now, talk fast, brother."

Logan looked up. "Raiders. Copter." He spoke between gasps, his strength fading again. "Took Surra, Hing, her babies. Surra bad hurt, still alive. One . . ." his voice slid into silence before he drew on the last of his strength. "Woman, Storm. Woman shot me." His eyes shut and his body went limp in his brother's arms. Storm checked the medkit frantically. No, all was well. Logan might be long in mending completely. But he'd survive.

He rose, lifting Logan to carry him to a bed. Then he permitted himself to consider the words briefly. It was possible. Arzor had rarely suffered pirate raids. It had little of portable value save for the cat's-eyes, and for those alone major raiding cost more than it could recoup. At a glance he'd seen at least two rooms had been looted of small valuables. They hadn't attempted to open the safe though, as real pirates would have done. And the raiders had also gone out of their way to take beast master animals. That argued they were tied in with the other deaths and abductions.

Yet if they wanted the animals why hadn't they seen by now that it was futile? The beasts died. Why would they continue? He shook his head. Maybe this time the raider boss had been lucky. Surra could die, that was quite likely if she was in their hands and away from Storm too long. The meercats would probably survive. He hated to think of small, affectionate Hing and her new babies in cruel or uncaring hands. She'd never known anything but affection.

There was no time to think any further of that. He reached for the com. Kelson at the other end was almost incoherent with haste. No time to talk. He'd be there with Brad and Tani in two or three hours. Storm should hold on and wait. He did so but it seemed far longer than the time promised before he heard the ranger copter slipping in from overhead. Tani was first out and straight into his arms.

Chapter Ten

Storm reached out to hold Tani protectively. He could feel the shivers which shook her. This was personal distress, not only a reaction to Logan's hurt and the abduction of part of Storm's team—fond as she was of her brother-in-law and of Storm's animals. His gaze met the worried gaze of his stepfather over her head. Storm's instincts told him there was something he hadn't heard as yet.

"*Asizi?* What else has happened?" But Brad was entering the house. He'd see Logan for himself. It was Kelson who spoke quickly.

"The raiders must have come on to High Peaks. They hit the Djimbut first. No, no one of the Nitra was badly hurt. But they seem to have had a double agenda there. They were after cat's-eye gemstones and beasts."

Tani lifted her head. "They took Minou and Ferarre," she wept. "They stunned Mandy but she got away from them." Her eyes glowed fury before filling with pain once more. "We killed four of them but they still got away with my friends."

Until now Storm had not completely reacted to the loss of Surra and Hing and her babies. Now that loss filled him. His arms clamped Tani to him and his head bent over hers. A silent moan of pain tore through him. Tani felt the echo of his grief.

"Storm, what is it, are you hurt?"

"Surra, Hing, and her babies. They took them as well." He felt her stiffen. She stepped back. Her face was transformed into an implacable rage. Her hands came up slowly from her sides, fingers crooked a little. The anger coming from her was so powerful Storm could feel it against his mind like heat.

He stiffened—there were times when he forgot that she had lived on Terra during the Xik attacks, lost her father to the enemy, and seen her mother killed. She'd fled her world to escape being mind-broken or killed and survived it all. Under the gentleness of her surface lived a woman who was descended from one of the greatest female warriors of her people. Six months earlier when courage was needed, she had not been found wanting.

"Surra, Hing and the babies, Minou, and Ferarre." Her voice was the long dangerous note of a warhorn as she roll-called. "We'll find where the raiders went." She turned on Kelson. "What do we know?" He restrained himself from stepping back at the intensity of that demand. At the rage which filled the small slender body. He spoke slowly, wanting to defuse that flaring fury.

"Whoever they were they had help on Arzor. The port manager swears no one could have breached security without aid. We're an outer world and security isn't what it can be on an inner world, but it's good enough. I acted on Tani's first call. We'd closed the port before they reached it. So they should have been picked up entering the gates. They weren't." He remembered manager Gauda's report on that and his own anger rose.

"They got across the permacrete landing area and entered their ship disguised as cargo handlers. To do that they had someone's help. The manager was certain of that much once she'd checked the security tapes. She's so furious she has accepted a patrol offer. They'll bring in an operator with a deep probe. She's made that known and thinks it may . . ." A series of urgent beeps sounded from the ranger copter. "Excuse me."

He pulled down the hush cover and talked, listened, talked again. Then he lifted the cover as a pleased look spread over his weathered face.

"Nice timing. One of the people involved has talked. It seems likely he's scared of what else the probe could uncover. He's a small-fry. Not really involved. Just bribed to leave coveralls and a couple of pallets in an unusual place and let the raiders know where and how to dodge the scanner for long enough to get a head start to their ship. But he knew who bribed him. That's the first mistake. He wasn't supposed to but he did. The peacekeepers are out picking up that one now."

Storm imagined Surra, injured, in pain, separated from the human who had walked beside her so long. She would not bow to others. She was a cat and it was not in her nature. She would fight them every step of the way. She would end up dead like the others the raiders had stolen. But Hing, so happy with her new litter and new mate after being so long alone. The kidnapers would take the babies as soon as they were old enough to be weaned. And Hing who needed her kind about her would be alone once more.

The pain of their loss tore at him. He thrust it down. He would be calm. He would hunt down the thieves and when he found them they'd talk. He'd have his team whole again or die in the hunt. He had no idea of the image he made. Nor how

Tani had merged her own fury, then control, with his. Together they turned to study the ranger.

"When are they likely to have this talker?"

"Anytime now, but Storm, they won't let you talk . . ."

"We'll take Logan down to the hospital. Then we'll see what happens."

Kelson surrendered. "Yes. Logan is most important right now."

They flew back to the city. Logan was wheeled away. A doctor paused to speak before he too followed the stretcher. "He'll be fine. Don't worry. Come back in the morning."

Brad hesitated. Storm laid a hand on his stepfather's shoulder. "Go with Logan. Tani will be with me. When we're done we'll go to the ranch house. We can hire a vehicle to return there."

"No need. The crawler's at the edge of the port. I left it there when Kelson collected me. Use that." Storm nodded and stepped back. Brad headed for the hospital doors and vanished as Storm turned to eye Kelson.

"Tani and I will go to the port. I want to talk to Port Manager Gauda there and I may be able to have a few words with others."

"If you mean the man who was bribed, they won't let you near him. Go back to the ranch. If the authorities want to talk with you they'll find you."

"I'd rather find them. Wastes less time." His tone was implacable and Kelson threw up his hands.

"Do what you want to. You will anyhow, the same as Logan usually does."

"And that's made him one of the best rangers you have," Storm returned. "Think about it. This bunch attacked a

Nitra clan camp. They didn't kill anyone, but if they had the Djimbut clan would have ridden to war. Worse still, if they'd succeeded in stealing the Thunder-talker's regalia other Nitra clans would have joined them." He punched the air for emphasis.

"Think. It isn't impossible even the Norbie clans could have united with them. An affront to the Thunder or a demand from it is one of the few things that could unite both the wild and civilized tribes. It did once before. A dead Nitra warrior or two is one thing. Stealing objects of power and desecrating them is a lot more."

Tani cut in quietly. "You know the patrol's attitude on settled planets where there's already a native people. Point out to them that the raiders could have begun war here. That makes it of patrol interest as well as ranger business. Causing war between native and human settlers is an interworld crime. What if the raiders do something like this elsewhere?"

Kelson's face had been hardening as he listened. He'd thought of the possibilities himself but had not considered the patrol in this. A year back, the lethal Xik-bred clickers had driven the wild clans from their desert lands. The patrol would have forced the human settlers to evacuate their ranches, then Arzor, rather than see a settler–native war. He nodded slowly.

"I'll talk to the patrol office here about this. Tani's right. If she hadn't figured out that the raiders wanted gems then we could be facing a native uprising. If the raiders pull something similar elsewhere the patrol could have a civil war on their hands. And to my mind this all ties in with what Tani's kin discovered from other worlds. Someone's trying to collect augmented beasts from beast master teams."

He stood a moment, his face thoughtful. Even with Terra a

burned-out cinder, enough of the fleet and command structure had survived. A new High Command had risen which governed the patrol and the reactivated survey section. Most often now they acted as a clearinghouse for information and as the arbiters of final decisions.

"This could bring in High Command. It could even be that the raids are another Xik brew."

Storm shook his head. "It doesn't feel like that."

"Maybe not. But do you know it isn't for sure?"

"Of course not."

"But if High Command gets involved you have a lever," Kelson said softly, a grin sliding over his face.

Tani chuckled. "He's got you there, my love. As a beast master they'd talk to you, get your opinion. Maybe let you talk to whoever the probe turns up here. Of course the Xiks could be involved."

Her love looked down at her. "Cunning little warrior, aren't you?"

"I learned from the best," Tani retorted ambiguously. "Now can we start for the port? Time is moving on."

The ranger turned. "I can drop you at Brad's crawler. After that I'll talk to the patrol officer. Her Office is at the port too. Check with me before you leave for the ranch. If I've heard anything more I can tell you then." He climbed into the copter and waited until they were strapped in. Then he lifted for the port. Tani and Storm exited the machine by the crawler.

"Where first?"

"The port manager. We may be able to tell her a few things. This way." Tani came with him, their linked arms giving mutual comfort and support.

The port manager's office was a whirl of activity. People

came and went, peacekeepers walked through the milling staff, and now and again they could hear the manager's voice cutting through the din. Storm forged a path in and leaned forward, resting his hands on the desk.

"I'm—"

"I know who you are." She raised her voice again. "Everyone out. I want to talk to these two. Out!" The office cleared, the last man out shutting the door behind him. Gauda looked them over and grinned, a tired harassed smile that nevertheless managed to be surprisingly sweet.

"What I want from the pair of you are times. My man admits he was bribed. He claims it wasn't done until the raiders had reached the port. I know damn well he's a liar. The man he's named doesn't know a thing. He's so furious about the accusation, he did what Hasset never expected him to do and submitted to probe to prove that. It did. Now he's with his lawyer and laying a suit for several million credits on Hasset." Tani giggled. Gauda smiled in reply.

"Yeah. Funny. But not for Hasset. It seems while working as a lowly cargo handler he's managed to build up quite a nest egg. Gambling, *he* says. But he does have a fair amount to lose." Her smile sweetened. "And somehow the man he accused has found out about all those nice credits. Not a million, but if even part of the claim is allowed it'd wipe Hasset out and garnish his wages for the rest of his life. We're trying to persuade Hasset that we can get the suit dropped if he talks. Loud, clear, and very, very fully. We want every question answered honestly with all he can tell us."

"And?" Storm's eyes were savage.

"He's thinking about it. If you can give me times we may be able to prove some of his lies back to him. If we do that we can legally probe him. Show him that and he'll crack." She leaned forward. "He's a little man. Never one to take big risks. He's in over his head with all this and he's scared to death. Every time I question him he's standing there sweating in panic. If we can show him an escape he'll take it."

"Sweating in panic?" Storm said slowly. "That isn't a man who's just scared of losing credits. That's a man who sees an immediate threat. Why does he? Because I think he knows if he talks someone will come after him." He paused, leaping to a sudden conclusion. "Or perhaps because they're already here! Where's he being held?"

Gauda was on her feet, hand slapping a switch. "Theo, check Hasset. I'm worried."

"The doctor isn't here, Manager Gauda."

Storm wrenched the door open and they were running, all three of them, Gauda in the lead. Down corridors until they came to the open door of a storeroom. Inside the doctor bent over the prisoner. Gauda stopped dead and groaned in frustration. It took only a brief glance. Hasset the liar lay sprawled, face blue, eyes staring, body contorted in a last agony.

Dr. Theo Blandaay looked up. "Too late, I'm afraid. He's taken farakill." Storm drifted silently forward as the doctor turned back to his patient. His hands went out to close on pressure points in the doctor's neck. Theo slumped.

"*Hoy,* that's . . ." Gauda was protesting.

"The man who killed Hasset, I suspect. Look, when you found Hasset you questioned him. Was this man there?"

"Of course. He's doctor for the port."

"Did you search Hasset before you locked him in here?"

Gauda nodded. "One of the peacekeepers did it. A good thorough job too."

"Yes," Storm said softly. "So where did the farakill come from?" He stirred Dr. Blandaay's limp body thoughtfully with one foot. "He'll stay out another twenty minutes or so. The question is, how did he know it was time? That we could have something to make that poor fool talk. Or was he just afraid the man would betray him as soon as the pressure went on?"

Tani had been silent; now she trotted away, back to the port manager's office. She returned, followed by Gauda's assistant. Before either Gauda or Storm could question that, Tani was asking questions of her own.

"Your name?"

"Falia Tedisco, I'm assistant to Port Manager Gauda." The young woman's stance was proud, her eyes defiant.

Gauda intervened. "Falia was promoted to be my assistant a year ago. I trust her as myself." She looked at the girl. "Falia, this is nothing against you. We've had another killing. Help Tani. Answer her questions." They watched as Falia relaxed, her stance now indicating a willingness to reply.

"You know Dr. Blandaay?"

"Yes. He became port doctor soon after I was promoted to assistant." Her tone was edged.

"But you don't much like him?"

"Weeell . . ." Falia was doubtful. "It's not that he's ever said or done anything to *me*. But he acts as if no one is as important as he is. And I heard him being rude about Manager Gauda once. He seemed to think she didn't do her job as well as others could." Her face flushed. "It isn't true. Manager Gauda is the best the port has ever had. Why, since she took over the port revenues have tripled. And without setting ship captains against us. She knows where to spend money and where to cut wastage and . . ."

Tani smiled. "And you think the doctor might not have always liked where the cuts were made?"

"No. Everyone knows he was taking money to help ship crews with sickness. Manager Gauda added that to the port log." Tani looked to Gauda for explanation. The middle-aged manager was looking both surprised and amused at the revelations.

"It seems I stepped on Blandaay's schemes without knowing it. And while 'everyone' might have known what he was doing, I wasn't one of them. It went like this: The man's been here on Arzor a long time. He didn't work for the port full time but he was paid a small retainer to come and see to the staff when necessary. I've never heard anything against him. So when I reorganized I hired him as full-time port doctor. That meant he was hired at a flat salary to tend any crew from a ported ship who might arrive ill and to clear ship crew after looking them over for any signs of illness. I had no idea he was taking extra payment for that. But, recently, when I rewrote the new port greeting for incoming ships, I included the information that he was the port doctor as a matter of record." She laughed.

"I can believe Blandaay wouldn't appreciate that. I ruined his extra income since all ships after that would know they didn't have to pay his extra fees. Falia, why didn't anyone mention this to me?"

"We all thought you knew. That you'd chosen that way of fixing the problem without stirring up trouble."

Tani nodded. "You probably would have done it that way if you had known. Now, Falia, today. You were in the outer office before myself, Storm, and Manager Gauda all came hurrying out. Who else was there?"

"No one." The girl looked puzzled. "You chased out all of the others. There was just me left. The doctor went off to check port records or something next door. He came out a few minutes later and went away. Then you all came running out."

"Next door?"

Gauda moved. "Thank you, Falia. Go back to your office now. I want you to call the patrol office once you get back. Make sure no one hears you. Tell Officer Versha that I request her attendance as soon as possible. Say it's code black." She waited until Falia left, shutting the storeroom door behind her. Then she stared down at the sprawled figures. "You were right. The record room next door is from the old administration when security was more casual. It opens to both Falia's office and my own. Blandaay had only to ease the door ajar and listen." Tani started to speak and was waved silent. "No, you didn't see that. You wouldn't. The door into my office isn't used much. With the renovations going on in the building there's a stack of interior lining sheets leaning across it on my side. But the door opens inward to the record office."

Storm saw. "So he could open the door a fraction, hear everything, and then make sure Hasset couldn't talk." Remembering events during his war years he sighed. "He may have told Hasset that he'd give him a pill. One which would help Hasset resist deep probe."

Gauda looked disgusted. "Hasset would certainly have been dumb enough to believe it. We were supposed to stay up there talking a while longer. Then we'd have come down, found Hasset dead, and had no idea that it was more than the suicide of a guilty man. This is a storeroom. Not a cell. There's no record of who enters or leaves."

She looked at Storm. "If you hadn't suddenly wondered

why Hasset was sweating so hard we'd have missed it all. Blandaay must have stayed just long enough to hear me say that with the times you two could give us and the amnesty I'd offer, I was sure we could break Hasset."

Storm's answering smile was ferocious. "So we can't break Hasset now. But what odds would you give me that our healer here doesn't know even more?"

"No odds," Gauda said cheerfully. "I never bet against sure things. Storm, make sure he doesn't come to again yet. Then watch him a moment. I know where there is a spare roller pallet. We'll take him up to my office. First we search him down to the skin. If he had farakill on him there should be traces somewhere. I suspect Versha will be on her way. Once we tell her all of this she'll act. Versha is something of a hothead. That's why she's on a backwater outer planet. She acted fast once before. She was right but she annoyed some powerful man who was embarrassed by her actions. She'll enjoy this."

Versha swept in with a uniformed probe operator in tow minutes after they wheeled Blandaay to Gauda's office. The patrols officer on Arzor was a round, plumply innocent-looking woman. But her black eyes in the dark-skinned face were sharply penetrating and intelligent. She listened to the saga, nodded to her operator, and herself helped them dump Blandaay into Gauda's chair, fastening his hands and feet firmly. Then she hitched a buttock onto the desk edge.

"Get on, boy. If we start before he's come properly awake he'll be under before he can start fighting it."

Storm and Tani said nothing. Doing it that way was illegal but neither planned to protest. Blandaay wouldn't remember, and if he was guilty as they believed then it was better he had no chance to fight his way to mindlessness. The probe lattice was slipped on, patches and sensors connected, and the questioning began. Kelson arrived halfway through. Falia ushered him in and left again. Her eyes averted from the thing which babbled in the chair.

Kelson opened his mouth, listened to what Blandaay was saying, and shut his mouth again. Blandaay was confessing that he'd been corrupted long ago, that he'd come to Arzor from his home world of Lereyne to escape a charge of negligence. That he'd been helped, had that complaint wiped back home, that the whole of his almost twenty years on Arzor he'd been in the pay of someone. First renegades, men who took quiet profit from the Xik. They'd fled after Storm had exposed the surgically altered Xik aper who led them. After that another had come who knew the secret. Blandaay had been offered a choice: The whip, or the carrot. A fat, very juicy and profitable carrot.

If aiding the enemies of humanity hadn't bothered him, then working for a mere Thieves Guild member had worried him still less. Blandaay had snatched at the carrot. It hadn't entailed much in the time he'd been on the payroll. Just allowing the occasional crew member in on the quiet, ignoring any irregularity his master didn't want noticed. A doctor is in a good position to notice things about others though. Blandaay had his standing orders for a profile on any permanent member of the port staff.

Then finally a more specific order. He was to approach a cargo handler and suborn him. Have the man sneak three people through the sealed port. Blandaay had protested. It was dangerous. What if the man was seen, what if he was taken and talked? That was discounted. He was a doctor wasn't he? Let him dispose of the man once his usefulness was done. Let

Blandaay remember what could be told to the authorities if he failed. The doctor had shivered—and obeyed.

Versha nodded slowly. "All right. Let him rest a few minutes. Search him now. If we find traces of farakill on him we can fully justify this interrogation. If not—" She grinned. "Well, I've been in trouble before." A short time later she was eyeing the result. Gingerly she picked it up, crushing the capsule. "Looks as if I've been declared right. That's farakill." The silvery crystals glistened. "Gauda, have your lab check if it matches the spectrum in Hasset's bloodstream. If so we're in the clear and this interrogation tape is legal as well."

She reached for the office intercom. "Falia, call the port lawyer. Tell him we are asking for a probe permit for a Dr. Blandaay. And check if he has a lawyer of his own. If he does, call him here too." She reset the switch, cutting off the girl's surprised agreement.

"I'm gambling it will match, and that call will leak as well. It'll take the lawyers half an hour to get into action. But the leak will probably be with this filth's boss in a few minutes." She grinned cheerfully. "Let's just get that question answered and start making him look presentable again." She signaled the probe operator.

"Blandaay. The Thieves Guild man, who is he? Tell us about him. Everything you know."

"M-m-m. Marrice."

"Yes, good. Marrice who?"

A silly smile spread over Blandaay's face as his voice shifted into the harsher accents of Lereyne. "There was a little fishy who lived in a net," he chanted. "Net, debt. Debt paid." He choked. His face congested, and he slumped down in his seat.

Versha uttered several words. "Too late. He was sealed

against betrayal. A very nice piece of conditioning—if it really worked. That last bit sounded as if it came right out of his subconscious. If we'd started the probe when he was completely conscious he'd have died the moment he tried to reply. He was only half conscious so he took longer for the conditioning to work. We just may have got something." She pounced on the switch. "Population lists? See if Falia can do a scan for anyone at all with the first name of Marrice."

Gauda shook her head, her hand stopping Versha from touching the switch. "No need. I think I can guess. There's a man named Marrice Plarron. One of my patrol friends from Lereyne was talking to me a while ago. Jared wondered where Plarron's money comes from."

Versha looked puzzled. "Plarron, what does that have to do with debts or fish?"

"Blandaay came from Lereyne." She saw light leap in Storm's eyes. "Yes, you've remembered." She looked at them. "On Lereyne there's a major port on the inland sea. I know the man who's port manager there. It's a fishing port. Specializes in canning, drying, producing dehydrated flakes. Just about anything you can do with fish for export. A lot of ships land there direct for cargoes." She took in a deep breath. "It's called Port Plarronet."

Versha moved purposefully to the intercom. "I'll have a word with the peacekeepers. I think with my authority that's enough to have him picked up. Probing may be a different matter."

So was collecting Marrice Plarron. Those who went to scoop him in found the net empty. There was a hunt, but Marrice Plarron was gone. However in his panic to get clear of retribution he'd left enough odds and ends of only partly destroyed information to be useful. It became a matter of putting the jig-saw together. In that, Storm and Tani could be little help.

Storm rode the basin lands and the ranch had never been so meticulously run. Tani spent time spacegramming her aunt and uncle. Kady and Brion had contacts in strange places. And it could be surprising what unworldly scientists sometimes learned. For the two who ran the ark, they'd even pass it on. Maybe if the net was flung wide enough something might be trawled up.

Logan was recovering slowly; Brad had him back at the main ranch in a month. Time dragged on and they were no closer to knowing where Surra, Hing, and her babies might have gone. All they could do was hope that the beasts still lived. By now the kidnappers would be reaching several planets. Once ported they could disappear.

Then there came a call from Gauda. They'd partly broken the false ID provided for the raider ship. Not what it truly was, but the world providing it. Trastor! And more, several linguists had listened to the record made of the brief words Mandy had overheard. The accent was lower merchant-class from the world of Brightland. Overlaid with a would-be upper-level accent. The combination rang bells with a peacekeeper chief at Brightland's largest city.

"He's sure it's a woman named Ideena. She calls herself Lady Ideena and travels with a man named Baris. They're a dangerous pair. Into all sorts of dirty crimes. He says Ideena is the worst. Both are vicious but Ideena has brains as well. They have no known connection with the Thieves Guild. Ideena likes to run things and it's unlikely she'd join. But they could have been used to get a guild member into Arzor and out again. It's a starting point."

"Do they have any idea where she is at the moment?"

"He's done some private asking about through personal friends and contacts. She was last known at Staril Port on Lereyne. It's thought she was intending to ship on to Trastor. Versha's passed all this on to her superiors. She'll take a patrol courier ship to Trastor in two days to make further inquiries. She says if Storm would be interested in helping with that she can find space."

Tani's eyes widened as Storm's eyes narrowed in suspicion. "Why? The patrol doesn't usually invite civilians."

"Versha says this time it's different. The raiders could have started a war. And I gather her immediate superior loathes the Thieves Guild. She's also hoping that you may be able to sense your beasts if you get close enough."

"In other words I'd be a ferret being put down a rat hole to see what comes bolting out."

"You've got it. Are you in?"

Storm nodded. He most certainly was.

Chapter Eleven

The circus had been pulling in crowds. Cover, it might be, but Dedran was delighted. Laris, too, was pleased. The animals were always happier playing to a crowd. They understood the approval, the shrieks and applause. Credits had flowed in. The whole circus atmosphere lightened. Dedran was even pleasant to Laris, who was surprised but hid it. She supposed that his boss, whoever that might be, preferred the circus to pay its way. And what pleased his boss pleased Dedran.

Prauo enjoyed seeing the performances through her eyes. He still spoke little most of the time but increasingly she was aware of his emotions. It seemed that he was aware of hers as well and sometimes when she was unhappy he'd transmit scenes from the better times. Or just the remembered feeling so that she laughed and felt happier. Their performances in the ring drew crowds, which always pleased Dedran. Prauo playing the ferocious predator, kept only in check by Laris, dressed in her boy's costume, with a whip and courage.

Dedran preferred it to appear there were more performers than there were in fact. So to that end Laris appeared in a different costume, makeup, and wig for each of the acts in which she was involved. She loved being in the ring. The feel of the animals' anticipation, their innocent pride in the applause and a job perfectly done. And she had no need to strike any of them, only to pretend she did in the tigerbat act. That pleased both her and Prauo.

She wondered when Cregar would return. He'd been gone just long enough to be due back if nothing much had gone wrong. It was nice staying somewhere for a while. There were times when she wondered wistfully what it would be like to have a real home. To be settled. To live on a ranch, say, on Arzor. To ride the land knowing it was yours to care for, to live on for the rest of your life. To love. She wondered what Storm and Tani were doing just now. And Logan. Particularly Logan.

She'd liked him. More than she wanted to admit. But she was bonded. There was no future for her there. Not until the bond was canceled, and not even then if he ever discovered her part in his brother's loss.

Oh, yes. There'd been a spacegram from Ideena's ship. Laris had managed a brief sight of it and been interested to learn that there'd been a good season for swingleberries and that Baris and Ideena had placed and received a very large order on Dedran's behalf.

Laris grinned wryly. Dedran wasn't so smart. He'd left that lying about briefly, believing it would tell nothing to anyone who read it. She'd done so, seen who'd sent it, and guessed the simple code. Cregar had made a real haul of beasts. They had to be some of Storm and Tani's teams. She mourned both for the humans she'd liked and the bewildered animals torn from their homes. They'd be here any day now and it would be her duty to keep them alive.

"Laris!" The voice was a whip-crack. She turned submissively and Dedran's look became approving. "Prepare the hidden cages. Cregar will be here tomorrow."

"How many do I prepare?"

His look was triumphant. "Three of them. Plan space for a pair of beasts of medium size, one of large, and a number of small." He stalked away, every line of his departing body shouting his pleasure in the catch. Laris watched him retreat, remembering. Not the birds, by the sound of it. She would guess at Surra, the coyotes, and some of the meercats.

Laris hurried off to prepare. She cleaned the cages again, strewed fresh bedding, checked the water and feed systems, and went over the gate mechanisms. The cages were ingenious. Each was built into the back of a cage used genuinely for some of the circus animals. A door could be opened at one end revealing stacked gear with hay, straw, or Tirevian peavines—the soft lengths of that vegetation being popular as cheap bedding.

But that stack of bedding was a decoy. It appeared to fill the rest of the space from floor to ceiling. In fact the wall was only one bale thick. If one operated a hidden sliding door at the other end of the cage back, there was room to enter. Behind the bales there was a space, large or small, according to cage size. Concealed holes let in air. Concealed lights could be left on at different levels. A pair of peepholes at different heights allowed anyone inside the hidden section to see out, both into the outer cage, and outside onto the circus concourse.

And the partition which closed the space off from the open part of the cage could be removed. When nothing was hidden this was done. On a few occasions Dedran had maneuvered peacemen into ordering the space emptied to check. He—or perhaps his patron—had then organized a complaint about overzealous security upsetting the animals and the peacemen had been reprimanded. On such worlds most peacemen now left the circus strictly alone. After all, it had been proven that the circus had nothing to hide.

"Laris?" She emerged from the last cage and stood waiting. "Is everything ready?" She nodded. "Good. I've had word. The ship lands in an hour. You'll be here to take charge of the beasts. Settle them in, feed and water them, then report to me. To me, you understand? If Cregar is with me you'll return later."

She wanted to ask if Cregar was now suspect in the shadowy world where they all lived. But she knew to say nothing. Instead she simply nodded again. Dedran produced a smile. It was a poor effort but then it was too rare to be anything else. She noted that too. He *must* be pleased.

"Run along now. Make sure the tigerbats are ready for their performance this afternoon. I'll call you once the animals arrive."

Laris ran. Her obedience would please her bond-master, and right now she wanted to please him. If she could care for the kidnapped beasts she might be able to help them. Make sure they remained alive and in good condition. The more Dedran approved of her the better the chance that she could do that and he'd agree to anything she might claim the animals required.

She kept an eye on the circus entrance, so was the first to notice the man who strolled in, closely followed by two people she remembered. Cregar was disguised; they were not. But she knew Cregar by his walk. She withdrew silently behind the row of cages, watching. Behind them came cargo pallets on lifters. There was no sound from them. They appeared to be stacked with bales of animal bedding.

Laris snorted. Dedran had a one-track mind with his secrecy, using the same tricks over and over. He'd better watch out. People who got into ruts were often buried in them. Cregar was looking about for Dedran who appeared quickly. They spoke briefly then Cregar and the other two strolled away. She allowed herself to be seen now. The circus boss waved her over.

"Laris, take this bedding to the supply area. Take care now. We don't want any wasted."

She understood the order. "I'll be careful, Dedran. I know this lot's in short supply lately." Her tone was very faintly sarcastic.

He gave her a sharp look and she reminded herself not to be too pert. Dedran could be stupid in some ways. But he was smart enough to keep a close eye on her if she angered him, and happy enough to beat her if he thought she was overstepping her status. She towed the pallet away, doing her best to look dumb and innocent.

Dedran stared after her thoughtfully. That reply had been a little too independent. Laris had come back from her holiday on Arzor a trifle too inclined to act as if she owned herself instead of belonging to Dedran. He watched, considering his options with her, as she and the pallet rounded the corner of the cage and vanished from his sight.

Away from the circus boss, Laris glanced about. There was no one in sight. She reached up to flick open the hidden latch at the back of the cage and shove the pallet forward into hiding. Then safely under cover inside the first cage, Laris unloaded drugged coyotes and cursed her quick tongue. She'd managed to turn slightly, to look back, as she moved the pallet. She'd seen that considering look. Please let him forget her words, she thought, let him write them off as just a pert bond-servant. She settled the unconscious coyotes and checked them. No injuries, and they did not appear to be thinner than they should be. It looked as if they'd been eating well enough.

In the next cage she unloaded Hing and the babies. She sat a moment cuddling them. They were so cute. So sweet. Maybe she could make real friends with the babies. Although most likely Cregar would have that in mind for himself. Still, the animals had met her. They might be prepared to respond to one they'd associate only with their own people. They might connect Cregar with their abduction. She left them reluctantly, watching for anyone who might see her as she exited.

Then she moved the pallet on. The last animal would be under the second false flooring. If it was Surra it would take Laris all her time to shift the big cat. She was almost to the cage she had ready when Cregar appeared quietly.

"I'll take her. You make sure no one can see behind this row. Shift a screen to block it off." She did so hastily, then held the door open briefly as the unconscious cat was raised and carried inside. Laris leapt in behind them and closed the door silently before flicking on the light.

"Get that door locked. Hurry." He carried Surra forward, placing her on the bedding with a sigh of relief. Now that she could look at the animal Laris restrained a cry of anger with difficulty. Cregar saw her face. He didn't want the child to think this was his fault.

"It wasn't me. That Ideena is an idiot. A space warp. She shot the beast master's brother and the cat came toward Ideena so she shot the animal as well."

Laris moved so that her face was hidden. Keeping her voice quiet and level by iron will she asked, "What about the boy? He was killed?"

Cregar shrugged. "Not then. He was alive when we left and

once we were at altitude I saw someone a few miles out riding toward the house. He should have survived." He stroked Surra's shoulder. "I hope so. Authorities are a lot less bothered about chasing leads if no one's dead. It's this one I'm worried about though. We've kept her asleep the whole journey. She's been fed intravenously but she has to wake up sometime."

"She met me. Maybe if I'm the only one to take care of her she'll stay alive," Laris offered.

Cregar grinned knowingly. "And maybe if you're the only one she knows she'd bond to you. I don't think so, girl; it doesn't work that way with a beast from a trained team. Besides, even if she did, you wouldn't want to go where she'll end up. No. You feed and water them all. Clean them out when it's needed. I'll be the one who works with them. You're not to have any more to do with them than you need while doing your work. Understand? I might not punish you if it happens but Dedran will and his hand's heavier anyway."

"I know."

He eyed her sharply. "Has he been beating you again?"

"Not much." She allowed her shoulders to move uneasily as if in memory. It had been weeks since Dedran had clouted her for anything but Prauo had reminded her of the plan. She knew Cregar disapproved of Dedran's habits. She'd added a set of bruises to her arm as well. Now she let her sleeve ride up so they could be seen. She shifted her shoulders again and winced.

"And Dedran said I'm to report about the animals to him." She invested the next words with significance. "When you aren't around."

Cregar looked disgusted. "Man's crats," he muttered half to himself. Then to her, "Do as he says. Don't get caught doing anything he forbids. And don't go poking around. Too long a nose can get cut off." He smoothed Surra's fur one last time and stood, pushing Laris before him out of the hidden cage. But not before she had seen the quick flare of rage in his eyes. He hadn't liked that last bit, or what it implied about Dedran's trust. "How are the tigerbats? You kept up their training?"

"Of course," Laris said indignantly.

"Don't get upset, I was just checking." He dug his hand into his pocket and produced something. "Here. You're a good kid. I know you stayed out of my stash too. I brought you something. Just don't wear it on Arzor if you're ever there again."

Laris cradled the ring in her hands, admiring it. She raised wide eyes to Cregar. "It's beautiful. Thank you. But why can't I wear it on Arzor?" Her face fell. "Oh, you stole it from the Quades."

"Let's say I happened on it around their place. Don't worry. It's pretty but it isn't worth much. That's ordinary silver and the stone's flawed. You might get a couple of credits for it at a thieves' market, that's all. I reckon it'd been sitting for years at the bottom of the box where Ideena found it. I doubt they've even noticed it's gone."

He was wrong about that. It had been one of the first items Brad Quade had missed. Raquel, his wife, mother of Storm by her first husband, and mother of Logan after her marriage to Brad, had owned the ring. But it had descended to her from her own grandmother. The silver and the stone had both come from the Navaho lands on Terra. Raquel's great-great-grandmother's husband had dug both, shaped them into a gift for his adored one. He'd engraved a cat's head on the stone because her name was Walks-Soft-as-a-Puma.

Raquel had died. But the ring waited for a new woman of the line to take it up. It was family custom that only a woman of the blood should wear it. The next one eligible would be a daughter of Hosteen or Logan. Of all the items stolen, Brad had noticed the absence of the cat ring first. The other jewelry he'd bought for Raquel. Most of the pieces were cat's-eye items and had come from Arzor. He was sorry they'd gone but they could be replaced if he wished and had any reason to do so. The ring was an heirloom, irreplaceable.

Cregar was right in that it had little commercial value. Its value was sentimental in both senses of the word. To the family certainly. But also on a market composed of many who had lost the world of their birth. Assured that the ring had come from Terra, that it was old, made from natural materials from Terra, there were a good number of people who'd have paid a very reasonable price for it. Far more than the silver and flawed stone would normally fetch.

Brad knew this. Ideena would have, had she realized where the ring had been created. He hoped that wherever it had gone, in whoever's hands it ended, they'd appreciate it. Without knowing any of that, Laris did. Now and again as she worked through the rest of that day she admired the green gleam of the stone, the brighter glow of the polished silver. The small cat head had been carved with consummate skill, the curves and hollows making it appear as if the tiny head was alive, the minute eyes watching her with interest.

Laris worked hard. At intervals she returned to check each of the drugged beasts. Hing and the babies had been drugged only lightly. They were the first to stir. Laris cradled the sleepy kits in her hands again, reaching out with her mind as she did with Prauo. They responded in thoughts which were formless as yet: only emotions of warmth, comfort in her hands, and a small, diffuse trust.

Hing's mind was clearer as the drug dispersed. But she too relaxed with Laris, to the girl's delight. After that she tried the coyotes again. She knew that Cregar had hoped the adult animals might bond with him since their beast master was not trained. One touch against their emotions and Laris knew he'd be disappointed in that. It was Ferarre who touched back. His mind was cunning and coldly angry, fixed on his own human and the demand for her.

Laris saw to the coyotes' needs and left them quietly to themselves. Let Cregar break himself against that will; she would not. Nor would she seek to break the animals to hers. But still she worried. Dedran would not heed what was said about the beasts' determination to accept no other master. He expected Cregar to succeed. If the ex–beast master failed, the circus boss would have no hesitation in taking samples, then disposing of the uncooperative beasts.

Out of interest Laris had read a lot on the beast master/beast team links. A human began with the ability to reach animals by mind-touch and empathy, but something in that continual touch created a bond over time. In training the bond was reinforced, both by the constant practice and by psychological factors as a gene-altered team and their human learned to trust each other and share their senses. However some of the bond's strength could depend on the abilities of the human. Laris could tell by Ferarres's obstinacy, that, untrained as Tani might be, still her abilities were powerful and her team was bonded to her very strongly. Storm, of course, had been trained with his team so that Surra and Hing would never accept another in his place. Dedran was *not* going to like any of that.

He'd soon be calling for her too. She hurried to check Surra last of all. The cat lay motionless, only the slow rise and fall of her flank betraying that she still lived. Laris squatted to study the injuries. They were healing. Clean, not puffy, no indication of infection. But the cat had retreated into sleep and clearly intended to remain thus. Well, Laris could give as good a report as possible. That might buy them all time.

As soon as she had finished her rounds Dedran demanded her presence. The evening performance would begin in an hour. Laris went to his office, already wearing part of her costume for the public performance.

She also wore the ring, hung on a chain about her neck under the high collar of her uniform. Better not to let her bond-master know of the gift.

"Well, you've seen all the new beasts. Are they well?"

"The coyotes are angry but healthy. The meercats are all well and prepared to be friendly. The cat is still asleep. The injuries heal. Better she sleeps now, she will heal faster," Laris reported quietly.

Dedran permitted the corners of his mouth to curl upward. "That's good. You think the cat will eventually recover?"

"I think she may, if she is left to herself and not distressed." That might give Surra a chance to survive if Dedran heeded. He was nodding.

"Tell Cregar to leave her be," he ordered. "Care for her yourself." He switched to a glare. "Make no attempt to bind her to you. If I find you have, you'll regret it and she'll be samples and ash. Now get out." She bowed acknowledgment of the orders, then departed quickly and quietly rejoicing. Surra had a chance. She'd keep the cat alive in hopes that somehow Surra could return to Storm.

Behind her eyes Prauo was there. *It is well, furless-sister. When the cat-one chooses to wake I shall aid you to speak to her.* He gave the chiming sound in her mind that was his mental chuckle. *Cat shall speak to cat. I think all shall understand each other.*

Laris found she too was smiling as she went about readying the tigerbats. The performance over, she changed to her oldest threadbare clothing and went to look in on Surra. There was no change and Laris sighed. Her hand went up to trace the tiny cat head on her ring. Somehow she felt that it would bring them all luck. In the camps she'd learned that luck often ruled lives.

But more often it is determination that calls the luck, furless-sister. Be strong. I sense a change approaching.

What?

I know not, but I feel movement in the ways that govern lives. He could explain no more than that. Laris wasn't sure what it meant but if Prauo was sure good might be coming, she'd hope along with him. She slept that night more peacefully than in several nights. She was up early to check the beasts. First those in open cages, then those in the hidden ones. Hing and the babies greeted her happily. The babies climbed about her person, exploring pockets in search of tidbits, while Hing sat in Laris's lap, churring a meercat's sound of pleasure as the girl scratched behind her ears.

From the doorway Cregar grinned as he entered. That widened to an honest smile as the babies deserted Laris to rummage through his pockets and stand on his shoulders chewing mouthfuls of his hair. He stroked and scratched them as they churred approvingly.

"Cute little lot." He sat, his face blanking as he reached out mentally. The ability had been mostly lost but he could still feel something occasionally. It was what gave him hope his gifts were not gone forever. "Too young yet to bond, but they will. A few months and they'll be ready." He eyed her. "Stay away from them. No, I don't mean physically," as she would have protested. "Feed and water them but don't try to build any bond. I know Dedran will have warned you."

"He did."

"Remember it." Cregar's voice was quiet and very sober. "He's got high stakes riding on this game. If you're the one to spoil it he'll see you pay, until death would be a blessing, for you and your cat both." She nodded. "Smart kid. Dedran needs you right now. If this works out he may be moved on. Then your bond runs out and if you vanish possibly no one will come looking. Dedran would never admit you'd know enough to be a danger. Until then keep your head down."

Laris nodded again in silence as Cregar gently detached the babies and left. It bothered her how much the man saw. Had he guessed that she hoped to help Surra, or her other plan to escape?

It's good advice for you. I think he has come to it independently. He has grown to like you; he does not like Dedran. It would amuse him to see that one fail in some way, just so long as neither Dedran's wrath nor that of his superiors falls on Cregar. Quite a speech for Prauo, and Laris took heed of it.

The coyotes were still angered: by abduction, confinement, and the loss of their own human. She cared for them but made no further attempt to touch or communicate with them apart from a few soothing murmurs. They sat in a corner of the cage, eyes fixed on her, but made no overtures. She could feel their anger and understood it. She did her best to show in her movements that she meant no harm and wished only to do her work.

They accepted that, moving to the cleaned part of the cage once she'd done the first half. When she left they were lying together, eyes staring at the walls.

Surra was still motionless in her hidden cage when Laris entered. *She lies,* Prauo sent mentally. *She is awake and watching when you do not see. She remembers your scent. She is clever this one. She has made her kills and plans to live to make others. She is weak. She must mend. Until then she will lie.*

Laris smiled at the pun. *Would she understand me?*

If I aid.

She moved up and dropped into a sitting position beside the still form. Then she opened her mind and reached out. At first she could feel nothing, only a wall between herself and the animal. Then Prauo slipped into link. Laris reached again. Now she could feel the glow of anger, the pain of wounds, the sullen determination not to yield that burned in the big cat. Prauo approved. In the back of the girl's mind he anchored her thoughts, strengthening the thread she spun out to touch. Cat eyes opened to study her. A thought formed without words, an emotion then pictures. A query.

Why? Laris could see behind it the events. Logan falling, the stench of blood. Surra's fury and her charge, and then red agony, blackness. There was also a sense of disgust with herself. She was battle-wise, yet she had forgotten this. Too long from the war-trail she had reacted in rage when the human-friend had fallen. Storm would have reprimanded her for her recklessness.

Laris understood both feelings and question. Patiently she strove to explain. She was as much captive as Surra. She would help if she could. For now the path the big cat had chosen was wise. Let old skills be recalled. Let her lie, as a predator waits at the den-mouth for prey. In time the prey will come out, the kill will be made, if only one is patient long enough. Surra did not understand time as humans did but still she asked a query which could have been translated that way.

Laris did not know. If they waited it might be that another would find them. Free them both and the team-friends with them. They must be patient. Over and over she repeated that together with the picture of a cat which waited. The prey came when the prey came. Who could set a limit on that time?

Storm? That picture was powerful. A compound of scent, sight, touch, and emotion. It could be expanded to mean: This one who is loved, trusted, who leads. Who is also equal. Laris clutched the ring in one hand. Then she gathered her will.

Storm searches for you. Agreement flowed between them. Surra knew. Storm would find the path, follow it to trail's end, and none would turn him from that. Surra would wait until she was strong again. All this time she had lain limp, eyes shut. Now she opened them to stare up at the human girl. Golden eyes, fierce and determined. Eyes without the knowledge of surrender.

And in that moment Laris knew what she had done. Perhaps it had not been by her hand. But she had stood by. If she continued to stand aside she would be responsible for events she could not accept. There was no way she could get word to Storm of where his and Laris's stolen beasts were held. But when the time came—and she was sure it would—she would be prepared. She felt her decision weigh her down. She could die if she challenged Dedran. Prauo could die.

I prefer to live, furless-sister. Prauo mind-sent in response to that thought. *Let us continue to work to that end. Let the sick one sleep again. And you also, you are tired.*

That was the truth. Laris stumbled to her bed and fell on it wearily. Yet somehow she felt good. She had made a crucial decision herself, had not had one forced on her by others. She belonged to herself still. It was a warm feeling. She reveled in it as she fell into the dark.

Chapter Twelve

On Arzor Logan healed slowly. The injuries had been severe and Arzor, like many of the more rural settled worlds, had little of the faster-healing technology. Storm fretted at the lack of news. Tani rode Destiny, retreating more often to the healing calm of the desert fringe. She was welcome in the camps of the Norbies. They knew her to be clan-friend to the Djimbut Nitra. What was good enough for the wild ones of the clans was better still for the civilized clans.

That she wore some of the jewelry of a Thunder-talker was impressive. The items meant that while she had not received the training, she had the potential. Because of it she was welcomed also in the tents of the clan's shamen. It did not hurt that none but she or Storm could ride Destiny. The filly was three-quarters duocorn. She bonded to her rider, accepting Storm as an extension of her human friend. She had not yet accepted a stallion. It was hoped that when she did she would produce colt foals.

This day Tani had ridden over to the Larkin ranch. Put Larkin had a small place on the edge of the basin where he sent mares due to foal. They had warmer weather and better feed than in the High Peaks, and cooler temperatures and fewer predators than on the edge of the Big Blue, as the main desert was known. Tani leaned on a fence with the middle-aged man, Destiny standing hipshot behind her, and admired the first of the still wobbly new foals.

"From Fate?" Once she'd taken Destiny and named her, Put had been amused enough to call the filly's half-brother by a matching name.

Put shook his head. "Nope, I don't reckon he should be used until next season when he's rising three. I used a crossbred colt I already had for the main herd. It makes them half-bloods with him and the mares both being half-duocorn. Enough to add that duocorn toughness. Not so much they bond to one person only." He grinned at her. "Not saying many riders wouldn't appreciate that. But it makes it hard for some."

Tani knew. Not everyone wanted to teach her own mount. And what about those ranches which needed their horses to be available to any who might need a mount?

"What about Fate and Destiny's dams?"

"Risked him there. Just two mares wouldn't spoil him. They'll foal later. Should be interesting to see what we get. But maybe I'll have to sell them to riders as can do their own training. They'll be five-eighths duocorn. They'll likely bond. Dumaroy's already interested." He laughed softly. "That won't go down well with any Nitra horse thieves. Mounts they can't ride and which could be too dangerous to even try stealing."

The girl agreed with that. Her filly, Destiny, had killed two men thus far. One, a Nitra who'd tried to ride her against her wishes. The other was one of the clan camp raiders who'd run into Destiny in the dark and struck out angrily to drive what he believed to be a loose horse from his path. He hadn't lived long enough to scream.

Tani lingered, talking casually. It felt good to be here in

the sunshine. She could feel her shoulders relaxing from the tense hunch they'd been in. The heat soaked through her. The foals' play made her smile. Later, the feel of Destiny's powerful body under her made her sing as they cantered for home. She missed Minou and Ferarre painfully but she'd learned to live with the loss—for the moment. She returned to an atmosphere which was tense but, as she realized in the first minutes, with information, not danger. She looked at Logan.

"What is it?"

"You know the raider ID came from Trastor? And there was a suggestion from Mandy's imitation of them that the raiders could be Baris and Ideena. Brightland thought they might also be on their way to Trastor." He spun it out and Tani squealed in mock rage.

"*Tell* me!"

"It seems that whatever else may or may not be right, that last bit was. They've been seen and positively ID'd there."

She sucked in her breath. "That's wonderful. It is—isn't it?"

"Not quite," Brad said heavily. "Trastor says that the pair have done nothing against its laws. It won't pick them up, won't hold them, won't do anything but question them politely if we insist on it." He looked at her.

"Now Terra's gone, most planets won't let another world tell them what to do. If they believe we're trying to give them orders they'll dig their toes in and we'll learn nothing. What's more, it would put that pair on their guard and almost everyone in authority against us."

Tani froze, her mind racing. People might well feel that way and she could accept it. But this world owed a debt. Trastor, where her father Bright Sky had died helping the people escape the invading Xik. Where he was buried with a memorial calling the whole planet to acknowledge the debt. She straightened, her face shifting into almost feral lines. The raiders had stolen Minou and Ferarre. They had tried to kill her kin, abducted Storm's team.

"The patrol officer, Versha? She said you could go with her to Trastor. I shall go with you. I'll talk to the government. I'll tell them what they owe my blood. If they forget I'll remind them. Make a fuss, *Asizi*. Just in the upper levels. Give them no time to spread the news. We're to be told when we're a couple of hours out from port." Her voice was crisp and Brad blinked.

He hadn't known his stepson's wife except as a nice young girl with beast master potential who loved Storm. He'd known her courage but forgotten that with her aunt and uncle she'd landed on many worlds. Often it had been Tani's job to order and check supplies for her kin's huge ship. To make plain to the suppliers that she would not be cheated or ignored because of her youth. He was hearing the voice she saved for such times and it startled him.

Storm gave his stepfather one of his rare smiles. "As Tani says. Tell the government we'd like cooperation." His smile turned into an intent expression signaling danger to any who saw it. "If they can't see their way to that, I may find and speak to this Baris myself."

Brad winced. Baris wasn't likely to survive that experience intact and the Trastor peacekeepers wouldn't approve. He said so, to receive in turn a flat blank look. Right now Storm didn't give a damn. Nor did Tani, or Logan—who was demanding to be permitted passage as well. Brad turned to deal with that.

"You still need to rest."

Logan eyed him. "I can. It's two weeks to Trastor even on a

patrol courier ship. I'll spend the weeks taking it easy. By the time I arrive I'll be fit to get about." He caught Tani's attention and looked imploringly at her; he had no wish to remain behind but his father might object. Tani understood his plea, responding by nudging Storm, who nodded.

"Let him come, *Asizi*. He saw the raiders face-to-face. He can verify that under probe if need be. If he identifies this Baris and Ideena we can put in an arrest warrant with proof to hold them. Versha would back that with patrol status. Once the patrol has them they'll probe. We find what they did with Surra and the others. Logan files charges of theft, assault, breaking and entering, and anything else we can legitimately bring. We may find out then who took the beasts and why. I doubt it was this pair—they seemed more interested in loot. Maybe the third one who was with them was responsible. But these two were only guns for hire, if what their world says is correct."

Brad threw up his hands. "Who runs two ranches while you three go galloping off halfway across the known worlds?"

"You, the same as always," was his younger son's retort. Logan laughed. "I'm no use to you in bed anyhow. Besides which, I ride for the rangers most of the time. Kelson's the one complaining about my being useless right now. By the time I get back I'll have recovered enough to start riding again. As for Tani, did you ever seriously think Storm would go alone when part of her team is out there somewhere as well?"

"Not really. All right. So I don't get any work out of the three of you for several months. You'd better come back in good health. I can't afford to hire new hands." Tani saw beneath the assumed gruffness and flew to him, hugging him hard.

"Don't worry. We'll be fine. I'll look after these two.

They'll look after me. Was there any more news or is that it?"

"Not exactly news." He turned to glance at Logan. "This is about that nice child from the circus. I promised I'd see what I could find from the camps about her."

Logan looked up sharply. "You found something?"

"A few minor items. She came from the De Pyall camp on Kowar. She was able to tell me approximately the date she was transported there. I checked incoming traffic for that time frame. She got there on the old *Sally Ann,* and I managed to connect to the captain. Still the same man and he has records. Not great ones but enough to say that the load she came in with were from the main De Pyall camp on Meril as she'd thought." Brad snorted.

"He copied me everything he had and you've never read such a mess. Barely half on computer, the rest on paper with portions crossed out, written over, then written over again. I've accessed those lists for Meril though. They have her on one. No real information. Still alone. No record of where she came from to Meril. I think she said her mother died at a camp farther back. But they do have the girl listed quite clearly on Meril. Somehow they lost most of the name in the next transit. She's only listed as 'Laris' on Kowar. But for Meril she's Shallaris Trehannan."

"Sounds like an English name," Tani commented. "The Trehannan bit anyhow."

"So I think. But Meril is quite sure that none of those refugees came from Terra. Which may mean either her family had lived elsewhere for a while, or that she'd been transferred in from yet another of the camps. Since she's sure she started out with her mother, there must have been at least one previous move. I think there may have been a number. They seem to have shuttled some of those poor damned refugees all over half the systems during the war." His face went bleak.

"If the circus is there when you arrive, let the child know what we have so far. It must be hard for the girl not to even know her full name. Tell her I plan to keep digging." Unspoken was the thought in all of their minds. It would help Brad to keep his mind occupied while the rest of his family followed another trail.

"I can let her know about the name," Logan offered. "It won't be too exhausting for a poor invalid."

His brother snorted. "I'm sure it won't." Logan flushed then grinned.

"So I'd like to see her again. No crime."

Storm's eyes were kind. "No crime at all. She may even have seen something. After all, a circus uses animals. It's possible someone could have approached them offering to sell beasts. See if Laris has heard anything."

Brad spoke quietly. "If you do ask, do it without anyone else hearing, son. I didn't take to that boss of hers. I'd say he wasn't the most honest man around. I doubt he'd take openly stolen beasts to use. Too much trouble could come of it. But I suspect a couple of those tigerbats of his may not be completely legal. They were all but wiped out on Lereyne. Since they've been preserving them in special reserves this last five years the bats are banned from being taken off-planet."

Logan looked puzzled. "So?"

"So Laris mentioned that the two females aren't related to the other three. They're only about two years old as well. He might just have bought them from a reserve or some private collector on a different world. But it's in my mind he could also have had them smuggled from Lereyne. There'd be plenty of collectors who'd be ready to sign fake papers for a price. But two unrelated females—they'd spread the gene pool, breed far better. Tigerbats are becoming so rare now that any he breeds would sell for high prices on several worlds with arenas we could all name."

Tani was thoughtful. "That's true. We could also have Versha talk to Lereyne wildlife officers about that. Lereyne may have some way of telling whether the two young ones were born there. If so maybe I can get Laris to take blood or tissue samples. If we prove the bats were smuggled then Lereyne will apply for their return. If they fine Dedran they might be able to confiscate the other three tigerbats as the fine. I think Laris would like that. She doesn't like them being in the circus. She says they aren't really happy there."

"Sounds like a possibility. All right. You three start to get ready. Versha commed while Tani was gone. She'll pick up any who are leaving at around nine-hour. Get moving. You don't have that much time if you want to eat, pack, and sleep before she arrives." They scattered at once.

Versha was on time, her teeth showing white against the dark skin as her face broke into a grim smile. "All three of you. I expected that. I heard the Trastorian authorities were being difficult but there's ways around that if you know the right people." She grinned with wicked amusement.

"I've talked to the patrol officer on Trastor. Jared trained with me until he transferred to the patrol. He confirms that the raider pair were seen again only a few hours ago. He's arranged a stop on their own personal IDs. If they try to board a passenger ship they'll be very politely turned away. I've taken a precaution or two myself. He's also identified their own ship. It looks as if they may be staying on Trastor a while." Her smile broadened.

"Oh?" Logan grinned back.

"Oh, yes. We don't want to spook the game before we reach them. But he's arranged a small party if it looks like they're planning to up-ship before we reach Trastor. After all, they have the ship registered under a false ID. And guess what?" She surveyed three amused faces. Storm was the first to reply.

"You've tied in the fake ID with some complaint."

"Exactly. So until they can prove that the ship the complaint is listed against is not their ship, then they stay right where they are."

"Won't they realize that it's a setup?" Logan queried.

"Possibly. But they may also assume that old enemies have caught up. Gods know they have them if Brightland speaks true. The Trastor broker could have sold them a fake ID to achieve just this. He'd deny it either way and once he hears about this mess—and Jared has arranged that the broker will hear first—he'll vanish anyway. We have a front-man making the very serious and convincing complaint. It can be tied in via Meril and if they get that far, to criminal figures from Brightland." Versha chuckled richly.

"By the time they've unraveled that rat's nest, talked to Trastor, Meril, and Brightland, found no one there is involved—that will acknowledge it or help them very much, and then traced back our front-man to Trastor again. We could have had enough time to arrive, decide the meaning of life, and arrive back on Arzor lifting on a ship traveling solely by pedal-power. Believe me. They won't up-ship until the patrol says so."

By now all four were grinning. It was bad enough trying to trace an error through the bureaucracy of one planet. Trying to sort out a mistake through the red tape of several was the sort of thing which sent the would-be tracer completely crazy. Experienced bureaucrats had even been known to turn green and resign on the spot at the suggestion. The usual method was to come to an agreement with one's opposite number. Cut out the whole loop and start again. Except that for civilians with suspicious antecedents this wasn't an option.

Storm had been thinking. If it was his problem he might just decide to act like a pirate. Cut out the loop, not in records but in real life. He hoped Versha had thought of that. Better to ask and find she had, than not ask and discover the raider ship had quietly vanished from under the authorities' noses. He asked.

"Hmmmm. You and I would think that way. Jared's a good man. But he's never been in the field. His whole career's had him flying a desk. I never thought to mention that chance. I'll check he's taken precautions. Boot up the com for me while I get the code settings."

Versha was back quickly, taking over the seat Tani swiveled toward her. "Thanks." She flicked a dial, moved a switch carefully, then spoke quietly. It seemed little time before a slow voice answered.

"Patrol Office, Trastor sector. Jared Anwar speaking. That you, Versha?"

"It's me. Listen, there is no time to waste. Have you done anything physically to see the ship we're interested in doesn't lift?"

"Physically?" The slow voice sounded startled. "But there's an injunction against departure on the ship."

"The owners don't seem to be the types to necessarily obey court orders. If they lift and clear Trastor how do you make them come back?"

"Why, I . . . well . . . I suppose we . . . Um. Versha, have you any reason to think they could try that?"

"Only that they're wanted on three worlds including their own under their real names. They've had charges filed for everything from piracy in the space-lanes to assaulting a spaceport official on Aubeare."

Jared was diverted. "Why did they assault the official there?"

"I gather he wanted them to file flight reports from their last couple of stops and as that isn't normally a legal requirement, they didn't see why they should. He tried to prevent them leaving so Baris shoved him down the ship's ramp."

"That's hardly a major offense."

"It can be on Aubeare; most of their officials are minor members of the royal family. But take a look at a few of the other charges. I've just spacegrammed a list. I think you'd better take precautions, Jared. If that ship vanishes, we may lose our best hope in years of getting a line into some of the crime the patrol's been investigating since the Xiks pulled their heads in. If that happens I can name you a whole list of our superiors who won't be happy about it."

There was a thoughtful silence. Then—"Just a minute." His voice was raised in a shout. "Namor, in here." After that they caught scraps of brisk orders being issued. Jared returned. "How much force is reasonable?"

"As much as you have to use. Try to keep that precious pair alive. They won't do much talking dead. But if it's the life of one of your people or theirs, then shoot and we can hold a post mortem later."

There was a moan at the pun. "You owe me a round of drinks to wash that down. All right. I'll put Jola in where she can overlook the ship."

"I want it stopped, not watched as it leaves."

"Oh, don't worry about that. She'll have a scramble-laser. One good burst in the right place, the ship's navcomp is wiped, and emergency set-down is instigated. It can't lift again until the navcomp is recalibrated. Those old-fashioned ships don't have shielding against a well-aimed scramble-laser. Jola's the lady to do it too. She was one of the Trastor's best first-in commando fighters until the Xiks quit."

Versha's tone was envious. "Just how do you rate a scramble-laser?"

"Heh, she liberated it from the Xiks before they pulled back. I slapped a requisition order on it when she joined. Officially it's both her own personal property and ours on permanent lease. That way it can't be taken off us, it belongs to her."

"And it can't be taken off a civilian because it's leased by a secure department," Versha finished. "Smart! If you run into any other civilians with a scramble-laser and an urge to travel, let me know."

"Will do. Now, I'd better have a word with my peacekeeper opposite. If we end up making a shambles of his area I'm sure he'll like to know why in advance."

"No!" Versha spoke sharply. "The pair have friends. They weren't doing this on their own. Our superior says keep events under your hat. We don't know who might be involved in planetary circles. You say nothing. If you have to kill this pair you refer him to me and say nothing until I arrive. I'm bringing people in to file official charges on Trastor."

"They won't listen to off-planet civilians."

"They'll listen to these. Get on with it, Jared. If you lose that duo our superiors may have my head on the block, but they'll have yours first and for sure. Versha out." She flicked a dial and the humming died. Logan stood carefully.

"Twelve days until we know if he managed to hang on to them. I plan to spend the time sleeping, eating, and exercising. Let me know when it's dinnertime. I'll start with that."

Storm nodded. "I hope Jared can hang on to the ship."

Tani turned to Versha. "About Baris and Ideena. I suppose no captain on a passenger ship would go against a patrol warning. How certain is it that the pair can't hop a cargo ship if the captain takes a bribe?"

Versha developed a wicked look. "Oh, fairly certain, I think. I had a confidential notice circulated, saying that the patrol discovered a pirate group has been getting spies aboard cargo ships. The spies either try to get a look around at defenses and cargos, or try to persuade captains or other officers into shipping them illegally. It is suspected they then help the pirates to take the ship and dispose of the crew." She smirked.

"There's a very clear description of Baris and Ideena included in the notice as possible suspects, and Jared's people will be ensuring every cargo ship arriving on Trastor receives that information. Under the circumstances I doubt any captain or officer, no matter how greedy, is going to touch that pair with a very long pole. But he isn't likely to say why either if it makes a pirate group mad at him personally. He'll come up with something moderately believable and wish them happy voyaging—with some other ship. Well?"

Tani was giggling and even Storm was smiling a little. "I'd give a lot to be there listening to any of that," Tani assured her. "I think you have it covered. But it's still going to be a long trip."

It was, but even the longest trip doesn't last forever. Twelve days after that conversation they were two hours out of Trastor's main port and signaling their arrival.

From there they could also pick up Brad Quade's discussion with the peacekeepers. Before that became bogged down in refusals to act against the Lady Ideena or Baris, Brad mentioned that incoming on an official patrol vessel two hours out was Tani, daughter of Bright Sky, the savior of Trastor. Tani believed she had suffered personal hurt from this pair the peacekeepers were trying to protect. The discussion and protection reversed abruptly.

Chapter Thirteen

There was a small committee—one man and his assistant—waiting to greet Tani when the patrol ship set down. As Brad had requested, it was not ostentatious, nor had information of her arrival been given to the press. Versha left her ship first and took up a position which made it plain she was acting as a guard. Then Tani walked down the ramp flanked by Storm and Logan, each a half-pace behind her.

"Gracious Lady, Trastor welcomes the daughter of Bright Sky, savior of Trastor." The welcoming official was a small man of innocuous appearance. From an angle where he could not see what she did, Versha's hands flew in the hand-signs used for communication between settlers and natives on Arzor.

"Cunning, do not underestimate, this one is an important man."

Without turning his head the small man suddenly grinned. "Thank you, Officer." His attention returned to Tani, his eyes studying her. He nodded once to himself and offered her a slight bow. "Let me stop being polite and start being cunning. This way." He ushered her to a comfortable hovercar, saw to the safe seating of the other three, then signaled to the assistant to drive. They moved off and the man spoke quietly.

"I am Under-governor Larash-Ti-Andresson. My friends call me Anders. I hope you will be friends. You would not know this, Bright Sky-Ti-Tani, but I was one of the people your father saved. Later, if it is your pleasure, I will take you to his memorial." He spoke almost lightly but both Tani and Storm could sense the very real emotion beneath the words. This man, whoever or whatever else he might be, did indeed remember and honor the man who died helping to free Trastor from the enemy.

"I have reviewed what information I have received so far," Anders continued quietly. "I will summarize. Patrol Officer Versha has requested we take into custody two citizens of the planet Brightland. These two, a Lady Ideena and a man named Baris, are at present on Trastor. They arrived openly, appear to have money, and own their own ship." His lips quirked. "It may be a rather shabby and obsolete model but it does belong to them. It is in spaceworthy condition and carries all emergency beacons and supplies mandated by law.

"They have committed no known felonies here, nor have any complaints been made against them by citizens of Trastor. Apart from this we have received no warrants against them for offenses committed on other worlds which we would recognize as—to use the old term—extraditable. However I am told they have committed crimes against you personally. You are here to make a formal complaint and request that we act as Versha asks. That we take these people into custody and question them rigorously. Is this correct?"

Tani simply nodded.

"But an ordinary complaint about something which occurred on another world does not carry over to ours," Anders said gently.

Tani met his gaze. "This does," she said flatly. "I am here as a representative of the Nitra on Arzor. Patrol Officer Versha is present to verify my complaint. I charge the people known as Baris and Lady Ideena with attempted insurrection of a native race against the humans of a 'settled world.' On behalf of the Nitra I charge theft of sacred items which I can identify."

She could see that Anders suddenly looked grave, as well he might. It was one of the few charges which could and did carry over to another world. No world with a native race wanted some fool out there starting a holy war against the humans. Still less did they wish the other nonhuman races with whom they allied to think that Terrans did not take such a complaint seriously. Anders opened his mouth and Storm cut in.

"I am here as a representative of the beast masters unit in which I held a commission. This may be verified on application to High Command. They stand prepared. I charge those known as Baris and Lady Ideena with acts of sabotage against a unit of the Terran Command. In the course of which acts they injured a civilian, committed theft and damage of property, and violated port safety regulations. The government of Arzor has filed charges over the latter. I carry the warrants for those and can produce them on request."

"Beast master unit? Terran High Command?" Anders's voice was horrified. Storm descended from the harsh emotionless attitude he'd assumed to impress the Under-governor.

"Anders." He leaned forward. "That pair attacked a clan camp twice. They stole some jewelry from the female shaman they'd stunned. The Nitra are leaving it to Tani to sort out—for the moment. She's a clan-friend."

"Isn't that unusual?"

"She's only the second in Arzor's history," Storm said tersely. "But the Nitra want satisfaction. They want the jewelry returned with Tani and the thieves provably punished. They'll settle for the thieves but not the sacred items alone."

"In other words they want satisfaction."

"Yes. As to the other charge, that could become worse. You had a beast master living here. Yes, I know he's dead," he added before Anders could interrupt. "We have reason to think this pair may have been involved with that death, or know who was. Listen." He spoke slowly as the hovercar floated silently along the path toward a series of office buildings. It halted as Storm finished speaking. Anders exited the car and found Logan at his side. The young man spoke very quietly and seriously.

"Anders, you said no complaint from a citizen had been received." He took a breath. "But isn't Tani an honorary citizen of Trastor? I'm sure her Aunt Kady said so once."

The Under-governor eyed him. "That is so. We decreed that Bright Sky was a citizen of our world. It was a posthumous citizenship but you're correct. It descends by law to any child of his living at the time it was granted. It also gives me an unimpeachable reason to act." He waved the others to join them, sweeping them with him to a large office. There he sat and reached for a control panel. Into the speaker above that, he snapped a string of brisk orders as he switched from office to office. Then he looked at the four.

"That will set things in motion. Officer, you have had your people here see to it that the criminals do not depart unexpectedly."

Versha smiled. "Oh, I think they'll still be around."

"So do I," Anders said dryly. "That was a statement, not a question. I've heard something about a complaint against a ship which may or may not be correctly identified. I've also heard about pirates." He leaned to the speaker panel and called for refreshments, then sat back. "Let us wait in comfort while we see if my preliminary endeavors bear fruit." He looked at Tani. "Do I gather two of the stolen beasts are yours? Are you also a beast master?"

"I was never trained. But yes, I have the gifts and the coyotes are part of my team."

"If you are not officially a beast master how do you come to have Terran animals?"

Tani settled back. "I am the niece of Brion and Kady Carraldo." She saw his look of half-recognition and continued. "I grew up on their interstellar ark working with animals and helping the scientists and my kin there."

The Under-governor's memory released the information that had been teasing him and the back of his neck went cold. Lord of Light! The ark was an invaluable resource for every human-settled world. It was run and ruled by scientists, but he guessed that scientific detachment did not apply where it came to this girl if they thought Trastor was ill-treating her. They might continue to assist Trastor, but there were many ways in which they could deny a world what it needed without appearing to flatly reject official requests.

Tani would not have dreamed of using that power, nor would her aunt and uncle have considered it. She did not even see the way Anders might be thinking. Storm did, but said nothing. If a man thought that way you wouldn't change his mind-set by arguing. If Anders believed that helping Tani and laying hands on Baris and Ideena would keep Trastor in credit with the ark, let him. He'd make sure Brion and Kady heard of the man's help. How they reacted was up to them.

Anders stood. "Please excuse me for a time. There are

certain things I must do. The burdens of government." He chuckled a little and left.

Versha stared after him. "Not the fool he looks even if he was jumping to a few conclusions there at the end." She dug a small comunit out of her pocket and spun dials. "Jared?"

"Jared here, Versha, where the Hades are you and what have you stirred up? Every peacekeeper, port official, and security beat-walker is out buzzing around. There's a hunt for our two like you wouldn't believe."

"Yes I would. Never mind that right now. Tell me everything you know about a man called 'Under-governor Larash-Ti-Andresson. My friends call me Anders.' Small man. Looks meek and mild, rather harmless. Until you say something important and see his eyes."

She heard a sort of gulp over the com. "Andresson? Oh, he's Under-governor all right. He runs the security for Trastor. Peacekeepers, port police, private guards, spies, anyone at all in those categories. He deals with anything that may imperil Trastor's safety, autonomy, or internal security. He isn't always soft-handed about how he does that either. But he's honest and he's very good at what he does. Particularly if he thinks what he does will help Trastor. He can be ruthless but he's a patriot. To him Trastor is first in importance, and other planets are nothing in comparison."

"Thanks. I think we've convinced him it's in Trastor's interest to help us. Don't go against him. But try to see that Baris and Ideena stay alive if that's possible. Versha out."

She snapped the comunit off and tucked it away again. "You heard that, Anders? You can come back now." The man who returned was the same until you saw his face with the meek mask of minor officialdom removed. His gait was firmly confident. His eyes showed a hard humor and wary intelligence.

"You knew."

"As you intended."

"Only if you were bright enough."

"Take it that I am," Versha requested. "And now that we both know who's who and what's what, how is the hunt going?"

"Mixed. They got to that ship of theirs. They started to lift and at a thousand feet someone hit them with a scramble-laser. Would you know anything about that, Patrol Officer?" Versha out-stared him. "I see." He continued.

"Their navcomp emergency system seems to have been ingeniously programmed. Instead of setting down right where they'd lifted, it swung the ship and landed in the next clear area. That turned out to be a park twenty klicks from the port—that's about fifteen of your Arzoran miles," he added for clarification. "No one was prepared for that trick. By the time my people reached the spot whoever had been in the ship had vanished again. We're questioning everyone in the area but there's no information coming in as yet."

He frowned. "Have they allies here, do you know? Anyone who might help them to hide or escape?"

Versha pursed her lips. "When they hit Arzor they had someone with them. Logan here never saw him, but Tani can verify that there were three people, believed at the time to be innocent tourists, whom the clan permitted to escape. We know three people also fled Arzor on that ship. So yes, they do have a colleague of some kind. Whether he's still here, who he is, or if he'd help, we don't know. But it's possible. Ideena isn't likely to stop at blackmail to get under cover."

Anders smiled dangerously. "We'll keep looking. Sooner or later someone will come trotting in to say that their neighbor is behaving strangely. Until then I'll make it clear to all the usual riffraff that it will not be business as usual. Not until I lay hands on this pair. Set scum to catch scum. The locals won't like having my men poking into every corner of their business. After a while when we don't let up they'll begin hunting for the pair themselves."

"But will they hand them over in shape to talk?" Logan spoke for the first time since they'd arrived in the office.

Anders nodded at him with respect. "They will if I make it clear that if our duo aren't alive I'll assume someone had something to hide and look even longer and harder." He straightened, stretching. "It's likely to take time though. Are you hosting your friends here, Officer?"

Versha glanced at her companions. "I think so. The patrol do have a suite for visiting VIPs. They can stay there until you want to talk again or there's news."

"It may not take long." His look was grim. "On Trastor it isn't easy to hide when I'm the one who hunts. We should have Baris and Ideena in a few hours, a couple of days at the most."

It was as well he'd taken no bets on that. Ten days later Baris and Ideena might as well have vanished tracelessly into a black hole and Under-governor Larash-Ti-Andresson was *not* a happy man.

Nor was Baris. He'd returned abruptly from a card game in which he'd been winning. His boots clattered up the ship's ramp and he'd yelled his partner's name in tones which could peel paint at ten paces.

"Ideena? *Ideena!*"

"For Ghesh's sake. What is it?"

"We're wanted."

Ideena raised an eyebrow. "That's so unusual?"

"Not what, who," Baris snapped, confusing her.

She stared. "Who? What? What the Crats are you talking about, you idiot? Make sense."

"That cursed Andresson has every peaceman out asking for us. We're wanted for questioning on interplanetary charges. If his people take us they can legally use deep-probe on charges like that. I'm getting out and I'm getting out right now! You can please yourself." He dived for the control room and Ideena followed.

"They have an injunction . . ."

"They can stick their injunction."

"That's the patrol you're talking about. They may have it backed by something," Ideena warned. She moved into the seat next to his, strapping down swiftly.

"I'll take my chances. I want out of here." Since that applied to Ideena as well, she said no more. Baris's hands raced across the controls, programming the navcomp and firing up the engines. Then he applied thrust. By now the port control office was uttering a string of threats and warnings. The chant grew louder and more indignant as the small ship began to rise.

". . . subject to penalties under law of not less than half the value of any cargo, and pending decision on value to be levied against the offending ship . . ." Baris slammed a hand down and the indignant voice faded as the ship rose.

"We did it," Ideena yelped. The ship shivered. The navcomp emitted an almost human groan and every light it had began to flash. From the panel behind it a voice alarm sounded.

"WARNING. WARNING. SET-DOWN ACTIVATED. NAVCOMP UNCALIBRATED. WARNING. WARNING. SET-DOWN ACTIVATED."

"What? . . ."

Baris was working furiously. He spared her a glance, his eyes half crazed with fury and terror. "A Ghesh-damned scramble-laser. They used a scramble-laser on us."

"Can they do that?"

"They just did. Shut up. I programmed something into the system they won't be expecting. I'm pushing the boundaries on that as hard as I can." He peered into a viewer. "We're landing about twenty klicks from the port. In some park. There're a lot of ornamental bushes dotted around. Grab what you want and as soon as we're down and the ramp drops, run like hell. The bushes will help to hide which way we go. With luck the pro-bies will be caught on their heels for a few minutes. If we move fast enough we can get clear." The ship was sitting on her tail, descending in a controlled emergency landing and steering with the small side jets. Ideena leapt across the control room, grabbing for emergency stashes of her loot.

"We can go to the circus. Dedran will take us in. If he doesn't and we're probed there's too much we could tell secu-rity about him."

Baris showed his teeth. "I know. Get the other two sets of fake ID. And anything light that's worth credits."

"Teach your grandmother to suck eggs. You get every weapon we can carry. Dedran may have other ideas about help-ing." By now both were stuffing pockets, shoulder bags, and the front of tunics. The ship's alarm was announcing that it was thirty seconds to emergency set-down. Baris hit the drop-ramp button, then, when it refused to obey, the override. The ramp dropped just as the ship settled. There was a grating sound as the ramp hit the ground and buckled. Both ignored it to race for the exit.

Ideena fumbled hovercab tokens from her pocket as they reached a line of the small robot-controlled vehicles on the far side of the park. Credits could be used but those who wished to use the cabs extensively during a visit often bought the tokens. They were in clearplas and weighed almost nothing. Nor could you spend them by mistake and find the cab refusing to accept larger amounts in notes. Thanking fortune she'd still a number of the tokens left, Ideena dug them from her pocket in readiness. They fell into the backseat and the door hissed shut. The hovercab spoke in a flat polite voice. "Where to, noble visitors?"

"To the Algona building."

"Two credits."

She pushed the token through the slot and leaned back. Baris started to question her choice of destination but she waved him to silence. They arrived at the building. Ideena cleared her throat and stayed put. The cab spoke again.

"This is your destination as requested. Do you have another?"

"Yes. Go to the Sharme intersection. Wait one half-hour for us. If we do not meet you in that time you are no longer required."

"That will be six credits, noble visitors." Ideena fed in the last of the tokens and hauled a bewildered Baris out the door. They watched the hovercab glide away as Ideena held her partner on the sidewalk. She spoke quietly.

"Those cabs are probably fitted with cameras. Andresson will be able to trace us here but not yet. The only way he can speed up getting that cab back is an emergency recall. And by the time he decides on that the cab's likely to be at Sharme. I packed disguises. We change here, walk several miles, and take another hover to Dedran."

Baris's look was sour. "They'll have cameras all over this building too, won't they?"

"Oh, yes." For the first time since Baris had burst into their ship, Ideena grinned. "I have an answer for those." She produced two small gadgets from her bag and turned, staring at the crowd. "I picked this up on Yohal a while back." She focused her gaze on two people moving toward them. "That pair look suitable."

The pair noticed were a tall thin male with an equally thin woman by his side. They were rapt in contemplation of each other and clearly unnoticing anything else. Ideena raised the first gadget and within it, there was a tiny humming. She opened it, removed the cassette, and placed it in the second small flat box. A tiny red light glowed momentarily. Ideena lifted the box to fit under a strap on her shoulder.

"Walk right beside me. Don't move away. The machine projects a holographic picture over us of the two I imaged. So long as we're within a couple of feet of each other all the cameras will see in here are those two." Baris eyed her with admiration. Trust Ideena to come up with something like that, it was one of the reasons he stayed with her, dominating as she was.

He took her arm and walked with her to the public bathrooms many large public buildings had on Trastor. There she entered, giggling wordlessly, with him in tow. She dropped a credit in the slot, dropped a towel over the camera, and signaled him to remain silent. Mutely she laid out disguises and they donned them with the quick ease of long practice. Baris produced a tiny pocket scriber and wrote swiftly.

"Won't they wonder why we blinded the camera?"

In reply she let out a yelp then a squeal. She opened her mouth and panted in a series of ascending gasps of apparent excited pleasure. Baris laughed and joined in. It was the perfect cover. Of course. They were merely two citizens in love and with no time to waste returning to wherever they lived. They kept up the pretense for long enough to be convincing. Then they exited using Ideena's box to foil the lobby cameras. Once in the street she shut off the box and they walked . . .

. . . No longer Baris and the Lady Ideena. Now they were an older man with his young son. Even Ideena's walk had changed, to the cocky swagger of a boy in his mid-teens. Baris became a more ponderous walker, a man of substance both financial and physical; an aging man who had never had to exert himself and whose reflexes had long since slowed. They took a hovercab in the direction of the circus. Several streets away they left the cab and strolled, two in a crowd, all heading for Trastor's newest attraction. There were guards at the circus gates.

Baris slowed. "Do we risk it?"

"No choice," Ideena hissed back. "We need to get under cover. Take your time. We'll look around the cages first. With good luck we'll see Dedran or Cregar without having to ask for them." They strolled, Ideena in character as a bored boy trying to pretend he was enjoying the treat his father had offered, Baris as the equally bored father only too happy that his lad was enjoying the show. From the corner of his eye Baris saw a familiar figure. His hand tightened on her arm and she turned casually to follow his stare.

Cregar was checking guard shields and locks on the cages. There was always some stupid child left unwatched who'd try to approach the cage front or sneak in the back to enter and pet the pretty animals. Most of the pretty animals would be delighted, some because they enjoyed being petted, others because they could always use an extra snack. He checked the next lock and held himself from a betraying movement as he felt someone approaching. A voice spoke very softly behind him.

"Don't turn around. This is Baris and Ideena. We're wanted. Ideena thinks it's about our raid on Arzor. Tell Dedran he gets us under cover or the probies have us and we talk our heads off. He'd better decide fast, they won't be far behind."

Cregar thought quickly. "Stroll about. I'll find Dedran. We'll slip you into the alley between cage rows. There're places there we can keep you where even the probies won't find a thing." He turned, looked at them briefly, and slid into the crowd.

He was back in five minutes with the worried-looking circus boss. Ten minutes later the fugitives were lodged undetectably if not comfortably in the secret part of the largest cage. Cregar and Dedran had talked and Dedran was both alarmed and furious but he hid his emotions from the fugitives. There would always be another time to act. For now he would have to wait and see what sort of a storm this stupid pair had raised. If it was too dangerous there were always options.

Chapter Fourteen

Inside the circus Laris heard nothing of the fugitives' arrival until Dedran sought her out. "The largest hidden place," he snapped at her. "It has occupants. Take them a jug of the local cider and see that it's cut with about half juice. I won't risk them getting drunk."

Laris snorted, "They'd find it impossible to get drunk on that stuff *without* juice added. And what if whoever it is blames me?"

Dedran's face was grim. "Tell them it's my order. Don't waste time, girl. Get moving and come straight back. I want to go over changes in the order of tonight's acts."

He strode away as Laris headed for the tent which held food and drink for the circus staff. She half filled a large lidded jug with the local cider and topped it off with a tart thirst-quenching fruit juice. She was wondering who Dedran had hidden. Cregar was nearby as she slipped down the alley behind the cages. He nodded once to her and went back to his work, which appeared to consist of polishing cage locks. Laris wondered about that, then thought perhaps he was checking security and seeing that no one followed her to the hidden room.

She opened the door with care, climbed in, and placed the jug on a small ledge. It was darker inside where the bright sun did not penetrate so her vision was blurred. She spoke quietly to the dim shape which lounged against the wall.

"I have brought you cider and fruit juice to drink. Dedran says it is by his orders." She moved to leave and was caught by the arm.

A half-familiar female voice purred softly. "Was it indeed?" A second shape moved up; as Laris's eyes acclimated to the dimness she stared and bit down fear. The speaker was Ideena with Baris behind her, and they looked unpleasantly pleased to see her.

"I don't much care for fruit juice," Baris said softly. "I'd prefer Fever brandy, wouldn't you, Ideena?"

"Much better than fruit juice," came the sweet agreement.

Laris twisted. "Dedran expects me back at once. He wants to discuss tonight's acts."

"Oh, but we'd rather you got us brandy. We're even prepared to give you a couple of credits and you can keep the change."

"Dedran—"

"Can wait while you go and buy us what we want." Baris took a firmer grip on her wrist. "Do you hear me? I want brandy!" His fingers dug into a bruise the girl had received earlier and Laris squealed at the sharp pain.

Cregar thrust his head in and scowled. "Never mind wasting time here, girl. Dedran's expecting you."

"Maybe we'd like her to stay?" Ideena's voice was half-questioning.

"And maybe we have work for her," Cregar said, looking at the woman. "There's an old saying: Offend not the host in his home." Ideena pouted but nodded to the man. Baris released his grip sullenly. He reached for the jug, drank, and spat in outrage.

"Fruit juice! Tell Dedran we want something drinkable. Merilian wine, even the wine they make here is drinkable. Anything but Ghesh-damned fruit juice. There's no kick in that for a man."

Laris scrambled out of the cage and left Cregar to discuss that subject. She wanted to be far away from the fugitive pair. If Cregar hadn't come when he did she had a feeling Baris would have started slapping her. And why *had* he come? How had he been about just when she needed him? She didn't know. She'd just be grateful he had been, and she hoped he'd be there if she had to tend that pair again. Behind her Cregar was speaking very quietly.

"Lay off the kid. She belongs to Dedran. She does a good job for the circus too. She's in four acts; Dedran won't be at all happy if she can't perform." His gaze became threatening. "Besides, she's not a bad kid. You start upsetting her and I might just take a hand. I haven't got a lot of time for your kind."

"Is that supposed to scare us?" Baris sneered. Cregar said nothing. He simply stood there holding the man's gaze with his own until the larger man dropped his eyes.

Cregar left. Baris made a spitting motion, then looked at Ideena.

"No one talks to me like that. There's always another day and next time it'll be my turn."

Ideena was thoughtful. "Yes. But not yet. First we need to get off this planet. The best way would be with our ship. I don't want to go back to finding another and fixing it up. Not if we can get this one back." She remembered the filthy jobs they'd had to take to afford even the shabby, decommissioned old patrol courier ship. It wasn't the killings she'd minded, nor the easier robberies. It was working for people who'd given the orders and treated her and Baris as if they were something scraped from a gutter.

She didn't want to do all that again. It was a pity they hadn't had a good chance at Cregar once they'd lifted from Arzor. But the man was cunning. Maybe now was a better time. Baris wasn't much for planning but he sometimes had ideas. She opened the discussion and waited to hear if this was one of those times. They settled to making plans as outside Laris was trotting for Dedran's office. He looked up as she entered.

"Where have you been?"

"Baris tried to make me stay with them." Laris hoped that a few words would convey more. It seemed to. Dedran's eyes went hard.

"What happened?" That was easy. She explained what the pair had said and done. Then that Cregar had come by, heard her cry out, and intervened. She exhibited the bruised wrist.

"He stayed?" was Dedran's question.

"I think so. I heard him talking as I left."

Dedran grunted. "Humph. Very well. I may have to speak to them if Cregar hasn't made it plain that I hire you to work with the animals. They don't qualify." Laris giggled and he shot her a look then half-smiled reluctantly. "They don't qualify as circus animals. Now, tonight we have some of the local VIPs attending. I want to shift the carra act . . ." They got on with work.

Later, after the show, Dedran found his man. "What happened with that pair and the girl?" Cregar was terse and the language he used was explicit. His boss frowned. "They're a risk. We may have to do something about that."

"All you have to do is say the word."

"Not yet. That could be a risk as well. I'll let you know."

"Want me to keep an eye on the kid? If they start anything with her and she screams there could be some outsider to hear and ask questions. That Ghesh-damned Anders has the whole city filled with spies. Baris plays some very unpleasant games I've heard, and anyway, if they rough the girl up too badly she can't work. She could even run away if they hurt or scare her too much. You don't want to risk any of that."

Dedran pursed his thin lips. "No, I don't. All right. Stick around anytime she's with them. I'll tell her she's to let you know beforehand." He changed the subject. "What about those beasts? The girl says the small ones are fine and quite friendly but the other two won't cooperate and the big one is still very sick."

"She's telling the truth. The meercats are friendly." He felt a warmth as he remembered how the small group welcomed him. The babies climbing his clothing to beg for treats and petting, even Hing accepted his physical touch—if not any mental contact as yet. "The coyotes eat and drink well. They are in good condition but they resist bonding very strongly. It will take time but I think they'll come around in the end." At least he prayed they would.

"And the cat?"

"That's a different matter. If Ideena hadn't shot her it would be a lot easier. As it is the animal associates me with her pain. Once she's healed further I may be able to convince her that I am a friend. It all takes time."

Dedran scowled. "I don't like having them here so long. There are too many snoopers prying. I'll make arrangements in case anyone does discover anything I'd prefer they didn't know." He broke off and looked at Cregar. "Let's just say that there's to be no evidence of any kind at all if a search gets too close."

He walked away, heading for the main tent and Cregar was left thinking about everything happening lately. He didn't like any of this. And what had that last comment meant? The possible disposal of Baris and Ideena didn't worry him. That Dedran might have the child disposed of if the authorities pressed too closely behind did bother him.

He suddenly felt an odd need to protect Laris. She was a good kid, she admired his training of the circus beasts, and she was good with the animals herself. He didn't remember clearly why he felt somehow protective of her. Only that somewhere behind the fog of years, from the before-time, when he'd had a team who loved him and a place of his own in society, he'd known a kid like her. On a planet destroyed by the Xik, he thought.

He dismissed his vague, trauma-blurred memories of the little sister he'd loved when he had parents and siblings and a world. But Ishan had been destroyed by the Xik and all he'd known and loved had gone with his planet. Over her years with the circus Laris had grown more and more to look like his sister. But Cregar didn't want to remember all the pain of loss again. He forgot again by an effort of will, his memories sliding back into the mists in his head.

In the security building Anders's assistant was speaking quietly into a comunit. He turned to Tani.

"Gracious Lady, it is requested that you join Larash-Ti-Andresson. I will drive you to the place where he waits."

"The three of us will be going," Storm said firmly. "Can we assume that after all this, our quarry escaped?" The assistant flushed unhappily and said nothing. Storm nodded. "They did. I see. All right. Drive us to meet Anders."

They met a man who under the mask of quiet competence was fuming. Storm was honestly interested. "How did they escape?" Anders evaluated the question and understood the genuine interest. The questioner had been in a similar business after all.

"They had an emergency override program. When the navcomp was blown by the scramble-laser the program kicked in. It allowed them to set their ship down in any open area within a certain distance. That distance was determined by how high they were when they had to begin descent again. The program uses a combination of height and side-jets to give a ship options in case of navcomp malfunction."

"Your people weren't allowing for the program?"

"Someone will be answering for that. It's a new system and the people I sent out to collect Baris and Ideena never expected a ship that old to have it installed." He paused. "In fairness to my people I should say that I would have thought the program too new and different to interface well with that ship's older equipment. But if I'd been out there myself I'd have still taken it into consideration just in case. They didn't and that gave Baris and Ideena a chance, one they didn't waste time in taking. We traced them to the street outside a building in the city. They were not seen entering by the building's security cameras."

"So they've vanished," Storm said flatly.

"For the moment." Anders's eyes took on a hard gleam. "Just for the moment. The governor has posted a reward for information. That's not for public consumption, by the way. We're just filtering it quietly through a few underworld informants. But every little criminal in the place will know about the reward by tomorrow. We'll have to sift through a lot of rubbish but someone who knows something will get to considering how much they know—and what it's worth. Then they'll make a call."

Tani looked up at him. "What if the someone hiding them is in as deep or deeper? What if they're the ones who hired those two from the start? They aren't going to come running to sell them to you. They'd be selling themselves at the same time."

She received a look of respect. "That's true. But there are always people who know small pieces of information and who aren't really involved. They'll talk, collect the reward, and immunity from prosecution for whatever minor crimes are on what passes for their conscience." He straightened, hands massaging the small of his back. "Don't worry. Baris and Ideena will turn up." He strolled ahead making for the hovercar, missing Storm's last comment to Tani and Logan.

"I'm sure they will. I'm just not as sure as he is that they'll be in one piece." From the looks of agreement the other two felt the same.

Anders wasn't as sure as he'd seemed. In reality he had thought of that himself. But he'd seen the full file on the fugitives. They'd been involved in much more than was apparent from their list of actual charges. In a secondary file there were pages of supposition and suspicion. Brightland alone suspected Baris and Ideena of involvement in everything from a couple of clever assassinations to several brutal robberies in which every possible witness had been eliminated.

It made it likely the pair could take care of themselves. Then, too, they could be valuable still to those who'd hired them. Anders thought that Ideena would be keeping a wary eye on those employers anyway. She'd know that often employees who became a risk were quietly deleted from the equation. She'd be watching for any hint that was planned. He thought that Ideena and her partner would turn up alive eventually. It was just a question of when—and where.

So he partly discounted the chance her employers would dispose of the two. Ideena would be alert and she'd keep the man alert too. The pair would most likely stay low, seeking a chance to get their ship back and get off-planet. He'd put a cordon about the ship to deal with one part of that. He'd pick them up if they appeared.

For the other possibility, that they might elude his men, he'd had the ship rendered inoperable. It would appear to be working, but there was a stop on the engines. Even if Baris produced a spare navcomp and had the undisturbed hours needed to replace the ship's system, the vessel would stay right where it was.

And the street-smart were talking. Anders had spies and contacts who owed him favors in many areas of the local crime network. Already word would be spreading. He had a two-pronged attack there as well. Firstly there was the reward. It was generous but with it went word that Anders would not appreciate his time being wasted for nothing. To help that along he had a section of his people rousting every game in town.

Each time it was carefully explained that they were searching for Baris and the Lady Ideena. Once they were found, this poking into every corner could stop. Anders gave a hard grin.

His efforts were infuriating half the big criminal groups in the city. Once they were annoyed enough they'd start doing his work. After that Ideena and her man were as good as in an interrogation cell.

At the circus Baris and Ideena certainly felt as if they were prisoners. The hidden portion of the animal cage was barely six feet wide and ten long. It held two very narrow bunks along the far end from the entrance. There was no entertainment but themselves so they spent much of the time eating, sleeping, quarreling, and drinking. None of it was completely satisfactory. The food was usually lukewarm and bland. Dedran would give them only weakened cider. And with the narrow bunks sleeping was not as comfortable as usual.

The quarreling was dangerous. They allowed themselves to do so only when the alternative would have been a physical attack. Neither wanted to risk that. Not on each other or on those who, for the moment, sheltered them. But Ideena knew her partner was becoming uncontrollable. Baris had never reacted well to imprisonment. The few times he'd spent short periods in jail he'd had to be sedated much of the time. She'd timed the visits made to them with food and the longer periods when they were left alone. Now she spoke.

"Let's get out."

Baris stared. "I thought it was too dangerous?"

"Staying here while we both go crazy is just as bad. If we disguise ourselves as father and son again we could have a while outside this rat hole. Dedran doesn't have to know."

Baris was scrambling into his outfit before she'd finished speaking. Once Ideena was ready they drifted out of the cage alley and joined the crowd flowing along past the sideshows.

They stayed out several hours, returning more relaxed to sleep well. After that they risked it again. Then again.

But apart from that, Baris wanted a decent drink. He'd have angrily refuted the idea that he was an alcoholic, and he never got really drunk, but he did like something strong and the fruit-juice-weakened cider which was all Dedran allowed them just wasn't enough to keep Baris happy. If he got his hands on that girl when no one was around he was sure he could scare her into finding him something decent to drink.

He hadn't seen Cregar and had no idea that the ex–beast master was watching any time the girl slipped away to take supplies to the fugitives. Cregar had seen them out however, and recognized them despite the disguises. He knew the risks they took. He was holding the information. If he had to stir Dedran to a decision he'd have the spur.

Baris lounged on the lower bunk. He heard the tiny click that was the latch and moved like lightning. Laris entered and his hands closed on her. One over her mouth, the other clamping her wrists together. But his victim hadn't grown up in the camps for nothing. Cregar would be waiting. Her heel slammed out. Not against Baris but against the door which was still ajar. It crashed open.

She kicked again through the opening. Cregar would see that and know she was fighting. Baris's hand gripped her wrists as he tried to kick the door shut again. From around the girl's neck a chain fell to dangle her ring against the rough tunic. Her attacker's eyes widened.

"Well, well. So that's who got this. Ideena, take a look. I guess I get a drink if I want one now." He swung Laris toward the watching woman. Cregar entered just as Ideena rose to her feet. She took one look at his face and sat again. Ideena knew when to back up.

"Let her go, Baris." Cregar looked bland and uninvolved until one saw his eyes. Baris wasn't looking.

"I do what I want an' right now I want a drink."

Cregar wasn't arguing. He placed a palm-sized needler against the man's neck and triggered. Baris slid heavily to the floor, eyes shut, body limp. Laris landed half under him with a gasp as his weight drove the air from her lungs. Ideena remained sitting as Cregar looked at her.

"Nothing to do with me," she said. He nodded acceptance of that as she continued. "If it was I'd mention a ring the girl has and I'd remember where it came from. Dedran won't hear about the ring if he doesn't hear about this." It was Cregar's turn to nod. "Soldier's oath?" He nodded again and Ideena relaxed. She'd never kept her word in her life if there was profit in breaking it. But she knew that those who'd been in the service prided themselves otherwise.

Cregar lifted the tousled Laris and helped her from the hidden room. She could stand, bruised and scared though she was. He surveyed her once they were safely outside.

"Did he hurt you?"

"Just bruises; he'd have hit me if you hadn't gotten there, though." The look she turned on him was honest gratitude and a deep admiration and it warmed him. He reached for the ring and dropped it back on the chain down her tunic neck. His hand patted her shoulder.

"Long as you're okay." Something stirred in Laris. Without thinking she turned her head to the side and, in a gesture old as the camps, kissed the hand which held her.

"Thanks to you. I won't forget. Camp oath on that." She

shook herself. "I'd better get going." She accepted the light push he gave her, grinned at him, and hurried away. Cregar stood considering the past ten minutes. He'd sworn not to mention Baris and his actions just now. He hadn't sworn not to tell Dedran a few other things his boss didn't know as yet. Such as that pair's habit of running about the circus in disguise, and maybe bringing the peacekeepers down on the circus. Cregar would wait just a little longer and he had no doubt that the pair of fools would stray so far over the line Dedran would have no choice but to eliminate the dangers they posed to his plans.

After her escape from Baris and Ideena, Laris worked busily, trying to smooth from her mind the few moments of fear. The circus with its people was becoming dangerously unstable. If things continued that way she might have to run. Trastor wasn't a bad world on which to get out. Their bond-laws were easier than those on some of the other worlds. She could prove she'd been illegally bonded. She had enough to pay her way for two years with the credits Prauo had brought her and the cat's-eye the Quades had permitted her to keep.

Better yet, she could no doubt find a trade to learn here in the city and buy in on an apprenticeship for a year. Depending on the work she chose, her time of service would be from three to seven years. But after that she'd have a trade and a guild. Maybe she could find something where her liking for animals would serve her. There was also Prauo to consider.

Laris felt his attention. *I wondered where I fitted in, furless-sister.*

You always will.

That is good. As for the ones whose minds I do not like. There was the sound in her head which was his laughter. *I think they will be dealt with soon enough. Too many have plans for them. They will not elude all. You do well. Continue to play the men, one against the other.*

He was gone again. Laris worried as she swept. She didn't want to go near Baris and Ideena even once more. And Dedran would expect her to continue. He knew nothing about Baris. Cregar wouldn't spill. He'd oathed. She thought wistfully of Logan, and of riding over the vast acres of the Quade ranch. If only she wasn't trapped here, if only she and Prauo could be free. She'd like to see more of Logan if only she didn't have his beasts on her conscience. Her thoughts wandered back to the humans concealed in the secret section of the cage. Cregar would keep an eye on her when she went there again, she hoped. He liked her and he didn't like Baris and Ideena—or Dedran. She liked him too, although it was a pity he'd ever gotten involved with the circus. She didn't think he was happy here. It was good for her that he was here though.

Cregar was thinking about the same thing. Sure, the circus had given him a place. But maybe it was time to get out. Cregar knew Dedran's boss; the man was a Thieves Guild patron and in the guild there were factions. Nhara was likely to be hard-pressed to hold his patron status with an expensive plan which had yielded nothing so far. If Nhara went down so did Dedran—and the circus. Very possibly any of the staff the guild thought might know too much would also vanish. That definitely included Cregar.

He saw a familiar face approaching and hid the startled feeling which shot through him. What was the boy doing here? Ideena had shot Logan, the circus held the beasts taken from the family; could the lad be looking for any of them here? At the least it wasn't a good omen that the boy suddenly appeared.

More than ever he felt it might be time to get away from the circus. He kept his face bland as he nodded politely. "If you're looking for Laris, she's grooming the tigerbats."

Logan grinned cheerfully. "Thanks. What's the season been like here so far?"

"Good. Real good. How is it that you're here on Trastor?"

"Oh, my brother and his wife had business here and I came along for the ride."

Cregar liked the sound of that even less. It was possible the business mentioned was the recovery of their animals; or had Baris and Ideena left some sort of a trail to the circus? He allowed his gaze to drift over the lad. A decent boy. Good family background, money, land, and animals. The girl could go farther and fare much worse. "You want to take off with her a couple of hours, tell her I said I'd do the work."

A hint of red showed across the boy's cheekbones. "I will, and thanks." Cregar nodded and turned away as if it was nothing. Once the boy was out of sight Cregar headed in another direction. Dedran should know the boy and his family were on Trastor.

Logan paced slowly along the cage rows looking for the tigerbat cage. He'd told Storm and Tani where he was going and they'd agreed.

"Brad did say to tell the girl her name and ask about the animals," Storm had commented. "Stars know Anders hasn't found out anything. You may as well see if there's anything to be found out about the origins of those tigerbats."

Tani had smiled gently. "Tell Laris her full name and that Brad's still looking. Storm and I will come by later on maybe."

Logan left. The hovercab delivered him to the circus lines

in a matter of minutes and then he had only to find Laris. He saw her first and felt quick pleasure. She didn't know they were on Trastor. She'd be delighted.

Sister! Laris felt Prauo's alarm. *The ring. Hide it, now. Quickly!* She obeyed at once. Seconds later she heard the voice.

"Laris, it's Logan. Hi!" She turned in sudden shock, thanking Prauo as she did so. Logan mustn't see the ring. He mustn't know. Her mind whirled as she smiled a shy, half-guilty welcome. What was he doing here? Did he know Storm and Tani's beasts were here? Why had he come?

Chapter Fifteen

Laris was suddenly and strongly aware of the ring down her tunic, the bright sunshine, and Logan's happy grin. They jumbled together in her mind in a wash of joy and guilt. She couldn't even return the ring. The circus had left well before the attack on the native camp and Quade ranch. If she tried to give the ring back Logan would know she knew who'd attacked him and stolen the beasts. He'd never forgive her. At the same time she knew she was smiling at Logan. Pleased to see him and showing it.

"Logan, what are you doing here?"

"I came with Tani and Storm." His grin left slowly as he told her much of what she already knew—and wished very hard that she didn't—of the raids on the Nitra clan and the High Peaks ranch house. Of his injuries and the kidnapping of Surra, Hing, and her babies. The loss of Tani's coyotes.

"The authorities think that there's someone killing beast masters and stealing their teams for some reason." He looked really serious by now. "I suppose it could be some new Xik idea. Storm doesn't think so though, nor does Brad; that's why we're here, to talk to the authorities. They'll listen to Tani on Trastor." He skipped the reasons the authorities were listening, no need to go into the whole tale of Tani's father.

He brightened. "I met a man on the way in." He described Cregar and Laris nodded.

"Cregar. He's a sort of second-in-command for Dedran when he's here." Oh gods, she shouldn't have said that. If Logan thought that Cregar was away from the circus sometimes he might wonder what the man was doing.

Logan wasn't even thinking of that. He had another idea. "So he's got some authority here? Good, because he said if you want to take off with me for a couple of hours, he'll cover your work. I've got something to tell you."

Laris considered fast, putting aside her guilt at her part in the recent events. Cregar was caring for the meercats and coyotes alone now—at his insistence. Laris still looked after Surra. If anyone else attempted that the animal promptly became worse. Guilt and sorrow at Surra's pain were eating at the girl but she dared not act. Not yet.

As for what Logan was saying it sounded as if the raid on Arzor was continuing to stir up too much interest. Dedran would want to know all about it. She could use that as an excuse. Feed Dedran small harmless bits of information while she spent as much time with Logan as she could. The thought made her happy. Then her feelings plummeted again. His requests for her company would last only so long as he didn't know she was involved. But she could be happy with him until he did find out.

"Well, if Cregar said so. That's kind of him. I'll just go to my cabin and put something clean on. Wait for me here, Logan. I won't take long." She had to get the ring stowed away. It wouldn't do to take it with her and have something happen.

She changed in a flurry with Prauo eyeing her from the bunk, purple eyes amused.

Take care, sister-without-fur. I shall watch what happens here for you, and listen also. You are wise to do this.

Laris was surprised at the last. *Wise, why?*

For a minute he said nothing, then, *Learn all you can. Dedran plans, Cregar also. And the two whose minds taste of evil. All plan. Yet it may be what you say and do that is the pivot on which all things hang. The currents of what-is move; ride them and live; let them crash over you and die. They do not know this. I do and I can see.* Laris wasn't sure she'd understood some of that but there wasn't time to discuss Prauo's words. It half made sense and she'd go with that half.

All right. I'll learn all I can. You stay at the back of my mind and hear it. Tell me if I should do anything. I've got to go or Logan will get tired of waiting.

The big cat yawned, fangs closing with a sharp snick. *That could be true—if he waited many hours. Since it is you for whom he waits, he is only impatient to see you again.* His eyes shut and he relaxed, then opened one eye. *Go, or do you dream of mating, go.* Laris blushed and went hastily.

Logan was admiring the tigerbats. He took her hand when she arrived. "It's so great to see you again. Tell me about this bunch. You work with them, don't you? How hard are they to train?"

She talked tigerbats. Logan was easy to talk to. He knew animals and liked them. Understood some of the ways in which they thought. She found herself telling him again how she wished Skreel, the lead tigerbat, and his tiny swarm could be free. Logan looked at her.

"Have you ever wondered about the last couple that arrived? Lereyne found out that tigerbats were almost extinct about five years ago. Since then they've put aside a special reserve for them. Dad says that it's been illegal to export them from Lereyne since then."

"But Dedran got ours just over two years ago." Laris was thoughtful. "Of course, other worlds have them in zoos. He never said where this pair came from. And some rich VIPs keep them to show off." She looked at the tigerbats. "If they were stolen from their home, Logan, that's awful."

"There's a way to know."

"How?"

"If you took samples Tani's aunt and uncle could check. You know they run the ark. All they have to do is match DNA with the existing gene pool on Lereyne. That'd tell them if the tigerbats were from there."

Laris wrinkled her brow. "But aren't all tigerbats related? Wouldn't the samples just match anyway?"

"Nope. Brad checked. It's been five years since tigerbats could be legally exported. But they were getting rare for years before that. Lereyne looked up the records. The last permit was almost seventeen years before that. They can run the DNA matches right down to recent generations. If your two show DNA that matches, then they came from Lereyne in their lifetime. I can't explain it all to you. Just take my word for it." His fingers tightened on her hand.

"I do, I am." Laris was flustered. "What do you want me to do, just take samples and get them to you?"

"Yes. I promise we won't make trouble for you." His tone became edged. "I'm sure Dedran will have an innocent explanation of how he came by them." Laris was sure of that too. "But if they were stolen from Lereyne, they'll be confiscated and returned. You'd like that for them?"

Laris had no doubts about that answer. "Yes. I would. I just wish they could all go back. They aren't happy in cages. They aren't like the carra or the dogs. They really love this life. The tigerbats don't."

"Then help us find out."

She nodded slowly. "All right. When?"

He swung her to face him, a broad smile on his face. "How long can you spend with me?"

"Cregar said a couple of hours. Anyhow I'd have to be back in plenty of time for the next performance. Why?"

"We'll go to the park and have something to eat. Then, when we come back if you think it's safe you can get the samples and I can leave with them."

By the time they returned, Laris thought, the other circus people would be busy getting ready for the ring. Dedran would be busiest of all. No one was likely to question what she did. But she mustn't let Logan know how often she took samples. She let him tell her how to do the job and provide the slides as he led her toward the park. At the far side of the green area were benches. They settled there, eyes on each other as they talked. Laris felt happy all over when he reached for her hand. His gaze on her was gentle, almost—she was afraid to believe what her heart told her—perhaps his gaze was loving, yet that could be wishful thinking.

They strolled a while, her hand still clasped in his. Laris had never felt so contented, but her joy was tinged with a bitter guilt—if Logan knew what she'd done he would hate her. In that hour she alternated between happiness, fear, and rage that she had been swept up in Dedran's schemes. Finally they returned to sit at the small cafe, ordering food and drink.

"Finish that bun and listen." Logan leaned forward. "Brad was able to get your records as far back as the camp on Meril. All he's got so far is your full name. No trace of your mother. You were alone on Meril. But we've got that far." He saw her face fall. "Brad says it all takes time but he's sure he can trace you farther back." He grinned teasingly. "Don't you want to know your name?"

Her face told him the answer. "Okay. You are Shallaris Trehannan. Brad looked that up too. Where the Shallaris came from, we don't know. But Brad says that Trehannan is a very old Terran name. When he found that he read an old rhyme to us. It goes, 'Tre, Pol, and Pen are the Cornish men.' "

"What does that mean?"

"Cornwall was part of the British Isles. It was one of the oldest lands settled there. Many Cornish families had prefixes in their names like that. It means that if you hear a name with Tre, Pol, or Pen at the beginning the family most likely came from this Cornwall."

"Trehannan!" Laris tasted the feeling. She had a name. A place of origin. She was Shallaris Trehannan and her family had come originally from Cornwall on Terra. Maybe not in her generation, but once. Her face lit with a smile of pure uncomplicated joy, and Logan caught his breath. It was wonderful to know he'd made her that happy. He saw a shadow slide over the delight.

"What is it?" If Brad had found out that much, Laris knew, he must also know what she'd hidden and Dedran had lied about. She was a bond-servant, not Dedran's ward. She summoned resolution.

"I'm . . . Dedran bonded me," she blurted. Logan smiled gently.

"I know. He lied. Brad says you weren't of legal age either. You could get the bond revoked. We'd help if you wanted that. Tani has a special status here. She'd talk to the governor for you. Trastor has bond laws and Dedran's broken just about all of them."

She sat thinking. They'd help. Would they still help her if they knew the rest of it? And what about the samples? What would happen to all of the animals if Dedran was discredited? If he was ruined because of her, he'd talk. About her, about the thefts she'd carried out at his order. How understanding would the authorities be over those? And what if Dedran insisted on claiming Prauo?

A tickle in the back of her head. *Tell him you'd rather wait until you can be sure the tigerbats are safe. He'll understand that.*

Laris reached out to take Logan's hand. "I know Dedran broke laws, but he hasn't abused me." She grinned wryly. "Well, just cuffs, a beating, and a crack of the whip now and again. He's fed me decently though, and I've been respectably clothed. It was my only way out of the camp. I don't like Dedran." The look in her eyes said that statement was milder than the truth. "Still, if I'm here until we know about Skreel, my lead tigerbat, and his swarm, I can make sure they stay put. That Dedran doesn't have them spirited away or killed."

"That's sensible so long as it isn't too hard on you."

"I'll manage," Laris assured him briefly.

"Then, Shallaris Trehannan, shall we walk?" He stood as she giggled at the alliteration.

"Why, we shall lope, Logan." She ran for the park's broad

acres of grass, laughing as he chased her. She danced. "Can't catch me!" The words ended in a squeak as he caught her arm and spun her into his arms. His lips touched hers with a tenderness that was pain. He wouldn't do that if he knew the truth. He wouldn't hold her like that. As if she would break.

Live for today, sister. Tomorrow may change all things. She gave her lips to Logan then, praying that it would.

They returned to the circus. Content to walk holding hands. Everyone was busy as they'd hoped and Laris drifted them along unobtrusively in the direction of the cages. Once there, she took the slides held out to her, and the small needle. She listened solemnly a second time to the muttered instructions before she took the samples, then stowed them away carefully for him in a bag. Laris watched him leave, with what was by now an almost familiar mixture of joy and guilt, before going in search of Cregar. Quietly she told him what she'd learned. Her eyes on him showed trust and he answered that with a warning hand on her arm.

"Don't tell Dedran about their theories. Nothing about dead beast masters and stolen teams and a conspiracy. Let him think they believe it's a one-off. Just a pirate raid and that they took the animals to sell to rich VIPs. Don't say any more on that. Not yet. Say you're getting the boy to talk but it's taking time." His look was thoughtful as he considered her information.

"Tell him everything the lad said about his side of the raid. Especially that he can identify Baris and Ideena. Tell him about Tani's father, the hero of Trastor. That the government will listen to her and they've got the ports sealed up. That the patrol's interested because of the attack on the native camp and the theft of sacred jewelry." Laris nodded obediently.

Prauo?

He speaks with honesty and care for you. I read that there is danger and he fears what may happen. What that may be I cannot read. Listen and agree. Laris nodded at Cregar as he spoke, his face earnest.

"You mean I should emphasize how dangerous it could be having Baris and Ideena here?"

"Exactly but be subtle. Then leave it to me. Just try to let me know when you're telling Dedran all this."

She considered. "He'll know where I've been already. Once the evening performance is done he'll want to see me. If you keep an eye out you could go in once I leave."

"Good girl. I'll do that. You take care." He moved then swung back. "If Dedran ever thinks the peacekeepers are after him, if they come here, you stay away from the cages. Particularly the ones with the hidden sections. Hear me. That's a true warning. I'm not saying more so don't ask. But you and your cat stay away."

He strode off before she could ask questions. He'd asked his own after that comment of Dedran's. He'd found answers he didn't like. The circus boss was ruthless, Cregar had always known that. What Dedran had done made sense in that way. But Cregar didn't have to like it. He sighed as he walked. A man did stupid things. Then he got in deeper and deeper. Until he'd dug himself into a hole too deep to climb out of.

So far the kid wasn't in any holes, Cregar thought. She was straight. That wouldn't last. He knew Dedran was using her and that big cat of hers for burglaries. A bond-servant couldn't be punished if she testified under probe she'd been in fear of her life or safety, or the life or safety of another. But how long before Laris succumbed to the lure of money, if only for the funds to escape? He'd seen it before. As for Baris, his smile was savage. Let Dedran hear the kid, then Cregar would tell him a few things. After that there'd be no more worries about Baris and Ideena.

He strode in the direction of the circus mess tent. He'd help things along with a nice jug of something for Baris to drink. He drew half a jug of the cider then added, not the innocuous fruit juice, but Fever brandy. A wicked mixture which would prime Baris well. With that inside him the big man would be mad to don a disguise and get out into the midway. When half drunk, Baris always looked for a woman other than Ideena. Cregar would watch to know when he went out. He looked grimly across to where the circus boss's tent stood. Everyone had plans, not just Dedran.

Tani was one of those who certainly had plans. She grilled Logan about what Laris had said about the tigerbats, collected the tigerbat samples, and saw preliminary testing begun on them. Matching the samples fully would take much longer than the basic tests, but with that begun she could speak to Aunt Kady.

"Send the second set of samples now," Kady advised. "Not to the ark, send them to Lereyne. See if the patrol has a ship going from Trastor sometime soon."

"Should I send any notes with the results?"

"No. I'll do that. I'll talk to a friend." She reeled off a name and address. "He's involved in the prevention of endangered species smuggling. I'll see to it that if the results match tigerbat DNA held on Lereyne, he'll talk to me before he moves on the information."

Storm, with a wider knowledge of how far evil would go to be safe, interrupted. "Make very sure of that, Kady. If samples indicate the beasts were stolen or smuggled and your friend goes in to get the animals too openly, the owner is likely to destroy the beasts so there's no proof against him."

"Officer Tarwyn will know that." Kady's lips quirked on the com screen. "It's hardly the first raid he'll have led over illegal animals."

"Better check footing than fall."

Kady chuckled. "So true. Love to you, Tani. Take care. And you too, Storm." Her voice and image faded into the static of the starlanes. Storm considered the samples and the basic results which had just arrived.

"I'll duplicate copies of these results and split the samples. I'll send our original results and half the samples to Lereyne, hold the other samples, and a copy of the results here. That way we have backup if we need it." He glanced at Logan. "I think you should spend as much time with Laris as you can. If those tigerbats are illegal, we don't know what else the owner could be doing. If things get nasty it would help if you were there to get her and Prauo out quickly."

"If you think so." Logan kept the exultation from his face with an effort.

"I do. Don't you, Tani?"

She nodded. Logan glanced at the chrono on the wall. "Then I'll go and see the afternoon performance tomorrow." He left so quickly it was more of a controlled run. His brother and Tani grinned at each other.

"Were we like that?"

Storm shook his head. "No, but then we met over Mandy. The first thing I heard from the pair of you was rude." Tani laughed. She remembered that. Her paraowl had been taught—by a disaffected worker on the ark—a number of rude phrases in several languages with a common word for each as the trigger. Storm had inadvertently spoken the trigger word and embarrassed Tani to blushing fury. She'd blamed him. But not long after that Arzor had been in danger, and they'd learned to work together to save the planet she'd come to love. But there'd been no time for walking in the park holding hands.

She sobered. "I think I preferred it our way. By the time we had leisure to talk we both knew what we wanted."

Storm hugged her. "I still know, dearling," he said, using his word for her which had become their own. "And if Logan is away tomorrow we can spend time by ourselves. Unless Anders has something urgent in mind. But it isn't likely he'll be laying hands on Baris and Ideena that soon."

For which mercy those named were grateful. They were not so happy about everything else. Still, life was improving fractionally, Baris thought. Their tiny quarters were quiet while the evening performance was on. Just as it became quieter he'd thought he heard a tap at the door. He checked the spy hole. No one. But by the door stood a lidded jug. It had probably been the girl. She wasn't risking coming near him just now. Baris slid the door open a little, grabbed the jug, and flicked the door shut.

"What is it?"

"Just fruit juice," he assured Ideena. He gulped a large mouthful and swallowed as he turned away. Unseen by his companion his face turned pink and his eyes bulged as the liquid seared its way down. Baris opened his mouth to correct his words and shut it again. Why tell Ideena? She'd only keep him from drinking too much of it. And after all this time shut up with her a man needed a bit of amusement. This stuff was good! He gulped again and smiled. *Very* good!

Ideena ignored him and drifted back into a doze. Quietly Baris got drunk. For two people the jug would have left both happy and somewhat dizzy. Perhaps inclined to sing. But Baris wasn't a peaceful or pleasant drunk, he was drinking alone, and several liters of the mixture inspired him not to sing but to find either a woman or a good brawl.

He drifted off into a brandy-fueled daze for a while. He'd had most of the jug. He surfaced again an hour after the performance in the ring ended and the people returning past his room woke him. Good. If people were about he could don a disguise and get out for a while. He dressed carelessly. He still looked like the ponderous, respectable, middle-aged man he had before, except that the man was now drunk, and contentious with it. He crept out quietly after finishing the last few gulps in the jug. That he took with him. Maybe he could refill it somewhere.

Laris finished her turns in the ring, then changed and settled the animals back into their show cages. Afterward she waited where Dedran could see her. He appeared at the entrance to his tent and waved her over.

"What did the boy have to say?" He finished shutting the entrance as he stared at her.

"He talked about the raid on the native camp. Then the one on their ranch," Laris told him. She elaborated and once she reached the identification of Baris and Ideena she saw his lips tighten. His eyes glittered with fury. She explained how Trastor's authorities, normally so reluctant to help with another world's problems, were listening to Tani and just why that was so.

It became unpleasantly clear to Dedran that instead of this fuss soon dying down, it would continue, probably even escalate. Discovery of Baris and Ideena hiding in the circus could ruin him, and possibly ruin his patron in the guild. And if even the slightest breath of trouble touched Nhara, Dedran would pay. He'd contacted Nhara about the men who'd posed as security, and had it confirmed that there was in-fighting among the guild patrons. Dedran was on a knife-edge now and he knew it. He hesitated. Laris finished her story.

"Do I keep seeing Logan? At least he's in touch with what Larash-Ti is doing and Logan tells me everything he hears." She pasted a bored expression on her face and hoped.

"Yes, see him as you can and work allows." Dedran had other things on his mind. He unlocked the entrance and stood aside for her to leave. Laris went, as quickly as would not be too obvious. She passed Cregar as he approached. He hissed softly in slurring camp dialect in case there were bugs or Dedran's spies were listening unseen.

"You'm say wha' we agree?"

"Es. N' more."

"Done good, girl." He entered the tent and the entrance closed again. Laris didn't wait around. Dedran's tent looked flimsy but it was made of an impervoplas which was nonflamable, soundproof, and had a few other advantages. Inside Cregar was talking slowly, building up to telling Dedran that his dangerous guests, far from being well under cover, were often abroad around the circus.

"You're sure of that?" Dedran was almost incredulous. He'd believe a lot of Baris but Ideena surely couldn't be that much of an idiot. But listening, it was certain she had been.

"I wasn't certain at first. They disguise themselves well. Then I spotted Baris in that pompous merchant outfit of his. When he went out again I had a word with several circus people. They remembered seeing the merchant a number of times." He halted with a definite air of having said all he needed. Dedran wavered. It wasn't that he minded killing, but could he risk it? Ideena was clever. It might not be easy to dispose of her without a fuss, especially with Anders's spies everywhere.

"I'll have to deal with it." He could speak to Ideena. "I'll go there . . ." he began when a small urgent voice began calling at the door. He ripped it open and grabbed. Laris catapulted in already in midsentence.

"Baris is out. He's in the midway. He's drunk. Any minute now he'll make a scene grabbing some girl. Quick, *do* something!" Cregar understood before Dedran did, but then he'd supplied the ingredients for the trouble. He nodded.

"Baris! I knew that pair were trouble. Dedran, you deal with Ideena. There's no choice. She won't listen if Baris vanishes. I'll see to that drunken fool. Laris, show me where." They were gone, leaving Dedran to spin momentarily.

If Ideena hadn't stopped Baris going out alone it suggested she'd been sleeping. She wouldn't know the man was causing trouble. And if she didn't know, she wouldn't be expecting trouble herself. Dedran raced for the ship. In a cupboard there he had a number of interesting and unusual items and he knew one which would be useful now.

On the midway Baris was stumbling along. After telling her bond-master about Logan, Laris had gone to Surra to tend the big cat and make her comfortable. She stroked fur grown rough with illness, repeating her promise. She would help, find Storm, free Surra, but not yet. Soon, she was sure. She sat stroking as she considered ways. Perhaps if she could get Surra away somehow, the way she'd arrived, in one of the lifter pallets. Or maybe she could send Storm and Tani an anonymous message.

But would they be satisfied with getting Surra back?

Wouldn't it just make them look harder for the other missing team members? She knew how she'd feel if Prauo went missing. She'd do *anything* to get him back. She wouldn't be in a rush to forgive someone who had stolen him, either. It wasn't as if she'd be returning Surra in mint condition.

With a final stroke of the cat's fur she rose and slipped from the hidden room. It was then she spied the familiar figure of Baris and fled for help. She pointed him out to Cregar after that and hastily retired to her own room with Prauo. The big male feline couldn't see anyone if Laris wasn't looking at them but he could read feelings. Particularly those of people either of them knew. It was how he'd warned her of Logan approaching.

Laris lay full length on her bed, Prauo sprawled beside her, her hand on his shoulder as she received his impressions. Prauo touched the minds of Cregar and Baris, felt their emotions, and shared them wordlessly with her.

Waves of giddy lust; indignation; a feeling that walls closed in on him, Baris reeled.

Taste of Cregar, old pain, new anger. Dislike focused on another. A thread of fear for the animals.

Baris again. *Recognition. Amusement. A surge of patronage. A lesser one approaches.

A hard-edged anger replied. A tinge of red. Pleasure. At last. No more pretense. A fractional flash of a girl who looked a little like Laris.

Baris stumbling. *Odd. World whirling. Legs folding. Blackness.*

Prauo spoke in her head. *The bad one is no more.*

Laris knew it for the truth. She could only hope Dedran knew what he was doing if Cregar had killed at his order. If the body was found . . . no, it would be bodies. Dedran disliked loose ends. Ideena would be gone as well. She curled up in her bed and slept. Tomorrow she'd check, very carefully.

Dedran and Cregar had no time to sleep. The idea for the untraceable disposal of the bodies was the circus boss's plan, but he required help. He'd have preferred to use the ship's engine turntable. But the engines were stopped for overhaul, seeing as the circus was staying several weeks on Trastor. If he started them again in the middle of the night, some snooper might ask questions. This other method would work. It had worked more than once before according to his sources. It should work again. And so it would have, but for a technical hitch.

Chapter Sixteen

If Larash-Ti-Andresson had not been happy about the disappearance of Baris and Ideena, their reappearance left him speechless—for all of ten seconds. After that what he had to say should have melted his plasteel building to the foundations. Then he was a whirlwind of action. Demands for specialist reports propagated like Terran rabbits.

Storm and Tani arrived just as the explosion was dying. Reports had begun to arrive. Anders read them and exploded all over again. His visitors listened until the fury had blown itself out.

Then Storm asked questions. "How did it happen, and where were they found?"

Anders snarled. "Ideena was poisoned. Baris was stabbed with a long and very thin blade. I doubt he even knew it. Here, look at this report." He dropped a hard copy before Storm and Tani, then continued talking. "The worst of it is that I suspect this method's been used to dispose of unwanted people before."

Tani raised her gaze from the report. "How did it go wrong this time?"

"Someone will be furious about that," Anders said grimly. "It was outside the murderer's control."

"Anders, what happened?" Storm had finished reading the preliminary reports.

"Trastor has a couple of moons as you know. There's a large mining dome on one and a smaller group on the other. Since they're so close it pays not to use the expensive type of ship. But we have to run a regular service. When the mines were opened we had several small, old-fashioned ships mothballed. We reactivated those. They leave every fifth day from a small separate port."

Anders gave a small snort of amusement. "That was what wrecked things. The ships are really old. They use the matter drive. In other words, at a pinch they can burn anything for fuel."

Tani smiled. "They may be old fashioned but there's still plenty about. The circus you have here uses a huge old freighter of that sort. And the ark has those engines. They're workhorses. No speed but a wide and low-cost range because they can use almost anything at all for fuel."

"Exactly. And they can cost little to run if they're being used for such short hops. So that's why we went back to them for the mines. Normally they're run on compressed fuel bricks. But some bright theorist suggested we combine operations. She purchased a compactor and is paid to collect unwanted garbage. That's compressed into bricks and sold to the mining company at a minimal price."

He grunted. "Bright lady. She makes her money coming and going. Not a lot at each end, but it's a cheap operation and the two amounts combine to make good credits. The system is run by her family. Her, a brother, and their older kids, with a couple of part-time oldsters doing the light stuff. If what I suspect is true, in the past anyone with a spare body to get rid of hauled it to the compactor, dumped it in overnight, and left again."

"They filled the compactor ready for the morning's start?"

"Uh-huh. The old chap who runs it would just have pressed the button when he got there the next morning. When enough bricks had fallen out into the loader he runs them to the next ship to lift and loads them into the outer fuel chamber. That's what did it. He pressed the button. The compactor gives a groan and dies. He calls the family. The brother rushes over to fix the compactor, checks the load in it first, and guess what he finds?"

Tani laughed. "I see what you mean. Bad luck for the killers. Did you ask how often the compactor breaks down?"

"I did. They said it's very rare. That was only the third time in the five years the system's been going. But—and listen to this—the other two times it was at the end of the day. They fixed it overnight and were running again by morning. In other words: It was unlikely anyone but the family ever knew about those times. The method must have looked like a sure thing for disposal. It never broke down."

A woman bustled in just then, laid papers on the desk, and departed in silence. Anders turned to leaf through them. He glanced up. "Nothing important. Interviews with everyone we could find at once who lives near the mining port. No one saw or heard a thing." He shifted a switch. "Is that pathology report in yet?"

"Not yet, sir."

"Crats." Anders sat back. "I asked them to do Ideena first. Maybe finding out what was used on her will give me a place to start." He looked as if he was about to explode again. "The *nerve* of them. I'm looking everywhere for that pair and someone kills them. Right under my nose. Then sticks them in the garbage." His gaze on them sharpened. "Do you think this beast master business could be the link?"

"I think so," Tani said thoughtfully. "We know they were involved with both raids. Mandy's imitation of the voice she heard was identified on Brightland. The authorities there were certain it was Ideena. Logan saw the woman who shot him and is certain it was her. The pair are known to have been working together for years. But look at their records. They don't steal animals."

Anders was reading swiftly down the list of ascribed crimes again. "No. They go for portable high value. I can see them taking your Thunder-talker's regalia. Green or white cat's-eye gems are worth a lot of credits in a very small package."

"But this time they grabbed whatever they could find of some value. Yet they also stopped much longer to pick up a pair of coyotes, a family of meercats, and Surra, injured though she was. I think it's the third man. He was the one after the animals. The other two were on contract with the right to loot."

"Makes sense." Anders propped his chin on one hand as he re-read Ideena's rap sheet. "That ship was hers. Since officially she and Baris were fugitives wanted for questioning on both crimes against a citizen and interplanetary crimes, my people have been tearing the ship apart. So far they've found some fascinating things which may clear up a number of the crimes Brightland has listed here. Nothing on your problem as yet. That may come.

"The man who specializes in the job says he's rarely seen such diverse ways to hide contraband. He's sure there are still a number of places he hasn't found. They'd have required damage to the ship and so long as we had no conviction we couldn't do that."

Tani smiled sweetly. "But now the ship's owners of record have been murdered. It's your duty to find out how that happened. If you have to tear the ship down to basic structure it's legal, surely?"

"Yeeess. Yes. It is." Anders was thinking. "After all, it's clear the owners were criminals. That's plain from things we've found so far. There's no record of any deed of gift or will disposing of the ship. We should make every attempt to satisfy court requirements. We have to find those who'd inherit."

"Apart from which, don't you have the Contingency Law?" Storm suggested before reciting: "Where the owner of a property has been involved in provable criminal acts and dies before conviction, the state may confiscate the property, provided no immediate or minority heirs exist." He pointed to the documents before Anders.

"Baris and Ideena were never legally bonded. Not to anyone else or each other, and they're both dead. They have no known children. Brightland says they come from respectable families there. Their respective parents formally and legally disowned them. Their siblings are all adults. Neither Baris nor Ideena have had any contact with their families in many years. So they can't have any legal responsibility to sibling offspring. So far as I can see the Contingency Law applies."

Anders nodded. "I'll speak to the head of the search team." He touched a panel. "Jyrin? Yes, Anders. Listen. We're applying Contingency Law to that ship you're in. Rip it apart. I don't care what you do. Just find everything there is to find even if you have to take it down to the hull plating." He nodded in reply to a question. "No. On my authority. We've checked records. No immediate or minor heirs. Go to it."

He turned to grin at them both. "Jyrin's a good man with

similar habits to a Trastorian burrower." He chuckled. "He looks a bit like one as well but if there's anything in that ship to find, Jyrin will dig it out. Once he's done the ship can be put back together again and join the mining fleet. The governor will be delighted about that. We've been needing a fourth ship."

Tani laughed. "Everyone benefits. Except Baris and Ideena. I keep wondering who the third person with them was."

"Speaking of a third person," Anders queried idly. "Where's your brother?"

"Where else? With Laris at the circus."

"Which reminds me, I had a spacegram from Brad Quade. Not long. But he's found out something more for the girl." He picked up a report and handed it over. It was as brief as promised. Tani read the few lines rapidly and looked up.

"He says they've traced her and her mother via two other worlds to Fremlyn. Her mother was listed in the camp there as Shalmarra Trehannan." Her voice went up, "And her father as Aylaris who was already dead. See, Storm? They combined their names for Laris. Brad says that the Fremlyn camp took in refugees from Bowlil, Meril— and Ishan just before the Xiks destroyed it. He thinks Ishan is the most likely, but not to tell Laris that until he finds out more."

Storm picked up the spacegram. "We could go now. Even if we don't find her we could give this to Logan to pass along." He allowed a tiny smile to warm his eyes. "I'm sure he'd enjoy that." He swept Tani up, bade Anders farewell, and once outside hailed a hovercab. They were borne in the direction of the circus.

"Why don't we just give Logan the report when he comes in tonight?"

"Because," Storm said slowly. "I've been wondering. Those raiders. They're stealing animals. Where's the easiest place to hide a tree?"

Tani blinked. "In a . . . I see. You'd hide animals among other animals. In a private collection or a zoo except that those don't travel. But a circus does. I've had a nasty thought too. Those raiders seemed to know just where to find me. Our High Peaks ranch, fine. That's all on record. They could have got into conversation with anyone from High Peaks district."

"Except that they didn't. Remember? They arrived and flew straight to the Djimbut camp then on to the ranch. No conversations."

"So who knew where I'd be? Brad has a big map of High Peaks on the study wall at the basin ranch. There's a sketch of the ranch house in the corner. Who's been to see that?"

Storm hesitated. "Laris was at the basin ranch with us. But how would she know about the clan camp?"

"What do you think Logan would have talked about? He knew I was going there to hunt for a ten-day once Laris was gone. I told him just before the circus left Arzor. I even said I might stay a lot longer if the hunting was really good. I know he'd have talked about the clan. He's proud of being a ranger and of me being the Djimbut clan-friend."

The reply was thoughtful. "That's all possible. But there's one thing there. The raiders came in as if they expected the Nitra to lie down for them. Laris would have known better if Logan talked so much. She'd know Nitra aren't Norbies. They're the wild clans. They're warriors who shoot first and ask questions of the body. Maybe she steered the raiders that way—if it was her—hoping they'd fail and be killed."

The cab stopped and the two of them climbed out. "Say

nothing," Storm cautioned. "Let her see nothing. She's bonded. She may have been forced into this but even so, she'd be a risk if she realized we're suspicious. We'd better find Logan first."

They found him at the side entrance to the main tent. The afternoon performance was on and he was watching the antics of the carras and Terran dogs. Storm gave him the report from his father and watched as he read it. Logan's gaze shifted to where Laris waited in line. The next act was the girl and the tigerbats. His gaze warmed as he watched her, his face shifting into softer lines. Tani caught Storm's flickering glance at her and nodded slightly. Logan was in love.

Once the acts were completed, customers filed out. Laris came running to Logan. "I have to change, then check all the animals, Dedran's gone into the city with Cregar for a couple of hours so I'm doing his rounds. I'll be back soon."

She was as good as her word. They accompanied her to the dog cage, then to spend a little time with the carras. Quietly Tani began to talk. She spoke of Minou and Ferarre, how she loved them. How much they were missed and how sure she was that they missed her and grieved for her absence. After that Storm took up the theme, telling tales of his war, of sabotage and reconnaissance missions on strange worlds, and how a team could be one.

Logan noticed nothing but Storm saw the girl's increasing distress. Her face showed little but the movements and the posture of her body all betrayed her.

Sister-without-fur. There is suspicion in their minds toward you.

Why? How could they guess?

I do not know. But they wonder. Now may be the time to enlist aid. Swiftly, distract Logan, when he is gone from your side a moment, speak to the woman. Be cautious in what you say.

Storm was wondering still more as he watched. The girl had been almost frantic with stress. Then, abruptly, her movements changed to those of one who listened to a voice unheard by the others present. He'd seen that posture in first-in scouts who had ear-implants. But this child couldn't have one. To what was she listening? Or to whom? She asked Logan to go ahead and see that no one was with the tigerbats. Storm could tell she was deliberately walking more slowly as they followed Logan. Storm waited, hoping.

Laris spoke carefully. She must make them understand how she was bound by Dedran. She must betray nothing more than that. Not yet. To Storm's puzzlement, she began talking about her cat.

"I found him at the edge of the spaceport. He was only a tiny kitten and starving." She remembered Prauo as he'd been then. His paws, too large for his little body, and his now distinctive black-and-gold markings had been softer shades of fawn and a darkish brown.

"I couldn't leave him to die but I was afraid Dedran wouldn't let me keep him. Once he'd seen Prauo he didn't mind though, he said Prauo might learn tricks and fit in, if he didn't he could always be sold somewhere." Storm saw the fear flare brightly in her gaze as she said that and he began to glimpse her problem.

"There's no proof you own Prauo?" he asked gently.

"None, and I'm bonded. On some worlds Dedran owns not only me, but anything I may have or earn as well. It was circus food which fed Prauo, a circus bed he slept on, Dedran owns it all. I have no ownership papers for Prauo."

"Nor does Dedran, I imagine?" Tani asked.

"That wouldn't matter, he owns me and anyhow, he can always get papers if he wants them." Storm heard her comment with interest. That Dedran could always obtain false ownership papers for an animal fitted in with their suspicions about the tigerbats. He'd mention to Versha what Laris had said once they were away from here. Laris was still talking.

"You don't know how fortunate you are, you have your teams within the law and they're Terran animals, they can't be harmed or taken from you legally anyhow. The only law which covers Prauo and me says that he isn't mine." Her gaze fixed on his, and there was both terrible fear and blazing passion in her voice.

"I love Prauo, he's my friend, I can't even imagine being without him after all this time. If anything happened to him I think I'd die. We're bound together—as much as your team is to you. I'd do anything I had to do to save Prauo; anything at all, no matter how bad it was."

Storm and Tani exchanged looks, understanding at last how Laris might have been coerced. If the girl had been entangled in the plot to steal Terran beasts it had been under duress, yet they would withhold their final decision on her true guilt or innocence until they discovered the extent of her involvement.

Tani had spent an earlier part of the day at the graveside of her father. Anders had taken her there. She'd stood and wept quietly as she read the words graven deep into the stone. Her father had given everything, his life, his team, his hope of return, to save an embattled people struggling against a merciless enemy. Now she looked at Laris. The girl had nothing, only the cat she loved. She would risk anything rather than watch him lost to her. In a way her decision was similar to the one Tani's father had made. Tani's voice was gentle. She needed to make a bargain clear but without saying anything which could be used against them later.

"We do understand. You know our grief. Maybe there is hope. A chance that Prauo could have title established. If so then maybe our grief would also be lessened."

Laris looked them both in the eye. "If Prauo was safe I'm sure it would be so. But I will take no risks with Prauo, he must be safe."

"We can find out what the law says and what can be done for you both. How would we speak to you safely?"

"I can tell Logan you are trying to secure Prauo for me. Dedran has encouraged me to spend time with him. Pass any word you have for me through him." Storm's eyebrows rose a little at that. So, the circus boss had a use for Logan's affection for Laris, did he? No doubt it had been where much of the information used had come from.

"Taking my name in vain?" Logan had returned.

Laris explained and he nodded eagerly. "I can do that. I think it'd be great if Prauo couldn't ever be taken away from you. He's beautiful."

The human has discernment.

He likes me.

Great discernment. A good beginning, furless-sister. I think they understand your dilemma, their feelings of distrust and anger against you have faded somewhat.

He was gone again and Laris returned to showing her visitors about, gradually relaxing with Logan's teasing. If there was word about the tigerbats they'd let her know about that too, she was assured. It might be possible to use that information, if the animals had been illegally obtained, to secure Prauo to her as well. How, they weren't sure. But a way might be found. She slept soundly that night. Her heart lifted with the beginning of hope.

Logan came the next day. Laris didn't mind seeing him alone and openly. Dedran was still happy for her to learn all she could from Logan. The boy laughed as he explained his early visit.

"Storm says I'd forget my head if it wasn't screwed on. I forgot to give you the official hard copy report on your family." He sobered. "Listen, Laris. You know who your parents were. Aylaris Trehannan was your father. He and your mother combined names for you."

"Which may mean I was their first child?"

"It's likely. You don't remember any other smaller kid with you?"

Laris shook her head. "I don't remember much of anything about my mother. I told Mr. Quade. I think I was about five or six when she died."

"According to this report your father must have died at least two years before that. There may not have been any other children. There was no trace of him in the two camps before your mother died. But in that last one Brad found your father's name listed as deceased. It sounds as if your mother knew how he died and had given the authorities the information so it could be correctly listed along with her, and your, details."

"But will Brad find anything more? That's the question."

Logan snorted. "You don't know my father. Once he's on a trail he's relentless. If there's anything at all he'll find it."

The girl took a deep breath. She'd thought about this all night and had talked it over with Prauo. She would gamble now with both their futures, trusting that what Tani and Storm had offered earlier was true. Logan liked her, maybe he'd see that promises made to her were kept.

"I have to tell you this, Logan. You know I'm bonded to Dedran?" He nodded silently, waiting. "He's made me break laws for him. Me and Prauo. We've had to do burglaries. He said that I'd obey him or he'd take Prauo away. When I still argued he said he'd sell Prauo to an arena, or kill him for his skin. I couldn't let him do that." Her mouth trembled.

"I always planned to get away. Prauo stole credits he found on some of those jobs and gave them to me. Sometimes Dedran threw me a few part-credits as well. We've saved for years. I've enough saved now to manage for a while once the bond ends and I'm free." She shivered, waiting. "Do you hate me?"

Logan remembered the things Brad had said. Bits and pieces about the De Pyall camps. One night he'd mused aloud, and quite graphically, on what it must have been like for a small girl left alone, shifted from camp to camp, struggling to survive. To Logan it sounded like horror. He could only marvel that Laris had survived and done so with her courage intact. He reached out, curled her into the circle of one arm, and looked down into deep brown eyes.

"I don't hate you. Brad told me some of what it must have been like in the camps. Even after all that you could find a half-dead cub and love him back to life. Care so much you'd do things you hated to keep him safe. Dedran's a lousy clicker."

A flash of amusement showed in the eyes which surveyed him. "More than that. He's guild, I think."

"*Is* he? Versha would be interested in that. No," he corrected as she startled. "We'll keep that quiet. But if all this falls apart it might help get her on our side." He hugged her hard. "Go and do your show. I'll see you afterward." They spent time together later as she cared for the animals. Once he'd gone she vanished to check Surra. Cregar would be taking care of the other hidden beasts.

In a secret room Cregar cradled meercat babies again, his heart filling with love. Hing blinked sleepily at him. The babies scrambled, churred, and trilled affectionately, ending up in a jumble in his lap. His hands slid over small, firm, warm bodies. The faint mind-touches from them were growing stronger. If battle-fortune favored him, in a few more weeks he would have part of a team again. At least two of the babies would accept him as their beast master.

His conscious mind worried at the problems they faced. Baris and Ideena were gone. But Larash-Ti was more energetic than ever. Dedran seemed to have no idea of how to deal with events. Worse, the local Thieves Guild patrons complained that all the peacekeeper activity was inhibiting their business. It wouldn't take much more before the local patrons leaned on Nhara to close the circus and provide a scapegoat.

Also Cregar had found a reason why Dedran seemed so smug about lack of proof. It wasn't that it didn't exist as of now. But when he wished it to stop existing it would. Cregar didn't like that idea. Not considering what it meant. He'd come into this business on a promise and a belief. It looked as if the promise was hollow. The belief was possible but without the promise, he'd still have little. So where did that leave him? He could think of answers to that question and he didn't like them any better.

He should act. But he wasn't sure which direction was the best way to jump. He'd wait a while longer. Observe, be ready. Keep an eye on the kid and her cat too. He didn't want them hurt and Dedran was a great believer in clearing away loose ends. Cregar stroked the meercats and allowed his mind to run free, to a time long ago when he'd been more than he was. When one had been many and many one. The enemy had slaughtered his team and Terran Command had refused him another. They'd claimed not to have enough beasts but he was sure they'd lied.

Driven by need he'd done something stupid and after that there was no chance for him to ever regain what he'd had. Then Terra was gone, and, as he'd feared, all hope of a second team with it. If he could have remembered how to pray he'd have prayed then. To have back, even for an hour, what togetherness had once been his. Belief, hope, consciousness faded. He slept as the furred ones snuggled close.

Chapter Seventeen

Two days later Storm woke to an urgent beeping. He rolled over and peered at the wall chrono. Great Spirit. It was barely four in the morning. What message had that importance? He touched the comunit to life and mumbled at it. The unit squawked cheerily in response.

"Up and awake, my lad. I'll be with you in ten minutes bearing news."

"Versha?"

"The same. Move it." The unit clicked off and she was gone. Storm groaned as beside him Tani stirred.

"I heard that," she said sleepily. Her eyes cleared as she sat up. She focused on the time. "Better do as she said. If it wasn't important she wouldn't have woken us this early after such a late night." She yawned widely. "Last night was worth it though. I enjoyed myself."

Storm could only agree. They'd gone to a place Anders knew. It served lightly frothed fruit drinks, tart and delightful to the tongue. The entertainment was provided by one of the allied alien races, a team of half a dozen who sang, juggled, and ran a very clever and amusing beast show. Afterward Storm and Tani had stayed a while talking to them and swapping animal tales. They'd had a wonderful time even if they had only returned three hours before Versha had woken them again.

Tani was moving swiftly, brushing her hair and watching the time as she hurried into her clothes. Storm followed suit. It was just on the promised ten minutes that both appeared from their room to meet Logan erupting blearily from his.

"Awake too, little brother?"

Logan surveyed him indignantly. "If that's what you'd call it. Do you know, Versha woke me just now and it's only four A.M." He sagged dramatically and gave a hollow moan. "I'm not used to this. It's too much of a shock to my system. I need restoring."

Storm's eyes were amused. Tani laughed. "You two. You'd think that you'd never been up this early before. At home you're often awake and away by dawn."

"Very true," Logan assured her. "But *not* after we'd only gotten to bed three hours earlier. If I'm riding at four I'm in bed by eight or nine. I like a decent length of sleep. This had better be worth it."

"I suspect it will be." Storm sobered. "Versha wouldn't wake us this early unless it was something important." He headed for the small kitchen attached to the suite. "I'll start drinks. Swankee for everyone?" He gathered the nods and began to spoon the powder into mugs. They heard Versha run up the stairs as he passed around the steaming drinks.

"Up and awake. Good. That swankee? Great. Give me a cup, sit down, and I'll tell you a few things." She was all quick movement, her eyes glowing as she accepted the swankee and spread papers on the small table. The others sat and allowed her to begin as they sipped the hot chocolate-tasting drink quietly.

"First thing. Those tigerbat samples that Logan got us, Lereyne contacted me directly about them a couple of hours ago. The pair checked were definitely obtained illegally. Samples indicated that the animals are the offspring of two of the tigerbats held in the reserve. The reserve people say that their records list when the animals went missing. At the time it was feared they had strayed somehow from the reserve.

"As you may know, the reserve there is in mountain foothills. An apparently natural break in the force-field fence was found and the reserve staff thought the young tigerbats had escaped and vanished into the mountains. They could find no trace of them but hoped they'd turn up when they matured sexually and came back to look for a swarm. It looks instead as if the pair were darted and stolen. Possibly the swarm was sleep-gassed and this pair chosen to order. Lereyne wants them back. *If* Dedran can prove he purchased them legally from the thieves without knowing the beasts were stolen, then he'll be compensated."

"If he didn't and we march in, they'll guess somebody's talked. I don't want Laris blamed." Logan was worried.

Versha grinned. "Quite true and I have no wish to get the girl into trouble. I'll go. You can be there already just visiting. But I have the readout for the tigerbat's DNA records from Lereyne. I plan to say that Lereyne has heard of the tigerbats, insists on DNA matching because tigerbats have been stolen, and that I'll have all of them cross-matched on patrol authority. I shall be very official when this pair show up as matching reserve records."

"Is that it?"

"No, I'm afraid it isn't." She sat fingering a sheaf of papers. "Storm, you were a beast master, and Tani, you were involved at the beast master breeding and recuperation center to some extent before you left Terra. Do either of you remember a man called Jason Regan? He was a beast master whose team was killed by the Xiks. He returned to Terran Beast Master Command but at the time they were short of beasts for new teams. They said he would have to wait but apparently he didn't want to do that." She snorted in exasperation.

"Instead the idiot convinced a trainee to try some trick called meshing. It was supposed to enable both humans to control the one team. They failed, the trainee died, and Regan's abilities were partially burned out. Regan was court-martialed but the court decided that the trainee had acted as he did of his own free will, and there wasn't any specific law to prevent Regan from doing as he'd done. However he was discharged, he left the service, and disappeared."

Tani wrinkled her forehead. "I remember hearing talk when I was small about what a dangerous thing it was to do that. I don't think I ever heard that name."

"Storm?"

He nodded reluctantly. "I didn't have much to do with him. He was older. Like Tani's father. They took beast masters where they could find them during the Xik war and there were never many with the beast master abilities. I did hear about Regan though. There was a rumor at the time that meshing could open you right up. Give you a team channel which was twice as good. Someone was supposed to have done it and got that result, so this pair tried and Regan was burned out."

"What does that mean exactly?"

"They weren't sure," Storm said slowly. "At the time it meant that Regan couldn't touch any of the beasts mentally. He couldn't keep working as a beast master. They thought that the channel might heal in time. You have to know, Versha. All this was experimental. It was war, they couldn't keep him and hope that in five or ten years he might be useful again. They offered him a commission in another unit. He refused. There was talk that he'd suffered some brain damage in the memory areas. He resigned from the unit and before they could con-script him somewhere else or order treatment he was gone." He waved at her papers. "Do they have any more?"

"Yes, and it's interesting. They finally discovered that he's been with Dedran's circus most of the time. Calling himself Jas Cregar. The surnames are just similar-sounding enough that he'd learn to reply quickly. Not give himself away. The few family records we've accessed from his time in the unit say that he came from Ishan. His grandparents emigrated there from Britain with the third settler wave.

"His parents had a daughter about ten years younger than Regan. No record of what happened to the family but they're all likely dead. As you know, Ishan was overrun by Xiks about fourteen years back. Most of the men and a lot of the single women died holding off the Xiks to get the other women and kids clear. The remaining defenders died when Ishan was incin-erated. So this Regan probably has no family we can use to appeal to him to help." She grimaced.

"We may need help. I've talked to patrol HQ. They've had a man in the guild this last couple of years. We've likely lost him now. He's gone silent. But before that he was able to reports rumors in the guild that a patron called Nhara has a scam going. What it is he's never found out but there have been hints the guild initially expected great things from it and it involves animals."

"The circus," Tani said. "They have illegal animals. They

have a burned-out beast master. Logan says Laris told him Dedran could get fake papers for any animal if he wanted them. Is there anything else which could point to the circus?" Versha picked out a paper with care and handed it to her. Tani read and handed it on so that Storm and Logan read it, heads together. Then they all looked at Versha.

"It isn't proof, my Arzoran friends. But yes. They found a tiny scrap of Terevian peavine on Baris's clothing. And the only place we could find that is currently using that is the circus. They use it as animal bedding because it's lighter than many other forms of bedding and it's edible for the animals in an emergency. Of course there's nothing to say Baris and Ideena weren't animal lovers, or fond of the circus and went to watch the show. But it's another clue."

Logan was thinking furiously. They had more than clues. Laris had told him she believed a guild patron was involved with Dedran and the circus. Dedran had her and Prauo burgling for him. And she'd opened up further about that the next night, once she'd seen he didn't condemn her. It looked as if Dedran was into stealing industrial secrets for resale. If the description of some of the items he'd had Laris and Prauo steal for him was accurate, such thefts could also tie into the guild. He didn't want to hurt or betray Laris, but this could be a chance for her and Prauo to get away. He spoke quietly.

"It's more than a clue. Laris talked to me after I told her her parent's names. Versha, she's terrified Dedran would manage to hold title to her cat. That he'd use the chance to kill it and punish her if he even suspected she'd talk. He's been using her to commit crimes by threatening to torture and kill Prauo in front of her. If you can get her clear with the cat and get her clear title to the beast she could give you a lot."

"Would she come in and talk to me?"

"No, not unless she was sure Prauo was safe first."

Versha sat thinking. "I was going to raid the circus for the tigerbats. What if, as an apparent afterthought, we collect the girl and her cat as well? Anders could say that we want to check her and the cat because there had been a minor outbreak of disease elsewhere which may have been started by a similar animal. Once we have her clear we should be able to sort something out. If she talks and her information's good we can hit the circus again with a full-scale raid. Anders would be happy to supply the men." She chuckled.

"He's still so mad about losing Baris and Ideena you can see steam coming from his ears when he thinks about it. We can take the tigerbats, the girl, and the cat, using just a couple of Anders's men, and get the animals and the girl out before Dedran knows that's what we're after. It should work if we make it clear we're confiscating animals suspected of being illegally on Trastor, and that so far as the girl and cat are concerned, National Disease Control is in charge. Logan, you find the girl. Tell her the idea. I don't want her thinking we're going to take her cat away for real and having her panic. Okay?"

"I'll go as soon as they'll be about. That's around seven."

"Good. I'll go and talk to Anders. Tani, I suggest you and Storm wander along to the circus around midday. That's when we'll hit them. It could be useful to have you there. Logan, don't tell the girl anything more than we're getting her and the cat out in payment for talking freely to the patrol. She isn't to know about Baris and Ideena, peavines, or a later raid. Understand?" He nodded agreement. "Right. I'll see you all in a few hours."

She hurried away, the papers clutched in one long-fingered brown hand. She also wanted more information on this Regan's background. If they could turn him into an informant she knew they'd find out enough to make a real dent in the guild.

Storm stood, Tani joining him as they headed for their room to dress for the outdoors. Logan was behind them. He'd dress properly then get something light to eat. He couldn't manage a real breakfast, he was too excited. He'd grab a snack, then make for the circus.

At seven Laris would be cleaning the animals' cages. She'd be busy with that for a couple of hours. The other staff had their own work and she'd be alone for most of that time. He'd showed up a number of times to help and just spend the time with her. No one would think it odd. But with no one around he could tell her not to worry, explain what was to happen, have her prepared to walk in at just the right moment with Prauo and be scooped up and away before Dedran could prevent it.

Laris was terrified of what her owner might do if he had any reason to believe she'd talked about his affairs. But then from some of the things she'd confided, Dedran was indeed both violent and a killer if he thought he was threatened. Logan wasn't exactly terrified of the man, but he did share Laris's belief that Dedran, cornered, would be very dangerous.

As for Cregar, Laris had made it plain the man had been a half-friend to her and Prauo. For that Logan was ready to hope the man wasn't involved. He ate slowly, thinking of how best to handle his actions at the circus, then, after clearing away the debris of his meal, he summoned a hovercab. It dropped him at the entrance to the roped-off circus area. The circus tents showed pale against the early sky as Logan made his way unobtrusively to the animal lines and found Laris sweeping. She looked up and her face broke into a wide, happy smile.

"Heyla. Come to help?"

"To help and to talk." There was a tone to that which warned her. She stepped to the cage door, glancing about.

"I know where Cregar is. And at this hour Dedran will be doing last night's receipts over breakfast. He won't be outside for another hour. If you help me do the next few cages we can stand where I can watch for anyone and we can talk. That way if Dedran or Cregar turn up I won't be behind with the work."

They worked industriously for half an hour. With the work well ahead of schedule Logan drew her to one side. She checked down the line of cages and nodded.

"No one in sight. What is it, Logan? It's important, isn't it?"

"Yes." He caught her small hands up against his cheek. "Listen to what I'm saying, love, and don't interrupt yet. First, we all know about Dedran using you and Prauo to steal. No!" he warned when her face whitened. "Listen to me, I had to tell them, but Storm spent time in one of the camps once as part of an undercover job. He knows what they're like. Brad worked with people who came to Arzor from the camp on Meril. We all understand that you had to get out and just how Dedran forced you to steal. You didn't have a choice, he owned you, he could kill Prauo, beat you half to death, and no one would prevent it."

Her shoulders hunched slowly as she half-turned from him. Logan reached out to pull her back into the curve of his arm. "I'm telling you, Laris. We understand how you had to get out of the camp, then how you had to obey Dedran. You've done a lot of reading, you know the law on a bond-servant. You acted as you did to save your life and if it came to a court they'd accept that."

"What about Prauo?"

"I have Versha's word that he will stay with you."

Laris eyed him with a flicker of hope. "Can she keep that promise—and will she keep it?"

"Oh yes. Versha's word is good, and on Arzor she's the patrol's assistant security head for the planet."

Laris's eyes widened. "Then she can say that, but you're certain she's agreed?"

Logan met her gaze, willing her with all his heart to trust him. "I swear!" he said slowly. "Storm had her write out a note of agreement saying you could keep Prauo just so long as it was proved you were the closest person to an owner he has. I saw the letter and read it, my word on that."

Prauo's mind voice cut in then. *He speaks the truth as he knows it, I would trust him.*

I think I do, Laris thought back, then she spoke aloud to Logan: "How do I prove Prauo is mine, though?"

"You told me once you'd do anything for Prauo. You may need to accept deep-probe to prove Prauo is yours. Can you do that?"

Laris took a deep breath and let it out raggedly. "I can do it. What else do you want me to do?"

"A couple of men from the Endangered Species Conservation Unit here will be arriving around midday. They will have a warrant to take the tigerbats. Once it's proved the two females are stolen property the whole swarm will be confiscated to be returned to the sanctuary on Lereyne. At the same time other people from the National Disease Control will collect you and Prauo. If anyone asks, they'll be claiming they need to test you both."

"Why?"

Logan grinned. "Because, as they'll tell Dedran if he asks, there's been an outbreak of a disease on another planet which may have been caught from a cat-like creature similar to Prauo. Disease Control wants to check out the two of you in case."

"What if Dedran doesn't want to let me go, Logan? He knows I could tell too much for his safety; he might try to stop them from taking me."

"Can you have Prauo make a fuss if they try to take him without you?"

Eyes opened again in the back of her head. *I will do that, furless-sister. I'll be so ferocious without you to calm me, they will insist on taking you with them.*

Laris smiled. "Prauo will do that if I signal him. Tell Versha to be ready."

"I'll make sure she knows." He picked up a broom again. "Let me help you finish. Just in case you can't get back to the circus for a while you might want to sneak off in a few minutes and have a bit of time to do things."

Laris smiled at him, relaxing. She had to admit that when he started this discussion she'd wondered. Almost all of her life she'd been used and she'd been afraid this was what would happen again here. But she trusted Logan, he was doing his best for her, and his family and their friends knew about her, all about her, and they still accepted her, understanding she'd done only what was necessary for her to survive and save Prauo.

Logan was right too, a little time now would be useful. She didn't want to leave her small hoard behind. If Dedran ran he'd run with the ship if he could—and her stash would go with him. Apart from her savings she didn't really have anything worth taking—except her ring, and once she'd told all she could to Versha, she'd have to give that back to the Quades.

Cregar passed just then with a nod to her, and Laris, her senses quick with her years in the camps, noticed the odd way

Logan looked at the man before he was out of sight. She knew that look. It said, "I know something about you."

She wondered what Logan could know and that brought another thought to mind. Cregar. He'd been kind to her. Saved her from Baris, trusted her over his own hoard while he was gone. She should warn him. If Logan knew something about the man then she'd guess the patrol did too. They could arrest him as well. He might prefer they didn't. And what about Storm and Tani's beasts? She swept so hard as she mulled over her options that Logan grinned.

"You'll wear out the cage floor."

"Less to sweep if I do," she laughed back. The work was almost done when Dedran appeared. He eyed Logan and grunted. No skin off his nose if the stupid kid wanted to work for free.

"Laris, we'll use the carras on the trapeze with you in the afternoon performance. I'm switching that act with Jonran and his knife-throwing."

"Why?" Laris asked in surprise. The act had been popular.

"The idiot was practicing this morning to add knife-juggling. He missed. He'll be out a while. I told him to pack his bags. We don't have time for fools who play about and leave me short-handed with the acts." He turned on his heel. "And don't forget the costumes."

Laris took the opportunity. "Logan, I have to go." Her voice lowered. "I'll see you around midday. I'll have Prauo with me. We'll be cleaning a cage by the tigerbats. That way I'll be just where Versha can see me." He hugged her quickly and left to tell the patrol officer all was arranged. Laris promptly darted in another direction. She found Cregar where she'd expected, just leaving the hidden cage with the meercats. She slid unobtrusively past, speaking to him in the soft slurred speech of the camps. Her lips were slightly parted but remained unmoving.

"Got'a talk. Danger you."

Cregar strolled in another direction, circled, and met her behind the cage line.

"What danger me?" Now he could speak more clearly but in his worry he'd reverted to underworld brevity.

Laris answered in kind. "Patrol comes. Logan say they know tigerbat illegals. Reclaim they. Take me 'n' Prauo too. Logan not say but think me he know something 'bout you. Look at you odd you pass us. Maybe you somewhere else sun-high."

Cregar sucked in a breath. Let the girl go and she'd talk. Looked as if it was over for Dedran. But the animals—Dedran had plans for them Cregar had never liked. His hands remembered the feel of small, warm, trusting meercat bodies. Of the first tiny itching of his mind-channels reopening. The meercats hadn't bonded to him as yet although there were signs they could, and might choose him if they did. But now at least he knew his ability had been only burned out for a few years. It could be brought back. Yet with what?

He remembered his team. Las and Lara, the mongeese. Keeroo, the Aubearan falcon. And Mali, the dune-cat, so like the sick beast in the hidden cage. He felt again the love flow across the bond. The trust, the place where oneness was. He'd loved them all. Mali had been half his heart, Las and Lara his laughter, Keeroo his eyes. With them gone he'd lost heart, laughter, and that inner vision.

Laris waited patiently as he pondered. Finally he turned to her. His eyes were different, she thought. It was as if life had flowed in to break the ice of indifference. Even his voice had changed. There was a clean snap to it, the slurring forgotten.

"Tell the patrol about the hidden cages. Warn them. I can't just open the cages and let the beasts go, there are reasons. And Dedran has the cages rigged to explode, destroy any evidence. I'll try to defuse that. Tell them, mount a full raid at midday. I'll try to be done in time."

"What about you?"

His smile was sad. "It's too late for me. You get out clean, girl. Take your cat and be free. I'll do my best for the animals. Tell the patrol to be careful in case I couldn't get all the hidden cages cleared." He walked away abruptly, leaving Laris standing there. Well, she'd told him. She bit her lip nervously. This business about the cages upset her badly. She didn't know much about such things.

Surely Cregar was wrong; he could simply open the cages, the meercats would run out as soon as the door was opened and Storm called them. The same with the coyotes. It would take only seconds for them to be safe. But not Surra. The big cat was weakened by months of drugs, illness, and her original injuries. She'd almost died but somehow Laris had helped her cling to life.

Cregar would have to clear Surra's cage first. But could he? On the other side of the circus Cregar was thinking he shouldn't take that risk. Surra's cage was right at the end of the line. Dedran could see it from his office tent. No, better to clear the other two cages first. Then if Dedran saw him he could maybe hold the man off long enough to save the dune-cat. The others would already be safe.

He checked the time. Not long. The cages had been cunningly rigged with the explosives. To clear both would take much of the time remaining before the patrol came calling. Cregar slid under the cage housing the meercats and began to work with hands suddenly deft. Yes, one cut here, slip this part from that. He'd been well trained by the unit once. It came back to him as he worked. Laris would wonder why he didn't just let the beasts go.

Dedran had been smarter than that. Tied into the circuits in the hidden sections of the cages was an electronic nerve-field. Dedran had these activated on the three cages holding the meercats, coyotes, and Surra. People could walk through the fields without registering their existence. A beast which tried suffered agony, dying from a burst heart. Dedran had the key to shut that off. Cregar did not. To get them out he'd have to disable the entire system or the pain would almost certainly kill the beasts. It was a failsafe against escape or theft. He worked on, sweat beads starting on his skin. One wrong move and he'd go sky-high. But so would the beasts, and even as he sweated, his hands kept working.

He cleared the circuits under the meercats. Best to leave them be. If he let them out now they might be seen and Dedran alerted. He inched along under the low cage until he reached the coyotes' prison. There he worked again feverishly. It was taking time, so much time. But now he knew how it went and he was a little faster. He glanced at his watch. Thirty minutes to midday.

In her suite at the patrol offices Versha was looking at information flow. Her investigator at Ideena and Baris's ship had cracked not only a very well-hidden safe in the ship wall but also the coded disks inside. Very interesting. More material had come from High Command. The last items from Regan's service file. A name in them was somehow familiar. Where had she heard it? She shrugged. No time to sit about wondering. Storm was reading the hard copy of the file over her shoulder. It meant more to him than to her and his eyes widened slightly. It was twenty-five minutes to midday.

In his office tent Dedran was considering recent events. It looked as if the patrol could be closing in on him. Nhara had sent a message. They'd found a spy in the guild. The man was dead by his own hand, too quickly for the guild experts to drain from him what may have been spilled. It might be safer if Dedran simply upped-ship. The *Queen of the Circus* was largely automatic. Liftoff at least could be done by one person alone. But first he'd stroll around the midway. See if there were any indications that he was being watched. He checked the time. Twenty minutes to midday.

Versha was on her way now with a six-peacekeeper squad, Anders, and Jared. In a hovercar behind rode Tani with Storm and Logan. They reached the midway, slipped into the crowd, and tried to blend in. Logan's gaze flicked about in search of Laris. He saw her with the tigerbats, Prauo sitting in the next cage, the door ajar. She saw them and nodded, leaving the cage to stand by Prauo, the big cat leaning against her shoulder.

Under the coyotes' prison Cregar sighed and slumped. One cage to go. He waited until the aisle between cages was empty of people, dashed across, and dived beneath the final cage. Above him Surra's ears flickered. She'd heard a sound. She could feel danger—and also in her mind there was the growing feel of her human getting closer. She was weak but not quite as weak as her warders thought. She dragged herself to lie by the door. Something was telling her Storm was near. She would be ready.

Cregar worked, hands flashing through the motion needed to defuse the cage. For Mali whom he'd loved. A parade of the dead and dying passed through behind his eyes as he worked. All the beast masters who'd fought Dedran's men. The beasts who accepted death rather than live without their human team member.

At first, locked in his agony of aloneness he hadn't cared. Had even been glad in a small mean way that they too should share his pain. But with the girl's arrival things had begun to change. She reminded him of someone; who that had been he couldn't remember. Only that he'd cared about her. He'd tried to stay aloof from Laris. But he'd diverted Dedran's anger or punishment from her more often than she knew. It felt right.

Then they came, Hing and her babies, and at last he felt something touch his mind and heart again. But each time he held them, felt channels open a fraction further, he felt as well the guilt for what he'd done. With emotion and earlier memories and teaching returning, he knew the pain he'd caused. Now his guilt for the things he helped Dedran do was all but unbearable. Superstitiously he feared that his returning gifts would be taken again if he made no repayment.

Maybe if he could save these, it would be counted for him. He could have his team again. He goaded his hands to motion. Faster. He had to finish and be away from here before anyone knew what he'd done. Boots halted beside the cage. In a soft, deadly voice Dedran spoke.

"Cregar? Care to tell me what you're doing under there?"

Chapter Eighteen

Cregar worked on for a moment before he replied. He could only think of one thing.

"I quit, Dedran."

"Do you indeed? But you know guild rules, once in— never out. If you didn't like it you shouldn't have joined."

Let the man keep talking, Cregar hoped. Let him tell me how clever he's been, how stupid I am. Anything. Just so long as I have time to finish this. Dedran didn't do the wiring himself. He had it done. If I finish he won't be able to repair it. The animals will live.

Dedran dropped to one knee, looking at what those racing hands had accomplished. He knew more than this idiot believed he knew. Well, well, he thought. So the fool really was trying to save the beasts. He chuckled patronizingly.

"A pity you've wasted all the work. But there's a deadman switch with each of the special cages. Too bad. And a dead man should go with it. You can't quit, Cregar. I'm firing you." He produced the tiny deadly needler he carried and pressed the trigger button. Cregar arched in agony as the spray of minute missiles struck. Then he slumped.

On Versha's watch, the display finally ticked over to show midday.

Dedran bent to peer under the cage. Blood all over, the needle's scorch in the chest. That was the end of a traitor. He straightened, resolved that it was definitely time to depart. If this wasn't a warning he didn't know what was. He'd go to the ship, close it up quietly, and lift before anyone including the port officials realized what he was doing. The circus had served its purpose.

He could blame the traitor the guild had found in its own ranks for any failure of his own and Nhara's plans. He strolled toward the ship and was out of the beast cage rows before something made him slow to stare around. That was odd. The usual crowds were missing. They'd been there half an hour ago when he'd come out to walk the midway. Where had they gone in that time? He advanced cautiously.

At the gates two peacekeepers turned back those who would have entered. Those who left stayed out. In the half hour Dedran had been oblivious to this, almost all of the people wandering the sideshows and animal cages had departed. At midday most planned to be home and were ready to seek the gates. The time of the raid had been chosen for that reason. With Laris's information Anders had made a decision. He'd have the midway clear. He wanted no list of dead civilians if a cage was accidentally triggered.

Twice, circus people noticing the odd emptying of the midway had sought out Dedran to mention it. Each time they'd missed him. The first had looked in the office tent and gone away muttering. The other circus employee had missed seeing Dedran as he moved between the cages. That second man had felt a warning chill down his own neck, gathered his meager gear, and sought the gates. The peacekeeper presence had reinforced his decision to be elsewhere while something was happening. He faded into the watching crowd by the gates and left hastily.

At the far side of the cages Laris waited with Prauo. Logan stood with her. Storm walked up to them briskly.

"Versha says that's most of the civilians out of the area." He turned to look up at Laris where she sat in the cage doorway. "My team. What do you know about them?"

She looked away, her voice a whisper. "I'm sorry. I was too afraid for Prauo to tell you before. Are you sure they have Dedran?"

"Not yet but they will." He frowned. "He was seen only a short time ago. He's still here. Don't worry, Laris, Anders will arrest Dedran the minute he's seen. So, talk to us. Where are my team?"

"In secret cages. Some of the bigger ones have special hidden compartments."

"Show me!" he commanded. Tani had arrived in time to hear much of this. She took Laris's freezing hands in hers, rubbing them gently. The girl was still so afraid of her owner, Laris needed to feel secure, to be soothed a little.

"Don't be afraid. We're all here. I promise, Laris, Dedran won't come near you, Storm will protect you. Are my coyotes unhurt? What about Surra and Hing and the babies?"

"Hing and the babies are all right. The babies are growing and everything. Your coyotes are fine, Tani. They were mad at me but I made sure they had good food and clean water. I kept Dedran away from them." Tears began trickling down her face. "Surra was so badly injured when they stole her. I kept her alive. I kept telling her that Storm would come for her. That I'd save her. I wouldn't let her die. She's in this end cage."

Storm would have looked under the cage for the circuits.

Laris pressed the back panel in the sequence which opened it. Before anyone could prevent it, Surra fell out into Storm's arms. She was skin and bone with wasted muscles and fur roughened by her illness, but she was alive. Tani was stooping by the cage.

"What's this? Storm, look here. Someone's been hurt. There's blood and a lot of it."

Prauo had leaned around Tani and sniffed. *Cregar, sister. He dies. Dedran shot him, I think. I follow the blood-trail.*

Laris gulped. "Storm. Prauo says Dedran shot Cregar. Cregar must have been defusing the cages. He said he would. We have to find them both. Cregar's hurt bad, Prauo says. And Dedran may do something awful still."

Storm was judging disconnected circuits with a knowing eye. "This one was cleared all right, and a job well done too. Let me check the next one before you open it, Laris."

Dedran had left quietly. With no crowd to provide cover he had slipped along the cage row and then darted behind the sideshow tents. Behind him Cregar stirred. The other beasts— still in danger, and the kid too. He knew she'd come first to try to rescue the animals. He forced leaden arms up to where the last circuits remained working under Surra's prison. The dead-man circuit was easily disarmed. Thanks be that Dedran couldn't resist boasting. Its greater danger lay in not knowing it was there.

Better not to emerge or try to stand. He dragged himself back under the cages and disarmed the switch beneath Minou and Ferarre. There. One last cage to go, then he could rest. It was strange. He'd been sure it was earlier in the day. But it seemed to be growing dark. Not that it mattered. Laris would come for the beasts soon. He must have them ready. He crawled, his breath tearing at his throat.

Laris was ahead, Prauo trotting now, tracing that painful trail and relaying it to the girl.

He grows weaker, sister. I think he dies. But he has some purpose. He goes toward the third cage now.

Tani had released the coyotes who frisked about her, leaping to nuzzle her hands. They sent satisfaction that they were free, assurances that both were well, and that neither had been ill-treated. The human female with the strange cat had been kind to them. In the midway Prauo gathered speed as he followed Cregar's trail; Laris raced after him ahead of the others. Storm, carrying Surra and distracted by Tani's reunion with her coyotes, was well back when Prauo realized where Cregar was headed. The girl vanished from Storm's sight as she dived between two large cages in a shortcut.

Cregar reached the last cage and stared along the ground. He felt the vibrations of someone coming. He peered out in time to see Prauo appear at the end of the cage row. Where the cat was, the girl would not be far behind. The last cage—it was still wired to that final circuit! She would try to free the meercats. He would be left watching as she and the small ones who'd trusted him died, smeared bloodily across the midway when the deadman's switch took its toll.

She was coming. He saw the small figure trot forward. Storm had rounded the cage some distance away, Tani and Logan at his heels. They saw a terrible figure appear then. Swaying, covered in blood, both new and part-dried, Cregar rolled from under the cage and forced himself to his feet. His eyes blurred as Laris moved toward him. His sister. She was coming. His small, much loved sister. He couldn't let her die.

Terror for her accessed the last of his strength as he tore open the cage panel. He leaned in scooping up the sleep basket in which Hing was feeding her babies. In his fear for them he was sending. Hing read the message, *Lie still! Danger!* and she chittered the babies into a frozen stillness in his arms.

Cregar paused a fraction of a second, then leaped backward with them. They passed through the alarm circuit. With it shut down there was no pain for the meercats. But the circuit noted they had left, the switch triggered, and the cage blew up in a great smashing explosion. Cregar had known it would. Even as he leaped he had spun, cradling the trusting meercats in his arms, his back hunched over them, his own flesh and bone between them and harm as he flung himself foward. One pace, another—then the explosion came and he fell.

He went down still curled about the startled meercats. The scythe of splinters slashed across the alley of cages but it met only their backs. Further down the row Prauo had read Cregar's knowledge in the last second and dived at Laris. They rolled entangled beneath a cage. Storm, carrying Surra, with Tani and Logan beside him, had been far enough back to miss the deadly spray. Now they came running as Laris and Prauo crawled out.

"Are you hurt?"

"No." Laris brushed him off. "Cregar, Cregar?" She reached the fallen man and would have turned him over but Storm had laid down his cat and now he caught the girl's hands.

"Don't. You could make the injuries worse." Hing squirmed chittering from under Cregar and scampered to her human. The babies followed. Storm scooped them up and handed them gently to Tani. Then he knelt, his hands checking with the experience of many battlefields. Cregar opened weary eyelids and gazed up at the blurred figure.

"Deadman . . . tied to . . . kill-bar circuit." Hing returned, patting his bloody face with small anxious paws. Cregar's memory turned back. "Las? Lara?" He appealed to Storm. "My team . . . are they . . . okay?"

"They are unhurt," Storm said steadily. The man was dying. Whatever sins he'd committed, so far as Storm was concerned, he'd paid for them with the lives of Hing and her family. "Rest easy, beast master. You saved them all. You've done well."

"Shal?" Cregar could see only a blur of light now. "Little . . . sister . . . Shal. I love . . . Shal?"

Laris was holding his groping hand in hers, tears pouring down her face. This was the one who'd saved her from Baris. The only one who'd been kind to her since she joined the circus. He'd saved the animals. Her grip brought him back a little. His gaze cleared and he knew her.

"Laris? My cache, yours." His eyes turned desperately to Storm. "You witness. Hers!"

"I witness. Whatever you have is to go to Shallaris Trehannan." He saw the man's eyes open in amazement. Storm nodded to the frantic question in these eyes. "Yes. She is. You saved her."

Cregar forced out the final words. "Good girl . . . not blame." He fell mute, appealing to Storm.

"We know. I'll see she's all right, beast master, it's Dedran who'll pay." Cregar heard the words. It was good. All good now. He'd saved his own blood unknowingly. Saved his team, saved his heart, laughter, the inner vision by which a beast master lived. Darkness was coming. Time for Jason Regan Trehannan and his team to hunt. He could see them. They were around him, with him. He could feel their minds holding him up.

Storm was silent, waiting. He saw the body stiffen a little, then as the eyes became blank windows staring up, it seemed to slump and flatten. Storm had seen it often enough. The man was gone, his spirit fled for judgment. Well, at the last Cregar had paid blood price. May the faraway gods open the Warrior Path to him.

Hing pattered back to Storm, swarmed up his pants leg, and cuddled close. Laris was on her knees still holding the limp hand. Logan was beside her. Tani, her arms full of meercat babies, was standing at Storm's back when a voice spoke.

"How charming. Now which of you is going to walk me to my ship?" Dedran smiled at them, needler rock-steady in one hand. Prauo appeared from under the cage behind him and departed the ground in one soaring black-and-gold leap. He landed, claws slashing away the needler. Dedran yelled as they included a generous amount of skin with that blow. Taken unaware and off-balance from the impact of almost eighty pounds of cat, he fell backward. The big cat landed sitting across the recumbent body.

Delicately he flexed claws, laid them across Dedran's eyes, and waited, watching Laris. *Sister? It will not keep him from talking to those who would hear.*

She hesitated. It would be sweet. The patrol could still drain the man of everything, deep-probe all his secrets. She looked at her friends. Storm was impassive. He'd accept her vengeance. Tani and Logan were less accepting. If she did this it would always lie like a dirt smudge across their friendship. Laris sighed.

Just stay there, Prauo. Don't hurt him. She brightened hopefully. *Unless he tries to escape.*

You mean that?

*I have to. But if he tries to hurt you or get away, then you can *shred* him!*

That I shall do. He settled down with the air of a cat which has no intention of moving anytime soon.

Storm had watched. Yes. Interesting. There was no doubt in his mind, even apart from the second file he'd seen just before they left the patrol office, that Laris had been Cregar's little sister's daughter. The ages would fit, and there was quite a facial resemblance if one looked for it. No one had before because the possibility had never occured to them. And only Storm had seen the last spacegram which had arrived from his stepfather minutes before they left for the circus. There hadn't been much in it, just the information that further old records had been checked for Regan. Those had noted that the man had reverted to his basic name and dropped the final portion. Originally he'd been Jason Regan Trehannan. So Laris came from a beast master line, and she appeared as well to be bonded to the big cat—or something.

Prauo's head turned toward Storm. Purple eyes studied him. An itch awoke in his brain; then words came.

Or something.

Storm opened his mouth in shock and would have said he knew not what, but for the arrival of Versha, Jared, and Anders. The woman was looking annoyed.

"We have everyone but that damn Dedran. He's vanished into thin—" Tani and Logan moved aside. Dedran was revealed with a smug Prauo still draped across him, a pawful of wickedly extended claws at the ready. Versha's face split into a wide, happy, and dangerous smile. "How nice. Fur packaged for safety." She turned to Laris. "Can we have him now, please?"

Prauo, time to get up. The nice lady is going to make Dedran almost as miserable as you could. Prauo yawned and rose. He padded over to Laris as Anders snapped arm-locks on the circus boss. Jared took charge of the prisoner and marched him away. Versha surveyed them.

"I think a conference in Anders's office would be a good idea. I'd like to know what's been happening." She glanced down. "Also if that man was Cregar, and who killed him? I see you have your animals back though. So—something of a happy ending." Her smile went hungry. "For us too. Dedran will talk, my superiors will be delighted, the guild will not be. A good result all around, I'd say."

Storm bent to lift Surra again. "Yes." Logan had persuaded Laris to let go of Cregar's hand and rise. He looked at the drooping girl. "We have loose ends to tie and things to talk about. Information to share as well. Laris?" Her head came up. "I don't want to jar Surra by carrying her all the way, any ideas?"

Given a need, Laris put aside her grief for a little. "Lifter pallets. There's one around in the next alley. Hold on." She darted away and returned with the pallet towed smoothly behind her. Over an arm she had a couple of blankets as bedding. Surra was laid on the blanket-cushioned lifter top. Laris produced a set of bars which slotted into the top. They formed a low surround to prevent Surra from rolling off. Storm pushed the pallet and it glided forward. The girl tucked the blanket edges over the cat and stepped back.

"Good. Thank you." Storm approved. She flushed and nodded.

The small cavalcade headed for the gates. Once there, a hovercar engulfed Storm and Surra, with Tani and her coyotes, who were still refusing to move more than a pace from her. Logan hauled Laris into the next vehicle. Prauo joined them, sitting comfortably between, to Logan's amusement. Versha and Anders entered his official transport and powered smoothly after the other two vehicles. Dedran brought up in the rear in a fourth car with watchful guards. They reached the Under-governor's offices and Anders halted them all.

"I think we should do best by taking a break right now. Go bathe, eat, drink, and rest. We'll meet tonight at eight-hour. By that time Versha and I may have answers to some of the questions you'd like to ask." He smiled at Dedran. "This does not apply to you, I fear. It is you who shall be providing the answers." He nodded to Dedran's guards. "Take him to the probe room and begin. I'll follow."

They scattered, to reassemble seven hours later, clean, respectably garbed, and hungry for information. Anders was waiting, his face alight with results.

"I'll make this fast. We have preliminary information which clears some of the mysteries. Briefly—Dedran's boss was a guild patron. They planned to use stolen team beasts and Cregar to build new teams. The guild patron intended to send these out as a sort of guild survey to find new usable planets. The whole circus was never more than a front. While they worked toward that plan they also used it in other ways." He saw Laris draw back slightly.

"Yes, he's talked about you and your friend there." He nodded to Prauo. "Before we began deep-probe Dedran tried to persuade us that the espionage, sabotage, and thefts were your idea. However I have seen the Kowar record copies. Dedran's acts began long before you joined the circus and you were twelve when you did so. Under probe he confirmed you were illegally bonded and under duress and his orders, not the reverse. I don't quite see you as the mesmerizing criminal mastermind he's tried to claim anyway."

Laris faced him, nerving herself. "I'll swear oath and take probe to back it. I was afraid for Prauo's life and my own."

"I believe you. I accept your oath but I'll have to have probe records for Trastor's governor and patrol High Command. Don't worry. For those who speak the truth, probe isn't dangerous—or even painful. We can do that now." He picked up papers and shuffled them. "Apart from that we had another informant in the guild's lower level. They confirm there is now considerable infighting going on. Dedran's patron has fallen. Other patrons would like to lay hands on Dedran. It's been made plain his best hope of life is to stay right here and talk about everything he's ever done or known."

"And?" Logan asked.

Anders grinned. "And once he understood that, the problem is going to be shutting him up any time soon. We're encouraging that. We have cheated him in one way. Somehow he'd taken the notion that if he cooperates he won't go to rehab. I'm afraid he's wrong. With even half of what we know he has done he already has a room booked. Or—if he chooses, a clean death. Either way he won't be merely jailed or let go."

Laris shivered. To have the personality wiped. To be a baby again and to relearn, then go free but never know who you'd been. That was death and maybe the worse sort. She shivered again. She guessed Dedran would choose a clean death in the end. At least if he did it would mean she'd never see even his body again. Anders moved toward the door.

"Laris, come with me. We can have this over in an hour. If you others would care to wait . . ." They did so. He was back with Laris in the promised hour, both smiling. Anders carried papers. He sat, handing the papers to Versha as he did so. The patrol officer took center stage.

"I've conferred with Jared and we agree. Laris, the probe confirms that all you did was done as a bond-servant under orders and under threat of death or injury to you or your beast. Therefore you are deemed guiltless. This, so long as it cannot be subsequently proved against you that you yourself were the deliberate cause, without legal excuse, of death or injury to any other." The words rolled out in solemn tones. Versha was giving the law as backed by the patrol.

"Storm witnessed the transfer of all property owned by the man Jason Regan, known also as Jas Cregar. It is accepted that this verbal transfer is a legal will and that you inherit as was the dead man's intent. No reason is seen why you should remain on Trastor. The probe clears you. You are free to leave when and to where you wish. Monies inherited may be transferred at your demand." She glanced at the papers and spoke again slowly.

"The beast known as Prauo is deemed to be your property until such time as you may decide otherwise. The patrol has no interest in laying claim to the animal. Nor has the circus, now listed as a criminal entity in and of itself, any rights in this matter. Your bond held by Aldo M'ranne Dedran is hereby canceled since proof has been advanced that such bonding was illegal. This judgment is the judgment of the patrol in the name and person of Sind Illisho Versha. So shall it be!" Her hand struck down on the table and she relaxed.

Laris sat there stunned. Logan grabbed her, lifted the girl to her feet, and danced her around the room.

"Don't you get it? You're free. Anything Cregar left is yours. No one can take Prauo from you." He slowed, looking down at her. "You aren't still worried, are you?"

Laris shook her head. "No. But Logan, I did terrible things. I helped Cregar steal Storm and Tani's animals. You were hurt because of me. And that isn't all." She fished under her tunic and began to draw up the ring. "Cregar gave me this. I guessed where it came from but I loved it so much. Take it, and if you don't want to know me, I understand." She dropped the ring into his hand. Storm took it from his brother.

"The ring of Walks-Soft-as-a-Puma. Brad will be happy to see that back again."

"I'm sorry," Laris choked. "I'm sorry." Prauo moved to stand with her. In Storm's mind words and images formed to combine a plea.

She has fought. Against the camps, her bond-master, those who would have ill-used her. Swift flicking pictures of Laris cowering under blows, the sensation of hunger, a blast of fear and pain. *Her life has been only strife until now. She had no place of her own. None save me to love for long and long.* Now a black cloud of lonely misery was sent, to pierce Storm with Laris's remembered emotions. *Do you now cast her out? What of your path? Has it been so free of wrongdoing. So smoothly perfect?*

No.

Then as the dark woman judged, do you also judge, with honor and mercy. Storm closed his fingers about the ring and his other hand was laid on Laris's arm.

"When the war finished I came to Arzor," he said softly. "I planned to kill a man I believed had betrayed me and mine. I found a man with honor but shut my eyes. Yet in the end I opened them to truth. Because of that man's mercy I stand now with my own family. With a place. Long ago a wise one of the people said that a gift should be passed on, not back." He turned Laris a little, so that she faced him.

"You kept Surra from dying, took care of Hing and her family well." He took in a deep breath. "For my part I forgive anything done against me in your name. It is dust on the wind. Forgotten."

Laris stared. Tani smiled down at her. "You cared for Minou and Ferarre. The clan accepts blood-price. Buy something of the sky here and gift it to them." She laughed softly. "I know where you could buy a meteor. A small black sky-stone. The clan would forgive much for that gift to the Thunder-talker. It is a thing of great power. They would forgive the debt. None of them were wounded and they took four bow-hands."

"I'd pay happily." Laris gulped. "Could I afford it?"

"Oh, indeed. You have not yet seen Versha's report on Cregar." She would save until later the news that the man had been kin. Tani held up a list. "Your friend was wealthy. In the hiding place of which you told us there was a disk. It holds bank records. I have spoken to one who knows. With all gathered together you inherit . . ." She spoke a sum which left the girl gaping. "You can afford a sky-stone. And land too, if you wished." With slow incredulous hope the girl moved to gaze at Logan. He held her.

"For my blood, you pay time. Come back to Arzor. Stay with the family three months. Ride with us. Know the land. If you choose then to stay or leave, any debt to me is paid." Storm swept Tani hastily out of the room after her final words.

"I think they'd like to be alone, dearling." Tani, catching one quick glimpse of Laris locked in Logan's arms, agreed.

It took time. Laris submitted to a longer probe session for information. Anders's friendly banker sorted out finances and transferred credits: A final sum which would buy a meteor—and quite a lot of land should Laris wish for the latter. Five tigerbats returned to semi-freedom on Lereyne. The Thundertalker's bracelets were found hidden in Dedran's quarters on the circus ship. Tani would return them along with a trophy lock of hair from the three: Baris, Ideena, and Dedran, and the tale of how they died. The clan would approve.

But before they took ship back to Arzor Laris stood alone on a hill and allowed ashes to sift through her hands. She knew now by whose hand she had been aided. Jason Regan Trehannan, who had taken his grandfather's surname to honor that old soldier when his grandson enlisted. Jason Trehannan who had become Jason Regan, then Jas Cregar, and who in the end had redeemed his honor. To the silence of the surrounding trees she spoke softly.

"Be free of your sorrow and pain, Cregar. May the spirits of your team find you now. Let them walk with you so you are no more alone. May you find also my mother, your sister who loved you, Uncle. And be doubly comforted. All debts are paid." She descended the hill to Logan's arms.

The ship seemed to move like a snail through space. They landed on Arzor at sunrise. Laris looked up to see the lavender sky lighting up the land as the warm air brought them the scent of falwood blossoms. The girl could feel her tension drain away.

The land took her to its heart, making her its own. She hunted with Tani, laughed, teased, and rode with Logan. Storm unbent sufficiently to show her the frawn herd.

Brad talked to her. Telling her of Ishan, of the people from Cornwall, Ireland, and Brittany who had gone there to bring back their language and some of the old ways. Then the Xik had come and Ishan was a burned-out cinder orbiting in death, but before that happened many settlers had moved to Du-Ishan, the new world settled from the mother planet. It was from DuIshan that Mandy, Tani's paraowl, came. One day perhaps, Laris could visit DuIshan and see her origins for herself.

Quietly too Brad and Storm attempted to find out something about Prauo. Was he a kidnapped cub from another race, or a gene-spliced experiment? Whatever or whoever he was none could deny his intelligence. It made no difference to the big cat. Home was where Laris lived. She was his sister; he would abide by the choices she made for them both.

Twelve weeks after her return to Arzor she rode out with Logan to sit her horse on the edge of the basin. In the far distance High Peaks showed purple as Prauo's eyes. It called to her. The rocks, the high hills, the dry scent of the desert fringe, the solitude, and the silence. Logan watched as she gazed over the scene. He spoke softly.

"I won't hold you if you feel you can't stay here. But if you wanted to stay and you liked the idea, we could buy land together." He kept his voice neutral, he'd not pressure her. "Do you want to leave?"

She said nothing for many minutes, allowing her heart and Prauo's to decide. At last she turned to him.

"Home is where you are. Why would I leave our home?" she said.

About the Authors

For more than fifty years, ANDRE NORTON, "one of the most distinguished living SF and fantasy writers" (*Booklist*), has been penning bestselling novels that have earned her a unique place in the hearts and minds of millions of readers worldwide. She has been honored with the World Fantasy Convention's Life Achievement Award and with the Nebula Grand Master Award from her peers in the Science Fiction Writers of America. Works set in her fabled Witch World, as well as the Time Traders, the Solar Queen, and Beast Master series, to name but a few in her great oeuvre, have made her "one of the most popular authors of our time" (*Publishers Weekly*). She lives in Murfreesboro, Tennessee, where she presides over High Hallack, a writers' resource and retreat. More can be learned about Ms. Norton's work and High Hallack at www.andre-norton.org.

LYN MCCONCHIE has written many books, including collaborations with Andre Norton, among them *The Key of the Keplian,* a Witch World novel, and *Beast Master's Ark.* She lives in Norsewood, New Zealand, where she writes and runs a farm.